MERCY KILL

A Cass Leary Legal Thriller

ROBIN JAMES

Chapter 1

PEOPLE WERE STARTING TO STARE. I wasn't one to care under normal circumstances. But everyone here knew me, and I'd had enough gossip aimed at me to last a lifetime. If that weren't bad enough, my waiter kept refilling my water glass to the point I'd never make it the five miles back to the lake house without my bladder exploding.

"You're sure I can't get you started on some appetizers, ma'am?" he asked. He was a sweet kid. Fresh-faced, good posture. But if he stuck that carafe in my face one more time, he might have to wear the contents.

"My friend is running late," I said. "I'll wait."

"It's just, the kitchen is going to stop serving lunch in about twenty minutes. I'd be happy to put your order in if you think your friend will make it on time."

"I'll let you know soon," I said. The kid finally took the hint and buggered off.

I picked up my phone and checked my texts for probably the tenth time. I'd only sent one asking what was up. For a second, I got the ominous three gray dots, but no answer in return.

Detective Eric Wray had never been late for anything as far as I could recall. This lunch date had also been his idea.

I jumped when my phone rang. I'll admit. My heart sank a little when I saw the caller ID.

"Hey, Vangie," I answered. My sister barked out a laugh on the other end.

"What's the matter?" she asked, recognizing my tone even though I tried to feign brightness.

"Nothing, what's up?"

"Well?" she asked.

"Well, what?"

"How was lunch?"

It seemed an odd question. I hadn't even recalled telling Vangie I had lunch plans.

"Uh ... again. What's up?"

She got quiet. "Just, um. Just checking in."

I smiled. "Nice try. Seriously. What's going on? How do you know I'm at lunch?"

"I called your office. Miranda told me you'd be out for a while."

"Still not buying it," I said. "And you're probably pulling at your hair right now. Admit it. Fess up. What do you know about my lunch plans?"

She sighed. "Fine. I just know Eric was planning on taking you out."

"Well, then you know more than me. He's not here. Stood me up." I checked my smart watch. Quarter after one. I'd been sitting here noshing on crackers for almost an hour.

"Well, I'm sure he's got a good reason," Vangie said. Too light. Too breezy. What in the actual blazes was going on?

"I'm sure," I said. "How was your boat ride? Did Matty get Jessa up on skis?"

My younger brother had made a summer project out of getting my nine-year-old niece up on water skis. He had about three weeks left before school started.

"She got up for about five seconds," Vangie said, laughing. "Then total wipeout."

"Sorry I missed it. She okay?"

"Oh, she's fine," Vangie said. "I don't think she'll forgive Matty for a while. He's trying to make it up to her by catching her a turtle."

Suddenly, I regretted not just taking the whole week off myself. Mid-August, and it was the hottest week of the year so far.

"I'll let you get back to your date," Vangie said. "Why don't you knock off early? You're the boss, after all. Joe's bringing Katie and Emma over later and grilling some brats."

"I *hate* brats!" I heard Jessa shout from the background. I shared her sentiment. That said, the crackers weren't cutting it.

"I'll call you when I leave the office," I said. "I need to handle a few things, then I think I will get out of Dodge."

"Good call," Vangie said. Then we clicked off. My waiter started circling again with a hopeful look on his face.

Enough was enough. I just hoped nothing dire happened in Delphi today. As the town's senior homicide detective, there was really only one reason Eric would have stood me up without a word.

Bad news.

"I'll tell you what." I gestured to the waiter. "Put in an order for a club sandwich and some of those sweet potato fries. Actually, make it two. If my friend doesn't show in the next five minutes, I'll take his to go."

Relieved, my waiter nodded. As he turned to scurry off to the kitchen, he walked straight into the more than six-foot wall of muscle that was Eric Wray.

"Whoa," Eric said, putting his hands up. He was quick, grabbing the water carafe just in time before *he* wore it.

"Oh, sorry," the waiter said. "I'll ... I'll, uh, get that order in. Oh, would you like to change it?"

"Whatever the lady said," Eric answered. "Never had a bad meal here."

He sidestepped to let the kid past with the deftness of an athlete. Back in the day, he had been. Quarterback. Captain of the Fighting Shamrocks All-State football team. Then, he'd been just as fresh-faced as the waiter now rushing to get our order in before the kitchen closed. Now, Eric had deep lines at the corner of his eyes and a healthy peppering of gray at his temples. His steely blue eyes caught mine, and I knew my instincts were true.

Something had happened.

"Do I want to know?" I asked. Eric usually made a point of not answering work calls when he was on vacation. A policy I'd helped him institute over the last year with the promise I'd do the same.

Eric sat across from me and reached for my hand. "I'm sorry," he said, his voice coming out a little ragged. "I lost track of the time." Hmm. I wasn't sure I bought the explanation. His eyes kept darting toward the door.

"You okay?" I asked. "Are they calling you in?"

"What? No. I just got caught up. Couldn't get to my phone. I didn't mean to keep you waiting. I feel like a jerk."

I bit my lip past the next question I wanted to ask. But I wasn't that girl. I wouldn't nag. If Eric said something caught him up, then it caught him up. Still, a few of the other diners kept staring. They were waiting for some drama to play out.

"You're here now," I said. "And I'm starving."

He reached for the cracker basket. Finding it empty, his face reddened even more.

"You should have ordered. How late was I?"

"Forget it," I said. It wasn't like him to be this forgetful, if that's all it was. "But are you sure nothing's wrong? You have that look."

His eyes flicked to me. "What look?" He said it oddly, almost rapid fire.

"That something's-going-on-but-I'm-a-big-strong-tough-guy-who-doesn't-bring-work-into-my-personal-life-except-I-always-do look."

Finally, the hint of a grin. "That's gotta be one hell of a look," he said.

"Oh, it is," I said. "It never works. I always know. See, I'm an empath. Which I thought made me an ultra-caring person. But it turns out it's a trauma response."

"Turns out?" Eric raised an amused brow. "You started seeing a shrink?"

"No," I said as the waiter brought our lunch. "TikTok told me."

Eric laughed. "TikTok. You're one of those people now?"

"Apparently so," I said, reaching for a fry.

"Well, warn me when you start doing those dances."

My turn to laugh. "I'm not *that* kind of person."

"You say that. I swear though, that app is turning people. Bunch of guys at work started posting their videos. People I'd never have expected."

"Don't knock it until you try it," I said, glad that whatever bad news darkened Eric's face seemed to have faded. Maybe I was just reading too much into a look. Only Vangie's call nagged at me too. I'd never told her I was having lunch with Eric. But her call had seemed ... expectant somehow.

"I'm thinking of cutting out early," I said. "Joe and the whole crowd are descending on the house later. There will be beer and brats. I think it's time to introduce you to another Leary family lake tradition."

"Oh?" He wiped a bit of mayonnaise from the corner of his mouth.

"On hot days like this, we take lawn chairs and just sit in the water where it's shallow. My grandpa used to call it our white trash air conditioner."

"Sounds genius," he said.

"You don't even know. Joe perfected it. He's got a floating cooler so nobody even has to get up to re-beer."

"That is genius," Eric said, then that dark look crossed his face once more. "Maybe next time though. There's something I have to ..."

He didn't get to finish his sentence before his phone buzzed. Eric froze for a moment then slowly took the phone out of his pocket.

Ice ran through my veins as he answered. His face turned to stone. He was holding his breath as his caller spoke. I watched as Eric gripped his phone so tightly his knuckles actually turned white.

After a long moment, Eric pressed a trembling hand to his face. I reached for him.

Eric Wray was strong. Physically imposing. Stoic. But that afternoon at a table in the middle of Linda's Diner on the east side of Delphi, he crumpled in front of me.

"Eric," I said. He squeezed his eyes shut and said the only thing I'd heard since he told his caller hello.

"I'll be right there."

Then he clicked off. He caught my hand and gripped it. "I'm sorry," he said. "I can't. I've got to go."

"Eric!" I said, loud enough to draw stares again.

He got up and had the presence of mind to throw two twenty-dollar bills on the table. I quickly gathered my things and went after him.

Eric stormed out of the restaurant with the force of a freight train. He pushed the exit door so hard I thought he might break the glass.

"Eric!" I shouted now that we were in the parking lot. He kept walking. Fumbling for his keys, he went to his car.

He was going to leave. He was going to climb in his car and speed off without so much as a word.

"Eric!" I forced myself in front of him. He curled his fists to his sides. I put my hands on his shoulders and peered into his face. He blinked fast, trying to push back tears.

"What's going on?" I asked.

He shook his head. "It's not ... I can't ..."

"*What* is going on?!"

"Wendy," he finally said, deflating. "It's Wendy. I have to go, Cass. My wife is dead."

The air went out of me too. I didn't move, barely breathed as Eric went around me and got into his car. I was about to follow when my own phone started blowing up with text messages. This was Delphi, after all.

I looked up. A few diners were still staring at me from their window booths. They knew. Of course they knew.

News travels quickly in the small town of Delphi, Michigan, population 16,524. No. 16,523.

Chapter 2

As I LEFT THE DINER, I didn't know where to go. I faced the choice of two different but equally invasive inquisitions. My blood family, or my office family. I chose the latter. At least among Miranda, Jeanie, and Tori, we might actually be able to find some answers.

I saw Tori, my newest associate, poke her head out the front door as I pulled into the parking lot behind my office building. No doubt, she'd warned the others of my impending arrival. By the time I cut the engine, Jeanie had the back door thrown open.

"It's true, isn't it," she said, phrasing it as more of a statement. "Wendy Wray's dead."

"They called Eric from the diner," I said.

"Who called?" Miranda asked. The gang had assembled in our usual space, Jeanie's first floor office. Tori sat on the couch near the fireplace, furiously texting. She barely looked up when I joined them.

"You might as well tell me what you already know," I said to Jeanie. She took a moment to at least feign ignorance, then waved it off.

"Have a seat. I don't know much. I got a call from a nurse friend of mine over at Maple Valley." Jeanie had spent time recuperating there after a cancer scare. It's where I found her when I first returned to Delphi more than three years ago.

"To gossip?" I asked, incredulous. "You're telling me she just randomly called to say, hey, did you hear Wendy Wray just died? How did she know whether her next of kin had even been told?"

"I suppose it's not worth worrying about that right now," Jeanie said. "And no. It wasn't gossip. It's got the place in a bit of an uproar."

"But why?" Miranda asked. "Poor Wendy's been ... well ... this wasn't unexpected, was it?"

"I don't know," I said. "Eric doesn't talk about Wendy very much. It's awkward. And painful for him. Her car accident was four years ago. It hasn't been easy to see her like that."

"I hate to say it," Miranda said. "But it's got to be a blessing. I know Wendy wasn't perfect. But she was so young. This has been a nightmare for her family. Seeing her waste away like that. It's just awful all the way around. In all the way that matters, she already died four years ago. It's just her body left behind."

"Are you okay?" Jeanie asked. I'd taken a seat in a leather wing chair in the corner of the room. It was hot. Sweltering. I fanned myself with the cotton cardigan I wore.

"I don't know," I said. "I just need to talk to Eric. I need to know if he needs anything."

I picked up my phone. He hadn't texted. I hesitated, hovering my finger over the keyboard.

"He'll call you when he's got something to tell you," Jeanie said. "He's probably going to be on the phone all day. You know. Getting a hold of Wendy's folks. Her brother. He's not local, is he?"

"I don't think so," I said. "California, maybe."

"Did she have her affairs in order?" Tori asked. "Is there anything I can do to help, do you think?" Since passing her bar exam, Tori had taken a keen interest in probate and estate law. She had a real knack for counseling elderly clients through uncomfortable topics and times of grief.

"It's just not something we talked a lot about," I said. "When the time comes, I'll mention it to Eric. I'm sure he'll appreciate it."

Miranda steered the conversation to other office matters, trying to get my mind off the bomb that had just been dropped in Eric's life. It worked for a while, then I retreated to my upstairs office.

A couple of hours later, new texts started coming in. I held my breath for each, hoping I'd hear from Eric. It was mostly my siblings, trying to coax me to come home. They'd started the barbecue without me. I didn't mind. I wanted to stay here. I wanted to be ready in case Eric reached out.

Just before six, Jeanie poked her head in. "How's it going?" she asked.

I shook my head. "Jeanie, I don't know what to do. If you'd seen the look on Eric's face when he got that call."

She pursed her lips and nodded. Not waiting for an invitation, she came fully into the room and shut the door behind her.

"It's an odd thing," she said. "That woman has been a living ghost for years."

"I know you didn't have a very high opinion of her," I said.

Jeanie raised a hand to stop me. "It's not for me to judge. I just know Eric was in a lot of pain over her long before she had her accident. Long before you came back into his life. I just hope Wendy's at peace now."

I nodded. Tears sprang to my eyes, taking me off guard. Jeanie saw and came to the side of my desk. She pulled me against her and hugged me. I hadn't realized how much I needed one, and new guilt washed over me. Why in the world did I deserve comfort over this?

"You love the guy," Jeanie answered, accurately reading the turmoil that must have fallen across my face. "Eric's a good guy. He tries. He suffers. And you can't fix this one for him. It's just going to have to play itself out."

I reached for a tissue and blew my nose. Jeanie took a seat in one of my client chairs.

"Yeah," I said. "I guess. I just want to be there for him."

"And that's probably the worst thing you can do. You've been discreet. You've been respectful. Hell, too respectful, if you ask me. But you hanging around right now wouldn't be the best thing for Eric when he's dealing with Wendy's family."

"I know," I said. "I don't want to hurt anybody. I just want to help if I can."

"Staying out of it is the best way you can do that," she said. "Trust me."

"I always do." I smiled.

"Now," she said. "Go on home. You're not doing Eric or anybody else any good moping around here watching your phone."

"I am not moping," I protested, but I couldn't stop my smile from spreading.

"It's Thursday," she said. "Take yourself a long weekend. I told you there's nothing you can do until Eric reaches out and asks. I have a feeling he will. The rest of us can hold down the fort around here."

"Thanks," I said. "I'll play it by ear, but I appreciate the offer."

My text alert went off for about the tenth time. Vangie.

"Are you okay?" she texted. Though one couldn't tell the tone of voice from a text, I sensed the news from Maple Valley had worked its way to Finn Lake. Everyone either knew Wendy Wray or knew someone who knew her. Everyone knew Eric. And me.

I grabbed my purse off the floor and slid my phone into the side pocket. "I better go," I said. "If anyone needs me, I'll be holed up at the lake."

"Worse places to hide out." Jeanie winked. As I stood, a soft knock on the office door drew my attention. Tori poked her head in.

"Cass," she said. "Sorry to interrupt. But there's someone here to see you."

"I don't have any appointments scheduled today," I said.

"It's not that," she said. "It's, um ... it's Deputy Craddock from Woodbridge County. He wants to ask you a few questions."

I heard heavy footsteps coming up the stairs. I passed a questioning look to Jeanie. Her expression turned dark. My heart dropped.

Deputy Gene Craddock was one of the oldest detectives with the County Sheriff's office. He loudly cleared his throat as he approached, as if the footsteps and Tori weren't enough to announce his presence. He had an ashen look on his face as Tori widened the door to let him pass.

"Miss Leary," he said.

"You know it's Cass," I said. Craddock had a deeply lined, craggy face and thick, steely hair. Jeanie quietly excused herself and took Tori with her.

"What can I do for you?" I asked.

Craddock motioned toward the chair Jeanie had just vacated. So, it was going to be a serious conversation.

"Miss ... er ... Cass," he said. He pulled a small notepad out of his breast pocket along with a stubby pencil. "I really just have one main question. Can you tell me where you were today between the hours of eleven a.m. and one fifteen this afternoon?"

"What?" I asked. I felt a little lightheaded. Like I'd just been hit by a boom. I sank into my chair.

"I'm sorry," I said. "What?"

"Were you in court? Did you have client meetings?"

"What's this about, Craddock?" I asked.

"Look, I'm sorry. I have to ask you. Can you just let me know?"

"My whereabouts," I said. My mind raced, refusing to land on the obvious meaning of Craddock's questions.

"Yes," he said. "Eleven to one, basically."

"I was here," I said. "I had client appointments until twelve fifteen, I think it was. Then I went to lunch."

"Where was that?" he asked.

My stomach rolled. He hadn't said it. Maybe he wouldn't.

"I went to Linda's Diner on Rance Street. You know it. I've seen you there a hundred times."

"Did you eat alone?" he asked.

"What? No. I had lunch with Eric Wray."

Craddock stopped writing. He chewed the inside of his cheek. "What time did you get to Linda's?"

"I can't tell you to the minute," I said. "Just before twelve thirty."

The corners of his mouth lifted in a smile. "Ah. You met Eric at Linda's at twelve thirty?"

Warning. Danger. It was as if red and orange lights flashed inside my brain. I fixed a smile on my face.

"Craddock, I'm sorry. What's this about? Am I under suspicion of something?"

He closed his notepad. "Cass, I'm just trying to tie up some loose ends. We can sit here and dance around it, but I know you know what happened out at Maple Valley Rehabilitation Center today. You know Wendy Wray's dead."

My throat turned to sandpaper. I folded my hands in my lap. "Yes," I said. "I've heard. I'm waiting to hear more. Are you trying to tell me there's something for you to investigate about that?"

"You were with Eric Wray when he got a call from a staff member at Maple Valley?" he asked.

"I was," I said. "Like I said, we were having lunch together."

"Right," he said. "Was Eric upset?"

"What? Of course he was upset."

Craddock considered my words. I could barely believe what was happening. He was trying to play it off. Routine. Just tying loose ends. There was only one reason the Woodbridge County Sheriff's office would care what happened at Maple Valley this afternoon.

"Is there anything else you need from me?" I asked. "Because Eric is a close friend of mine. I'm also his lawyer. He's going to need help making arrangements once the shock of this all has worn off."

"Right," he said. "I don't want to keep you. You've helped."

"I should hope so," I said. I had to bite my tongue. My protective instincts flared. What in the actual blazes had happened out at Maple Valley?

Craddock rose. He stuck his hand out to shake mine. "You mind if I take one of these?" he asked, helping himself to one of my business cards from a holder on my desk. "Just in case I've got a few more questions?"

"Of course you can," I answered. "Let me show you out."

Craddock raised a hand. "No need. I don't want to keep you from your work. You have a good night, Miss ... er ... Cass."

He left, shuffling his feet a bit as he went. Craddock played that quiet and unassuming. But I knew his game, and I knew that look in his eye. Something was wrong. Very, very wrong. I needed to get in touch with Eric. Now.

Chapter 3

ERIC DIDN'T RETURN my calls or texts that night. On a
hunch, I called his office the following morning and got his
voicemail. I couldn't work. Couldn't think. I left at lunch and
told Miranda I'd be gone until at least Monday.

Eric lived on a quiet street in one of Delphi's newer
subdivisions. He had a wooded lot in a cul-de-sac. The perfect
kind of house for a young, married couple looking to start a
family. Ten years ago, that's who he and Wendy were.

I parked in the street and went up the walk. His shades were
drawn. Two houses down, one of Eric's neighbors was
mowing his grass on a lawn tractor. He waved when he saw
me. I keyed myself in.

"Eric?" I called, though I already sensed he wasn't home. No
lights. No open windows. Silence.

I walked through the foyer into the kitchen. I turned off his
house alarm before opening the door to the garage. Empty
save for Wendy's red Mazda. He drove it a couple of times a
month just to keep it running, but hadn't wanted to sell it. Yet.

I went back through the house. The green light on his dishwasher blinked. I opened it. He only had a few cereal bowls and some spoons and cups inside. I emptied it, stacking the bowls on a floating shelf above the counter. He didn't eat here much. Lately, we had dinner together three or four nights a week and lunch yesterday.

I walked upstairs to Eric's bedroom. His bed was still made, the sheets turned down. It was Friday. His cleaning lady came on Thursdays at ten. It meant Eric hadn't slept here since at least the night before last.

"Where are you?" I whispered. I sat down on Eric's side of the bed. I never slept here. The few times I'd spent the night at Eric's, I used the guest room. We weren't there yet. Because ... I closed my eyes. Because of Wendy. I don't know what made me do it, but I reached for his nightstand drawer and opened it.

He kept a small, dog-eared Bible inside of it. That surprised me. A bottle of pills. Prescription antacids. Finally, a .38 handgun. I slowly closed the drawer.

I lay down on the bed. Eric's scent calmed me. Clean. A hint of his aftershave. I rolled over and found myself face to face with Wendy's nightstand. Sitting up, I opened the drawer.

I found a pad of paper with a phone number written on it in pencil. A time. Thursday. 2:15 p.m. What had she meant to remind herself of over four years ago? I wondered if Eric had ever even looked in this drawer since her accident.

Beneath the notepad, Wendy kept her eReader, a jar of foot balm, and an emery board. Normal things. Mundane. But a piece of her. I closed the drawer.

Beneath my feet, the floor vibrated as Eric's garage door raised. My heart skipped. I straightened the bed and headed downstairs.

"Eric?" I called out, not wanting to startle him. Though he likely would have already noticed my car parked in front of the house. Still, I had no idea what kind of mental state he was in.

I got to the top of the stairs as he entered the foyer. He looked up at me. My stomach dropped. He'd aged a decade. His hair, normally combed, stood out in peaks. He stared at me with hollowed-out eyes rimmed red.

"Eric," I said as I slowly walked down the stairs to him. I made it as far as the final step. He met me on the landing. It brought us almost nose to nose.

The sight of him made me stop breathing. I reached up, running a finger along the line of his stubbled jaw.

"Are you okay?" I asked.

He straightened his shoulders and closed his eyes.

"No," he whispered, then pulled me into his arms.

He broke. His body wracked with sobs, my spine bent as he leaned against me. I held him to my chest, running my fingers through his hair.

"Let's sit down," I said. "Let me fix you a sandwich or something. When's the last time you ate?"

He stiffened. When he pulled away from me, he'd gotten a hold of himself. "I don't know. Hadn't thought about it."

"Come here," I said, taking his hand. I led him into the kitchen. Eric sat quietly at his kitchen island while I brewed some coffee and whipped up a fried egg bagel with cheese for him and one for me.

We sat quietly eating for a moment. He'd take a breath, and I thought he'd say something. He didn't. I waited until he finished, then reloaded the dishwasher.

"Eric," I said. "For God's sake. What happened? Where have you been?"

He ran a hand through his unruly hair. "I need a shower and a shave. I've got to check in with the office ..."

"No, you don't. Wendy died. Nobody expects you to be at work. I'm not trying to nag. But I've been worried sick about you."

"I'm sorry," he said, looking out toward the woods. "I was with Wendy's family. I didn't think ... I mean, I barely had a second alone."

I sank onto the bar stool beside him, feeling like an ass. "I'm sorry. I didn't mean to make it about me. Ugh. Of course. Her parents."

"Her brother too," he said. "His flight got in from San Diego late last night. They wanted to help with funeral arrangements. Wendy didn't ... she didn't leave formal instructions for anything. That's been an issue for years."

"Did they say what happened?" I asked.

He shrugged. "She stopped breathing. Her body just quit. You haven't ... you haven't seen her. She was wasting to nothing, Cass. You knew Wendy. Before ... She was strong.

Athletic. Hell, she ran five miles a day. Lifted weights. Some days I could barely keep up with her. She weighed eighty-two pounds now. They told me ..."

I put a hand over his. "I'm so sorry."

"They had to feed her through a tube."

"Of course."

Eric's words spilled out of him. In the years since I'd been back in Delphi and had Eric in my life, he rarely spoke about Wendy's condition. Or about Wendy at all. Now, his torrent of grief washed over him.

"Her brain was mostly spinal fluid, they said. On her last scan. They showed me. It was all this dark space where Wendy's mind used to be. She was smart, Cass. Quick. Too quick. She had all these ideas. All these projects. It was all just gone. Atrophied."

"Oh, Eric. I'm just so, so, sorry. I want to help. Let me have Tori help with some of the arrangements."

He nodded. "It's just so strange. Like I don't know how to feel. I always thought it would be a relief. It is ... God. Does that make me awful?"

"No," I said. "It doesn't. But that doesn't mean this isn't awful."

"Cam and Dar ... Wendy's parents, they're not handling this well. I'm worried about them. It's good that Jeff is here, her brother. That's why I've been AWOL. I was just trying to keep Cam and Dar in one piece until Jeff could take over. They don't have anybody else. All their nieces and nephews have moved on."

"Of course," I said. "Eric, Gene Craddock came to see me. He had ... questions. He's investigating Wendy's death. What's going on there? It seemed like he suspected foul play."

Eric's eyes flicked back toward me. I knew him. He was holding something back. "He's just doing his job. Wendy was unattended when she died. He's just trying to make sure it wasn't abuse or neglect or something."

"I see," I said, but wasn't satisfied. "Then why did he want to talk to me, though? He was asking me alibi questions, Eric."

His expression darkened. "He what?"

"He asked me where I was between eleven and one yesterday. He's establishing the timeline of Wendy's death. Have you talked to him?"

"I'll handle Craddock," he said, practically spitting out his words. "That son of a ..."

"You'll handle him how, exactly?"

"He's out of line," Eric said. "Cam's behind this. Wendy's father. He's wanted Wendy out of that facility for a while."

"I see," I said. For the past few months, I'd sensed some conflict between Eric and Wendy's parents. I hadn't wanted to pry. "So you think Cam suspects they weren't properly caring for Wendy?"

"I'll handle it," he said once more. "What did you tell Craddock?"

"I told him the truth, of course," I said. "You know where I was."

"Right," he said. "Cass, I'm sorry. I'm not thinking straight. This whole thing has been a mess. Trust me. Cam Maloney is friends with Sheriff Lubell. I'm sure Craddock made some promise to Cam that he'd look into this to make him feel better. It's a formality. There's nothing going on other than Lubell wanting to secure Cam's campaign contributions. He's up for reelection next year. He's a worm. Trust me."

"I do," I said, wanting to press. Eric's theory made no sense in light of Craddock's questions of me. He wasn't fishing for information about Wendy's nursing home. He'd been fishing for information about me and Eric. Despite Eric's assurances there was nothing to worry about, I knew in my bones he was dead wrong.

Chapter 4

One Week Later

WENDY MALONEY WRAY had been beautiful in a way I used to envy. I'll admit. Sleek dark hair that hung so straight it looked ironed, though I knew it grew out of her head that way. Always toned, tanned, and wearing whatever the latest fashion was. No. Wendy Maloney had set the fashion trends at Delphi High School twenty-plus years ago.

She'd been two grades ahead of me. Beloved. A cheerleader. The Homecoming Queen. Class president.

Back in those days she had also been a bully. She and her group of friends looked down at my Eastlake lack of pedigree. Made fun of my clothes. All the normal, horrible things an insecure kid can do to another insecure kid.

Now, as I stood in the back of the funeral home crowded with the people who loved and admired her, I just felt tremendous sadness.

"She was so pretty," Vangie whispered beside me. I strained to get a look through the throngs of people. Eric stood at the front near Wendy's closed casket, shaking hands, trying to take in their expressions of grief. A large formal photograph of Wendy stood on an easel behind him. It had been taken about five years ago before her accident. She wore a sharp, blue blazer and smiled with gleaming white teeth. The picture had adorned her business cards. Wendy Wray had become one of the top producing real estate agents in the tri-county area.

"She was," I said.

In the corner, blocked from my view by a large floral display, I could hear the quiet sobbing of Darleen Maloney, Wendy's mother.

The line slowly moved forward. Vangie gave me a nudge when I didn't move with it.

"You go ahead," I whispered. "I'm just going to hang back."

I felt a hand on my back. Jeanie came to my side and offered me a sad smile. "Quite the turnout," she said.

"Which one is he?" Vangie whispered to Jeanie. Jeanie put a discreet hand over her mouth as if she were covering a cough. Then she pointed with a pinky to a blond man in a dark suit sitting at Dar Maloney's left.

"Stop it." I gave my sister a tight-lipped whisper.

"I'm just asking," Vangie said. "And I'm sorry. It's weird."

The man in question was Owen Corbett. Rumors had swirled for years that he'd been Wendy's Other Man. The one she'd been planning to divorce Eric over before she wrapped her car around a telephone pole after leaving his house in the middle of the night. Now, Corbett sat consoling Wendy's mother while her actual husband stood near her casket greeting guests.

"It's sure as hell awkward," Jeanie said as she left me to move up into the line. After ten minutes, she reached Eric. His shoulders sagged with relief as she hugged him. He was pretending, putting on a brave face for all these people. With Jeanie, there was no need for any of that.

The funeral director asked us all to find a seat or line the wall. Jeanie made her way back to Vangie and me. We found some folding chairs in the very last row. I lingered for a moment, standing while the others sat. Eric found me in the crowd, giving me a barely perceptible nod to let me know he was glad I was here.

Dar and Cam Maloney went to the front of the room and took seats beside him. They made a concerted effort not to lay eyes on Eric, however.

A pastor came to the lectern and said an opening prayer. After that, a few of Wendy's friends and co-workers stood to eulogize her. My heart twisted as Eric came to the lectern.

"Thank you for coming," he said. "Wendy touched a lot of lives. She was ... it's a cliché maybe to say she brightened any room she entered. But she did. You all know it. I'd like to thank you all for being here. She wouldn't have been able to believe it. Wendy was always harder on herself than anyone else could be. People mattered to her. You mattered to her. So thank you for coming. We've arranged for some refreshments in the adjoining hall. Please join us. Um ... thank you."

He shook the pastor's hand. He came back to the lectern and directed the crowd which doors to exit from. Eric weaved his way through the people and found Jeanie, Vangie, and me.

"You okay?" I asked.

He shook his head. "I just want to get through this day. We've got the graveside service just for family in an hour. After that ..."

"After that, you know you're welcome out at the lake."

His face dropped. "Yeah. Okay. I honestly don't think I can go back to that house right now. There's still so much of her there. I told Cam and Dar they could come over and take anything they want."

"You've taken the only thing that matters!" A sharp voice came from behind Eric. He turned. Dar Maloney stood red-faced, gripping her husband's shoulder.

"Dar," Eric said, beleaguered. I got the sense he'd had similar confrontations with her before.

"Is this her?" Dar asked, pointing to me. "She the one you threw Wendy over for?"

"Dar," Cam Maloney said to his wife. "Not here. Not like this."

"Is she?" Dar asked. She got aggressive then. She pushed past her husband and jammed a finger into my shoulder. I had enough fighting Leary in me that I took a ready stance. I had enough of my mother in me that I kept my hands at my sides.

"Dar, let's go," Cam said. "We'll go find a table in the hall. People are going to be looking for you."

"You couldn't make her happy," Dar said. She took a step toward Eric on unsteady legs. It was then I realized the woman was under the influence of something. I didn't judge her for it. No matter what else was going on, she would bury her daughter today.

Mercifully, Cam succeeded in pulling Dar away from us and toward the hallway. Most of the crowd had already left the viewing room. It left our small group oddly alone with Wendy's casket.

With the Maloneys safely out of earshot, I turned to Eric. "I'm sorry. I shouldn't have come. I had no idea things were that rough between you and Wendy's family."

"I didn't either," he said. "It's new. And everything's so raw. I don't plan to hold it against them."

"They want someone to blame," Jeanie said. "I've known Darleen a while. She's fought her demons. It's a bit of a miracle she's more or less upright today."

"You need friends around you," I said to Eric. I noticed that most of the mourners gravitated toward Dar and Cam. I didn't have to guess the flavor of the things Dar was saying about Eric. Then there was Owen Corbett, hovering close by.

"Wouldn't be a funeral without family drama," Eric offered.

"Still," I said. "I should ..."

"No," he said. "It'll help me most to know I've got somewhere to escape to later. I'll put in my time here. Then I'll leave the Maloneys to whatever they need."

"They're treating you like this was all your fault," Vangie said. "You've done everything you can for Wendy. Even after what she did to you. Eric, we all know what really happened."

He put a hand up. "I appreciate that. Really. But not here. And none of it even matters anymore. What difference does it make now?"

"It's just not right," Vangie said. "And I'm not afraid to say it. Owen Corbett has been flapping his gums all over town, saying how he and Wendy were going to get married."

"I'll see you back at the lake," Eric said. "And thanks, you guys. It really does matter to me that you came."

I hated to leave him. It felt like throwing him back to the wolves. Eric was right that this wasn't the time to air dirty laundry. But Vangie was also right: Eric had been just as much a victim in this as Wendy. There was no win. It was all just horrible.

"You need a ride back?" I asked Jeanie.

"If you could drop me off at the office," she said. "My car's parked there."

We left. The Leslie Brothers Funeral Parlor was just six blocks from my office. When I pulled into the front lot, a second car had parked alongside Jeanie's. Though we were closed for the day, the driver of said car waited for us behind her steering wheel.

"Is that Detective Lewis?" Vangie asked from the back seat.

"Officer Lewis," Jeanie corrected her. "She got demoted after her work on that last homicide."

That "last homicide" was my last criminal trial. At the conclusion of it, Delphi Police Detective Megan Lewis faced a demotion for dereliction of duty. There were those in town who thought she'd be better off just taking a job somewhere else. There were others who blamed me for coming after her hard on cross-examination and exposing the mistakes she had made in her very first murder investigation. I respected Megan for taking her lumps and trying to work her way back up. I knew she did not, however, respect me all that much these days.

"Jeanie," I said. "Can you drive Vangie home? I have a feeling Lewis just wants to talk to me."

"Should we check her for sharp objects?" Jeanie teased. It was just a joke, but Lewis's eyes did seem to hold murder in them.

"I think I'll be okay," I said. I waited for Jeanie and Vangie to pull away before walking over to Megan's car.

"You're alone," she said, staring straight ahead. Her lips formed a white line. Though her car wasn't running, she stayed behind the wheel.

"What were you expecting?" I asked.

"I assumed Eric would be with you."

"He's still at the funeral home," I said. "Is there a message you want me to convey? You do have his cell phone, I assume."

Megan finally got out of the car. She slammed the door behind her and faced me.

"Look," I said. "I know you pretty much hate my guts. Someday I hope you can accept that I was just doing my job in the Mathison case. Your instincts were good, you just cut too many corners. We learn from our mistakes, though. It's how we get great at our jobs. And you will be ..."

"Save it," she snapped. "I'm not here to rehash any of that. And I'm not here to apologize. In fact, this is the last place I want to be. But there's some stuff happening. Stuff I'm not supposed to know about or say anything about. But Eric's my friend. He's stuck his neck out for me enough times that I need to return the favor. If anyone sees me talking to him, like this, they're going to know who tipped him off. So ... I figure I talk to you instead."

She looked over her shoulder. The street was empty. Still, Megan was clearly on edge.

"Come inside," I said. "I can put some coffee on. Are you on call? I can even make it something stronger."

I got my door keys out and Megan followed me in.

"I can't stay long," she said. "I just need to know you'll try talking some sense into Eric."

"About what?" I asked.

Megan had a large purse slung over her shoulder. She pulled out a thin file and handed it to me.

"The official report will come out in a day or two," she said. "Before you go accusing me of anything underhanded, Eric's next of kin. He's entitled to a copy. I'm just giving him a small head start."

I opened the file. The air seeped out of me, deflating me. It was Wendy Wray's official autopsy report.

"He's not taking this seriously enough," Megan said.

"Craddock at the sheriff's department questioned me the day after Wendy died," I said. I was afraid to look at the last page of the report. I already feared what it would say.

"Did you tell Eric that?"

"Yes," I answered, though it felt like a betrayal.

"He played it off, didn't he? Said it was routine. Said it was just Wendy's family rattling swords and the sheriff's office throwing them a bone."

"Campaign contributions," I said.

"Yeah. He ran the same number on me when I saw him coming out of an interview room with Craddock."

"Eric was interviewed already?" I asked.

"He didn't tell you?"

"He did not," I answered.

"Something's going on with him," she said. "He's not acting like himself. We've all tried to get him to reach out. He's closed off."

I opened the file. Taking a breath for courage, I read the last page. One line at the end of the report.

Cause of death. Homicide.

My knees buckled. I leaned against the lobby counter.

"Bruising on her cheeks," Megan explained as the words in the report wavered and swam in front of me. "Consistent with somebody putting their hand over her mouth and squeezing her nose shut. They think somebody suffocated Wendy."

"My God," I whispered as the gravity of the situation settled over me.

"Eric hasn't seen this?" I asked.

"I'm pretty sure he suspects," she said. "Craddock's had deputies canvassing Maple Valley for days. You might want to call your friends at the prosecutor's office. They won't take mine." She left off the last part, thanks to me.

"Megan ... what's going on?"

"Judge Niedermeyer is signing an arrest warrant as we speak," she said. "Cass, Eric is going to have about twenty-four hours to turn himself in after that."

"This isn't happening," I said, setting the report on the counter beside me. "He didn't. He couldn't."

"I hope you're right," she said. "And I hope you're prepared to fight for him as hard as you do everyone else. Otherwise Eric's going down for murdering his wife."

Chapter 5

ERIC SAT on Jeanie's office couch, his fingers digging trenches through his hair. Each page of Wendy's autopsy report lay before him on the oval, cherry wood table. I watched his face go through a kaleidoscope of emotions. He was a homicide detective. You can't shut that part of your brain off. He was also someone who'd shared an intimate life with the woman described on those pages in cold, calculating, devastating medical terms. Finally, he was the man soon to be accused of killing her.

"This wasn't Wendy," he said quietly, speaking from the part of him that was still Wendy's husband.

"We have some time," Jeanie said. She sat in the corner chair. I sat beside Eric. Tori leaned against Jeanie's desk, taking notes when she could. "I've already talked to Sheriff Lubell's office."

He looked up. "I didn't ask you to do that."

"No," she said. "But you should have. It's understandable, but you're not thinking clearly."

Eric clenched his jaw. He grabbed a page of the autopsy report and crumpled it into a ball. "This is crap. This is your new prosecutor bowing to political pressure and Maloney's money. Nothing's going to come of this. I didn't kill Wendy."

"Of course not," I said. "But you have to take this seriously. You need representation. You of all people know how this works."

"Oh, I know how this works. Craddock wants to run for sheriff after Lubell retires. And he should. As a detective, he's worthless. I'm not afraid of him. I'll bury him if this gets to a courtroom. I'll relish it."

"Eric, what's going on with you and the Maloneys? Before all of this. They were treating Owen Corbett as if he were the bereaved widower yesterday. I had no idea they'd become close."

"It's new," he said. "Owen probably smells dollar signs too."

"It's more than that," Jeanie said. "Eric, we love you. We're on your side. But if you don't stop acting like a detective and act more like a defendant, this could get out of hand real quick. Let us do what we do."

Eric tossed the crumpled page back on the table. "All that does is prove what Cam and Dar haven't wanted to admit for over a year. Wendy was gone. Read what it says. Her brain weighed a quarter of the size of a normal female brain. There was nothing in there. She wasn't in there. They started bringing in all these quacks. Holistic practitioners. They put stones on her. Played wind chimes and burned sage. The last straw was when I caught that psychic Louise Lathrop at her bedside. She had Dar convinced Wendy was talking to her telepathically."

"Lord," I said.

"She didn't want this," Eric said. "Wendy was vibrant. Active. She was a pain in the ass too. I've never hidden our problems. But her treatment was my decision. About six months ago, the doctors started talking about end-of-life options. She was never going to get better, only worse."

He pointed to a page that showed an anatomical drawing of Wendy's body. The ME had reported bed sores in various stages of healing.

"We were starting to have conversations about letting Wendy go," Eric said. "Dar didn't want to hear it. I understand. Wendy was still her baby. I was trying so damn hard to be sensitive to that but also honor Wendy's wishes."

"I had no idea," I said, putting a hand on Eric's knee. He'd kept that part of his life from me. There had been so many times when he'd gotten quiet. I knew the days he went to visit Wendy. I could read the look in his eyes when he came back and knew something had happened. I never asked. It had been an unspoken pact between us. When Eric was ready to talk about it, he would. Now, it was being forced from him.

"This has to be wrong," he said.

"We're going to find an expert," I said. "A second opinion to look over these findings."

"In the meantime," Jeanie said. "Eric, we have to make arrangements for you to turn yourself in. Lubell's office has asked for a twenty-four-hour window."

His face drained of color. His right hand began to shake and Eric covered it with his left.

"It'll be temporary," I said. "We'll get you through as quickly as possible. You have a lot of people on your side in there."

"Not Craddock," he said. "Maybe not the entire Woodbridge County Sheriff's Department. You know there's always been a turf war between them and Delphi P.D. Craddock's probably salivating at the thought of seeing me in handcuffs."

"That's not going to happen," I said. "You'll turn yourself in on your terms. I'll say to you what I say to everyone else. We'll take this one step at a time. And it's going to be okay."

"Cass," Jeanie said. "I need to speak with you in private."

Eric didn't look up. His eyes stayed fixed on that autopsy report. He barely registered my movements when I got up to follow Jeanie into the lobby. She closed the door to her office behind us. When she turned to face me, she gave me a withering look.

"What?" I said, crossing my arms in front of me.

"It's time for you to step away from this."

"What?" I said, louder this time.

"You can't be part of any further discussions with Eric in the room," she said.

I shook my head as if that might clear it and Jeanie's words would make new sense.

"Forget it," I said. "I'm not taking a back seat on this one. No way."

The door opened behind me and Tori stepped out to join us. I glanced over my shoulder. Eric had gone back to the posture of carving his hands through his hair.

"He's not thinking clearly," I said. "It's going to take all of us to muscle him into what he has to do."

"You'll have a role," Jeanie said. "But you're not his lawyer. You're a material witness."

I curled my fists at my side.

"Cass," Tori said lightly. "You've combed through Wendy's death certificate and autopsy. You know the timeline. They're going to try to show that Wendy died between twelve and one p.m. on August 17th. When he was supposed to be sitting at a lunch table with you. And you're going to have to tell them the truth. You had no idea he was visiting her before your date."

My head started to throb.

"That's ridiculous. Eric didn't go murder his wife, then stop to get a club sandwich with me. It's absurd."

"Maybe," Jeanie said. "But worst-case scenario, this goes to trial. Hell, if it goes to prelim. Rafe Johnson's going to put you on the stand. You're going to have to tell the judge that Eric was late for that lunch date."

I started to sweat. "He's in denial," I said. "Can you blame him?"

"Kiddo, so are you. Right now, I'm going to need you to trust me. Let me take care of you."

"I don't need you to take care of me," I said, my anger rising. I wasn't mad at Jeanie. I was mad at the world.

She shot a look at Tori. Tori cleared her throat and pulled a folded piece of paper from between the pages of her notepad.

"Now don't freak out," Jeanie said. "If you take a step back and try to look at this objectively, you'd know this was coming."

Tori handed the paper to Jeanie. She unfolded it and spread it flat on the reception desk. It was Sunday. Miranda had the day off. The space was empty and quiet.

Gritting my teeth, I stared straight ahead. As if not looking could stave off the inevitable.

"Cass," Jeanie said.

Letting out a breath, I looked. The piece of paper bore the court caption that turned my heart to ice. The People of the State of Michigan versus Eric David Wray.

"A subpoena?" I asked, snatching the paper.

"They're going after your phone," she said. "They probably already have a record of your texts back and forth with Eric. They would have pulled it from his."

I got hot. Stifling. My clothes started to itch.

"They're going to try to use me against him," I said. Of course they were. I'd known it the second Megan Lewis told me he was under suspicion.

"He didn't do this," I said through tight lips.

"Tori," Jeanie said. "Can you give us a minute?"

"Sure," Tori said. She seemed relieved for the reprieve. She hustled herself upstairs to her office.

"Look at me, Cass," Jeanie said.

I wouldn't. She waited a moment, then gently placed her hands on either side of my head, guiding my gaze to her.

I felt like my lungs had filled with tar. The room started to close in.

"He didn't do this. He can't have done this."

"He loved that girl once," she said. "And she was suffering."

I pulled away from Jeanie's grasp. I shouted a whisper. "He didn't kill her, for God's sake. That's not ... he's not ..."

Jeanie stared at me with laser-sharp eyes. I knew the question she held in them, unspoken.

Was I sure about that? Could I swear with absolute certainty that Eric Wray wasn't capable of killing someone?

There was a secret we shared, Eric and me. One I'd buried so deeply, thinking of it now almost felt like a surprise. That it wasn't real. Except it was. I was the only person on the planet who knew that Eric could and had killed to protect someone he loved. He'd killed for Wendy before. Long ago, she'd been abused by someone in a position of power. Eric made that someone go away before he could hurt anyone else.

As Jeanie stared into my eyes, I knew I was wrong. Jeanie missed nothing. She saw everything. Without saying a word, she had just told me she knew Eric's secret too.

"He's in trouble, Cass," she said. "Deep trouble. But I can help dig him out of it. You can't fix this one. You need to trust me on this."

My tears came. "I have to fix this."

"You can't," she said more forcefully. "You can only make it worse. Your need to fix everything and Eric's need to try to protect you from everything is exactly what will bury the both of you. I'm right. You know I am. So let me do what I can. I have a plan."

A sob escaped from deep inside of me. "Jeanie ..."

"I know," she said as she held her arms out and I went into them. Jeanie Mills stood only four foot eleven, but in that moment, she felt like a giant.

We stood there for a moment. Me crying. Her taking it. A few minutes later, her office door opened and Eric stepped out.

I quickly wiped my tears and found a smile. He came to us. He took my hand and one of Jeanie's.

"What time did you tell them?" he asked her.

Jeanie straightened. "I told them to give you tonight to get your affairs in order. But that I'd drive you to the sheriff's department myself at ten a.m. tomorrow."

"Eric ..." I said.

He put a hand up to quiet me. I wondered how much he'd heard of my conversation with Jeanie. Enough. None at all.

"All right," he said. "Tell Lubell's office I'll be ready."

Chapter 6

JEANIE MADE me wait in the car when we drove Eric to the sheriff's department the next morning. She had to practically tie me to the steering wheel to do it. It got increasingly harder to detach my defense lawyer brain from my overprotective girlfriend brain.

The Fixer. That's what Jeanie had called me. Only now I had to rely on other people to help me fix this one.

"I'll be all right," Eric had said. When he tried to smile, it made it all worse. Two deputies stood at the entrance waiting for him. The miserable look on their faces probably should have comforted me. Turf war or not, Eric Wray was one of their own.

"Is that a promise?" I asked. I knew how bad this could get. Eric would spend most of today in a holding cell being processed. But we couldn't expect a bail hearing for a few days. This was a murder charge. Even with the best outcome, he would spend several days in jail. And he was a cop. He could play it down all he wanted, but someone, somewhere, might try to earn points inside by hurting him.

"Be careful," I said.

He laughed. "Try to blend in? Sure."

"Eric ..."

"Enough," he said. "You can help me by doing what Jeanie says. I'll talk to you when I can."

"I'll be there at your hearing," I said. He thumped on the side of the car and left us.

"Jeanie," I said. "I don't know if I can deal with this."

"You can," she said as she rolled up the window and pulled away from the curb. "Now it's time to go get some help."

She took the main road out of town and hit the highway, heading for Detroit.

"Why aren't you telling me who we're going to see?" I asked.

"Because it's not up for debate. No matter what else happens over the next few days, I'm not going to put up with you second-guessing me."

"I won't second-guess you," I said. "But I'm not going to sit back and do nothing."

"Well," she said. "For the first time in your life, nothing is probably the most helpful thing you *can* do. Besides, if this were you getting locked up for something you didn't do, I'd be heading to the same person. Now zip it and enjoy some music."

She picked a classic vinyl station and within seconds, Steely Dan blared through her speakers. She laughed when I grumbled.

I did my best not to think about what Eric was going through every second as we drove away. He'd be fingerprinted. There would be a mugshot. Within a few minutes, the news outlets would have it and plaster it online. No matter what else happened in his life, it would follow him. It could not be erased.

Almost an hour later, Jeanie took a Bloomfield Hills exit and drove us toward the most affluent row of office buildings. When she pulled into the parking lot of Slater and Slater, Attorneys at Law, I'll admit, I was impressed.

"Norm Slater?" I asked.

Jeanie put the car in park but didn't answer. She grabbed the green file folder we'd started in Eric's case. I sat frozen for a second as she shut the door and handed the keys to the valet. I forgot myself for a second, then scrambled out of my seat, running to catch up with her.

Norman Dale Slater was once the most famous defense lawyer in the state. He'd made a name for himself defending a plastic surgeon accused of murdering his wife. The book based on the case won a Pulitzer back in the eighties. But none of those things were what impressed me about Jeanie's choice. Though she'd never confirmed or denied it when I asked her outright, rumor had it she and Norman had a law school fling. In the book *he* wrote about the case, Norman Slater had mentioned Jeanie in the acknowledgements. It read simply, "For Jeanie M. and the summer of '74."

Slater and Slater occupied the kind of office space I used to have. The top of a high rise with mirrored windows on the outside. Marble floors and brass hardware on all the doors.

We approached a reception desk. Jeanie merely smiled and slid her business card across to the young kid sitting behind the desk with an earpiece in. He picked up the card, smiled, then pointed down the hall. "You're in conference room six. I can get a page to show you."

"We'll find it," Jeanie said. "Thanks, kid."

"Eric will hate this," I said. "He'll say we went to the bloodsucker pond."

"Do you hate it?" she asked.

"No," I said. "I just didn't realize Norman Slater was still actively practicing."

"He's not," she said. "Norm's just of counsel these days. Last I heard, he spends most of his time sailing on his yacht in the Florida Keys. We're here to see ..."

"Ms. Mills!" A deep, strong voice came in from my left. I turned. He wasn't especially tall. Maybe five nine. He had thick, chestnut hair slicked back and bright brown eyes. The suit was Armani, probably several thousand dollars. I saw a flash of gold from his watch band as he extended a hand to shake Jeanie's.

"You're Keith?" she asked.

"Yes. Man, it's a pleasure, an honor to meet you, Ms. Mills," he said. It seemed genuine. I'd only seen Norman Slater in pictures. There was one Jeanie kept in a desk drawer that she didn't think I knew about. They were on the deck of a cruise ship together. She wore a flowing black dress and sandals. Young. Vibrant. Chic with an ahead-of-her-time, Liza Minnelli sort of style. Norman stood beside her, with an arm around her waist. This man, vigorously shaking her hand now, was his double. Norman's son, no doubt.

"Keith Slater," Jeanie said, confirming it. "I'd like to introduce you to Cass Leary. My law partner."

Keith Slater's eyes lit up. "I know you by reputation, of course. Thanks for meeting with me here. I figured it's better to meet outside of Delphi when we can for now. Come on, let's get you settled in the conference room."

Keith ushered us into conference room six. It was your standard, big law firm set-up with a giant round oak table, and law books lining one wall that nobody really used anymore. It had a nice view of the downtown area from the floor-to-ceiling windows. I took a seat and Jeanie sat beside me. Keith moved to the opposite side. We waved off his assistant when she came to offer us refreshments.

"So," Keith said as the door shut a final time, leaving the three of us alone. "I've heard from the clerk's office. We've got Detective Wray's arraignment and bail hearing moved up to the day after tomorrow. I've sent my initial discovery requests to your prosecutor, Rafe Johnson. You're welcome to convey all of that to him if you speak to him before I do."

"Wait," I said. "What? Have you already filed an appearance?"

Keith shot a glance toward Jeanie.

"I have," he said, not waiting for a reaction from her.

"You've been retained? When?"

"I met with my client late last night," Keith said. "Thank you for handling the logistics of getting Mr. Wray to the sheriff's department. I'll head down there myself in the morning."

"Detective Wray," I corrected him. They'd done this behind my back.

"Of course," Keith said.

"I'm sorry," I said. "I was under the impression that we came here to interview you, Mr. Slater."

"Cass," Jeanie said, with an edge to her tone.

"You're here as a potential witness," Keith interjected. "I know you're close with Mr. ... Detective Wray. But he has retained me to represent him in this case. I don't have to tell you how serious the charges against him are. He asked me to meet with you personally. We felt it best to set some ground rules going forward."

"He's handling me," I said. "You're handling me."

"He knew you'd try to take over," Keith said. "And he also understands how problematic that might be. You're a defense lawyer, Cass. From what I understand, a great one. There may come a time or two that I'll need to pick your brain. But you're a witness. So ..."

"Pick *my* brain?" I said. "I'm sorry. Keith ... is it? I've barely even heard of you. With all due respect, I know your father's reputation. And I'm very concerned you've gotten where you are by trading on it. Jeanie, I'm sorry. Eric needs someone who hasn't nepotized his way into a corner office."

He straightened. "I've been a lawyer longer than you have. And I've tried more criminal cases than you have. Certainly more murder cases. Though I will admit, the majority of my cases were in Florida. I've only recently moved back here to Michigan to join my father's practice. Actually, to take over my father's practice. You're welcome to look me up. I spent ten years in the Dade County Prosecutor's office. I spent another eight in a private defense firm. Forty-two murder trials. Nineteen of those were capital cases. You ever defended a man from death row, Ms. Leary?"

"You ever defended someone who matters to me?" I shot back.

"Cass," Jeanie said. "Eric teleconferenced with three lawyers I recommended. It was his choice to hire Keith."

I seethed. He never told me. He never even asked for my opinion.

"Now," Keith said. He took the green file folder we brought but didn't open it. He had a legal pad on the table and slid it closer. He clicked a pen open and poised it over the pad. "Tell me about the lunch you had with my client the afternoon Wendy Wray died."

"What did he say about it?" I asked.

"I'm asking you," Keith said. "I know you've already talked to Deputy Craddock about it outside the presence of counsel. I've seen his report. Now, I'd like to know what was said from your point of view."

I hated this. There was an accusation in Keith Slater's eyes. He was asking me what I might have said that made Eric's situation worse.

"I told him the truth," I said. "That Eric and I had plans to meet for lunch. Linda's Diner downtown. We ordered club sandwiches. In the middle of that, Eric got a call that something happened to Wendy."

"Did you tell Craddock about the texts you sent Eric during said lunch?" Keith asked.

"Did I ... No. He didn't ask me about texts. He just asked me where I was during the hours of eleven a.m. and one p.m. I told him."

"Good," Keith said abruptly.

"He'll see them anyway," I said. "Craddock has subpoenaed my phone records."

"I'm aware," he said. "You want to save me some time and just show them to me?"

I pulled out my phone, brought up my messaging thread with Eric, and handed it over.

Keith read at a furious pace, his eyes flicking back and forth as he scrolled upward, going earlier and earlier in the timeline. I knew there was nothing much to see. My texts with Eric were always short and to the point. He hated texting in general. Most of the time, we just made plans to meet and told each other if we were running late.

"Good," Keith said. "This is good. I'm not seeing anything here of a sexual nature."

My back went up. I felt violated, even as I knew these were necessary questions.

"You don't talk about Wendy," he said.

"No," I said. "We rarely did. Eric keeps ... kept most of that to himself."

"Sure," Keith said. "Kind of awkward to talk about the wife with the new girlfriend."

"Listen," I said. "I've always respected what's going on in Eric's life. There are boundaries where Wendy's been concerned."

"Eric and Wendy were barely living as a married couple years before Cass even moved back to Delphi," Jeanie chimed in. "If Eric's trying to be a gentleman, let me set the record straight. Wendy had been cheating on him for years before her accident. Years. The whole town knew it. But he never did. He stayed loyal to her. Eric Wray is one of the most honorable men I know. To a fault, if you ask me."

"Were you sleeping with him?" Keith leveled a hard stare at me.

I wanted to tell him to go to hell. I wanted to storm out of his office. At the same time, I knew why he wanted to push my buttons. Rafe Johnson would if he put me on the witness stand. Would I get angry? Would I crack? Would I do anything to make a jury hate me and by association, hate Eric?

"No," I said calmly. "Eric and I are close. I won't lie and say our relationship isn't romantic. We are more than friends. But no. Our relationship is not sexual."

"Is there anybody who can prove you're lying on that?"

"No," I said.

"He ever spend the night at your place?" Keith asked.

I squirmed a little. He noted it. "Yes. And I've spent the night at his."

"And left your car in the driveway overnight where his neighbors could notice," Keith said.

I breathed a little fire through my nostrils. "Yes."

Keith wrote something down on his legal pad, scratched his chin, then looked back up at me.

"Thanks for your candor," he said. "I expect I'll have a lot more questions before we're through. For now, I've got to get ready for Wray's bail hearing. So far, the prosecutor's office is planning to argue against it."

"Against bail?" Jeanie and I said it together. White heat shot through my chest.

"They can't be serious," I said. "Keith, this trial could take months. Eric's a cop. He cannot do time pending the outcome. He's not safe."

"All things I plan to bring up. My question to you though, if it comes down to it, is how likely is it he'll be able to meet his bond conditions if they're set? Can he afford it?"

"We'll find a way," Jeanie answered for me.

"Noted," Keith said. "Now, if you ladies will excuse me, I've got another meeting in a few minutes. I'm sure I don't have to tell you how important it is that you don't discuss this case with anyone. If the prosecutor reaches out to you, I need to know about it."

"You're right," I said. "You don't have to tell me. What you do have to tell me is what you're doing to prove Eric's innocent? Don't give me burden of proof crap. I'm not convinced what happened to Wendy was murder. But if it was, Eric didn't do it. So who did? Is that an avenue you're exploring?"

Keith Slater's eyes went cold. "I need to make something very clear. None of that is your business right now."

"Like hell," I said. Jeanie put an arm on me, but I shrugged her off.

"Cass, Eric is my client. You're going to have to respect that."

I rose. "Eric matters to me. And this is my town you're about to step foot in. You aren't going to win this without my help."

Keith's nostrils flared. "Well, you did warn me, Jeanie."

She looked away.

"You talk to me, not her," I said.

"Fine," Keith said. He met me nose to nose. "I'll lay this out. You're a liability right now. You go digging, it'll be noticed. And it'll make it that much harder in court to clean up after you. Eric may matter to you. And Delphi is your town. Conceded. But ... you're one thing more than anything else. Do you get that?"

"What?" I asked and was instantly sorry. His words would hit me like a blow to the chest. I knew it. I understood it. But when I heard them, I forgot how to breathe.

"You're Eric's prime motive for murder."

Chapter 7

NOTHING COULD HAVE PREPARED me for the sight of Eric as they led him into the courtroom in an orange jumpsuit and ankle chains. It cut through me. Even as the heavy metal clanked with each step he took, he kept his head high, his back straight.

I stayed in the back of the courtroom as Keith Slater had asked. It mattered that Eric knew I was there. Vangie sat on one side of me, Jeanie on the other. As Eric passed us, Vangie's hand shot out, gripping my knee. I stiffened, sending her a silent message to keep a hold of herself.

Keith waited for him at the defense table. Rafe Johnson, Woodbridge County's newly installed prosecutor, entered the courtroom practically sprinting to the front. He went straight to Keith and the two of them exchanged a quick handshake. Rafe gave Eric a grim nod, and as much as I wanted to gouge his eyes out, I recognized it as a sign of respect. Rafe had gotten to know Eric in our last murder trial together. I wanted to believe he didn't relish his job today.

A moment later, the bailiff called the courtroom to order. I rose and tried to keep my hands from shaking.

"I hate this," I whispered. "I want to do something."

"I know," Jeanie said. "Just hang in there, kiddo. This isn't your fault."

The office to the judge's chambers behind the bench opened. Bill Walden, interim District Court judge, stepped through.

"That," I said, "*is* my fault."

Bill Walden was one of the longest-practicing attorneys in Woodbridge County. He was two years from being aged out of running for a judgeship in his own right. When the last permanent District Court judge ended up in jail, I'd turned down the offer to replace him. Bill took the job instead.

Beneath his robes, I knew he wore an ill-fitting, wrinkled suit with a tie likely encrusted with this morning's scrambled eggs. He'd combed his unruly mop of white hair this morning, so that was at least something. "Do the right thing," I murmured.

"Okay, let's get this moving," Walden said. "I've got a full docket today."

Already I wanted to murder him. Detective Eric Wray's arraignment was big news. The highest profile case Walden would likely ever get his hands on. Also, everyone in the county assumed he'd lose that seat next year when the general election was held.

"People of the State of Michigan versus Eric Wray," he said. "Mr. Wray, you've been charged with one count of first-degree murder. Your plea has been entered. Our main order of business is bail. Mr. Johnson, let's hear your motion."

"Your Honor," Rafe started. "The state is asking that bail be denied in this case. The victim in question was a member of our most vulnerable population. She was killed in cold blood by a person we believe whose ultimate responsibility was to protect her. He was her patient advocate. So due to the nature of the crime and the flight risk the defendant poses, we'd like to see Mr. Wray bound over until trial."

"Flight risk?" Walden asked. Even in my mind, I had a hard time referring to him as 'the judge.'

"Mr. Wray, as the court knows, is a member of the law enforcement community. There have been a number of local fundraising efforts started for his defense. We've gotten word that one of these online efforts has resulted in some chatter about helping Mr. Wray skip town once he's out on bail."

My blood heated. I turned to Jeanie. She shrugged her ignorance on the topic. At the defense table, Eric leaned over and whispered something to Keith. He made a downward gesture with his hand, perhaps silencing him.

"You have proof on this?" Walden asked.

"Of course," Johnson said. He had a stack of papers in his hand. Even from here, I recognized them as screenshots. He walked over to Keith and handed them to him.

"What's he talking about?" Vangie whispered to me.

"I have no earthly clue," I answered.

Rafe brought a second copy of the papers to the bench after asking for permission to approach. Walden peered over his reading glasses and leafed through them. He shot a concerned glance at Eric as he set the papers down.

"Your Honor," Rafe continued, "As you can see, we've become aware of a clandestine, online effort to fund Mr. Wray's flight from the county if he's granted bail. This is disturbing, to say the least. Mr. Wray also has family out of state, so in addition to the means to leave, he has somewhere to go."

"Mr. Slater," Walden said. "You have anything to say about this?"

"We absolutely do." Keith rose. "This is the first my client and I are hearing about any online message board advocating his flight. Mr. Wray, as you know, is an upstanding member of this community. He's lived here his whole life. He has dedicated it to upholding the law, just as you and I have. We, of course, maintain that he is innocent of the crime he's charged with. You can't possibly hold him responsible for online rumblings that were neither incited nor endorsed by my client. Mr. Wray has never once run afoul of the law. He doesn't have so much as a parking ticket on his record. The idea that he poses a flight risk or that he's in some way not eligible for the consideration of reasonable bail is frankly ludicrous. Given the fact that Detective Wray has served with the Delphi P.D. for nearly twenty years, his safety in custody cannot be guaranteed. You know it. I know it. Mr. Johnson knows it. We respectfully request that bail be set at a reasonable amount pending the outcome of this case. It's the right thing to do."

Jeanie squeezed my hand. "I told you. He's good."

It didn't matter how good Keith Slater was. It only mattered how good Bill Walden was. In my numerous past dealings with him in this very courthouse, I was worried.

Walden let out a sigh. He flipped through the pages in front of him and rubbed a hand over his brow.

"He's putting on a damn show," I whispered. This hearing was getting some local press coverage. It would serve Walden to get his name out in public as much as possible ahead of his election.

"These documents are highly disturbing," he said. "I tend to agree with the prosecution that Mr. Wray could pose a significant flight risk."

No. This wasn't happening. This could not be happening.

"Your Honor!" Keith shouted, stunned, just as I was.

Walden banged his gavel. "Mr. Slater, I know you're new to my county. But the same courtroom decorum rules I assume you're familiar with in Wayne and Oakland County apply here. Now sit down as I issue my ruling. If I need to hear from you again, I'll ask."

Slater sat down hard. From my vantage point, I saw the tips of his ears turn purple. His anger made me feel better for about one second.

"As I was saying," Walden continued. "I find the state's argument on bail compelling. Therefore, I'm denying bail pending the outcome of this case. The defendant will remain in custody."

He banged his gavel a second time, shattering my heart with it.

Chapter 8

"THAT SON OF A ..." Jeanie started. At the front of the courtroom, Eric rose. Rafe Johnson turned and started to exit the courtroom. It was just a moment. A split second. But I saw the look of shock cross his face. As he strode through the gallery and out the doors, he didn't look my way.

Keith said something to the two sheriff's deputies sitting behind him. Whatever it was, it resulted in another handshake.

Eric rose and followed them. Like Johnson, he didn't look my way. Slater did.

"You can have a few minutes," he said to me. "The deputies are going to let me confer with Eric in the jury room next door. Five minutes. And I have to be present."

"Of course," I gushed. Heart racing, I followed Slater out, leaving Jeanie and Vangie in my wake.

I practically sprinted out of the courtroom. The deputies had already put Eric inside the jury room. They waited sentry as Keith held the door for me.

"Eric," I said, dry-throated.

He sat in a chair against the wall. His face a mask of stone.

Keith shut the door. "We'll appeal this," he said. "Walden's out of his mind."

"He's worse," I said. "He's campaigning from the bench. He knows damn well this will probably get picked up by some national news outlets. All press is good press as far as he's concerned. Only no press is bad."

"Cass," Eric said. "I need you to stop worrying about me."

"Right," I said. "Not happening."

"Like I said," Keith said. "I'll file an interlocutory appeal."

"Even if you win," I said, "that will take weeks. Months. You've been doing criminal work for a long time too. You know what happens to cops in jail."

"Keith?" Eric said. "Do you think you could wait outside for a few minutes? I want to talk to Cass alone."

Keith let out a grunt but nodded. "You've got about two minutes."

He opened the door and left us. I went to Eric. I knelt in front of him and put my hands on his knees. His scent had changed. An odd thing to notice, but the jumpsuit he wore, the chains, they had a foreign odor to them.

"I need you to do what Keith says," he said. "I trust him."

"Do you?" I asked. "Because …"

"Cass," he said. "I'm not going to get through this if I'm worried about you too."

"I'll worry enough for the both of us," I said. "I just need you to keep your head down in there. Please."

"I can take care of myself," he said. "It's going to be okay. Keith's good. What happened out there wasn't because of him. You're right about Walden."

"Well, thankfully Walden won't be the one presiding over your trial if it gets that far. And I have no intention of letting it get that far."

He looked up. "Cass … what are you planning?"

"The same thing you'd be planning if our roles were reversed. We both know you didn't kill Wendy. I'm not even entirely convinced she was killed at all. But that's Keith's angle to work. So far, you're not getting any help from Craddock or the sheriff's department. Have you heard anything from Delphi P.D.?"

His expression became pained. "Radio silence," he said. "I'm plutonium right now."

"Not to me," I said. "Eric, I'm going to find out who did this. I swear to God."

"I need you to stay out of trouble for once," he said.

"I know how to take care of myself too. I've proved it enough times, haven't I?"

"If Wendy was murdered," he said. "Then someone out there will fight to protect themselves. A killer, Cass. If I were out on bail, it might be different. I can't back you up from here. It's not safe. Let Keith hire someone."

I raised an eyebrow. Eric pursed his lips and shook his head in frustration.

"I'm better than some lousy P.I." I said.

"Cass, it's dangerous."

"I'm not going to let you rot in jail, Eric. Not happening. No chance."

"You're so freaking stubborn," he growled.

I smiled. "Yep. Lucky for you."

His lip curled into a smirk. I sat back on my heels.

"You already have a theory, don't you?" he said.

"More of a starting point. I want to talk to some of the people who work at Maple Valley. Someone has to have seen something. Why they're not talking to the police is what has me stymied."

"Promise me you'll be careful," he said. "God, I hate this. I *hate* this!"

"Me too," I said. "Just be glad I'm on your side."

He rolled his eyes. "Trust me, I remind myself of that just about every day."

A little of the old, sarcastic, infuriating Eric came through and it brightened my heart for the first time. Before I could say anything else, there was a soft knock on the door. Keith came back in.

"Time to wrap it up. They're going to take you back, Eric. Keep your head down. I'll work the appeal angle. I'll set up an appointment to visit you in a couple of days. We'll have a scheduling order and a timeline."

"Work with Cass," Eric said. "She's got some good ideas."

"Cass is a material witness," Keith said.

"She's also good at this," Eric said. "Trust me. I know. And she's the only person I trust completely. I need her. You need her."

Eric got to his feet. The deputies came back in.

Eric reached back and squeezed my hand. I squeezed back as hard as I could, knowing we might never be this close again for months. He kept his head high as the deputies led him back out into the hallway, his chains rattling behind him.

"Why do I think I'm going to grow to hate that look on your face?" Keith said when we were alone.

I smiled. I went up to him and lightly patted his cheek. "I think you might be catching on," I said. "Come on. We've got a lot to talk about. I have an idea."

I laughed after Keith's next words. "Why do I get the feeling when you say 'I have an idea' the people who love you know to take cover?"

"You *are* catching on," I said, holding the door open for him.

Chapter 9

THE FOLLOWING MONDAY MORNING, Keith Slater moved into the conference room adjacent to my office. He fought me on it at first. But it was the only suitable office real estate in Delphi for the moment.

"You don't come in here," he said, standing in the doorway as I sat at my desk. "I mean it. I cannot have you involved in my trial prep. Consider yourself walled off."

"Fine," I said. "That doesn't mean I can't do research of my own."

"Cass," he said with a tone of exasperation I engendered in a lot of people. Keith Slater was quickly learning how far that would get him with me.

"The phrase you're looking for is thank you," I said. "This is my town. You need me."

He shut the door to the conference room and came fully into my office. "It's a problem if you start making big waves with this case."

"Fine," I said. "So I'll make little ones. The problem you have is people in this town don't like outsiders. Half of them barely like insiders. You come at this head on, you're liable to get a lot of doors slammed in your face."

"And you won't?" he asked. "I know how to do homework too, Cass. You don't make a lot of friends with the people you defend. People idolized that murdered basketball coach. They never found his killer. You want to try convincing me people don't still hold that against you?"

I couldn't. He knew it. There were other secrets about that case that I could never tell him. That I could never tell anyone.

"I won't argue that point," I said. "But you of all people know how this game works. You're on the same side of the fence as I am. Were you the most popular kid in Fort Lauderdale or wherever it was you hung your shingle before this? Besides. If you know about my work on the Drozdowski murder, you know I'm an asset to you. Use me."

He gave me a charming smile. He was neatly dressed in a tailored dress shirt and tie. Shoes freshly polished. A splash of color with red socks that matched his tie.

"Oh yeah," he said. "You gonna tell me all your tricks, Leary?"

"I'll start with just one, Slater. The jury won't relate to you looking like that," I said, gesturing to his clothes. "Write down your sizes and I'll have my sister head over to the Suit Warehouse in Jackson and pick some things out for you that won't turn them off."

"The Suit Warehouse?" he said, wrinkling his nose. "I don't shop anyplace with the word warehouse in the title."

"Exactly," I said. "You walk in there with that kind of attitude, you'll have already lost a third of the jury on the down stroke."

Another exasperated sigh.

"That little tidbit is free. I might charge you for the next one. And I'm not kidding," I said, pushing a notepad and pen to the edge of my desk. "Write down your sizes."

I got a harrumph, but he did what I asked.

"You're already cooking something else up," he said. "Eric warned me you would."

"Maple Valley," I said. "I hope you've memorized the police report and supplementals by now."

"Of course," Slater said. He pulled a chair up at my desk.

"I find it strange that no one besides Wendy's charge nurse, treating physician, and two nurse's aides were questioned. Don't you?"

"It bothers me, yeah," he said. "But Eric's strongest defense is that Johnson can't actually *prove* he killed Wendy."

"I get that. But how hard did Craddock really try?" I asked.

"What's his story?" Slater asked. His frustration with me seemed to fall by the wayside. He sat at the edge of his seat now and gave me a different look. A hungry look. He'd put on his investigator hat.

About time.

"I don't know Craddock very well. Just by reputation. I've never actually gone to trial on one of his cases. This one's a bit of a coup for him. I mean that he's taking lead on it. Most of the time, there's a lot of coordination between Woodbridge County and Delphi P.D."

"Except this time, Delphi P.D. is the main suspect," he said.

"Right. So ... I'd try to crack him a little on cross-examination. Delphi P.D. is more elite. It's going to be a sensitive topic for him."

"Good," Slater said. "That's good."

"See? This is why you need to listen to me."

"You need to listen to me too," he clapped back. "Because, I gotta be honest, I know Rafe Johnson. I've tried a couple of cases against him."

"So have I," I said. "And won. How about you?"

Slater smiled. "Seventy/thirty. But you tried *one* case against him. I know how to get under his skin. That's one of the reasons Jeanie came to me in the first place. Did she tell you that?"

"She didn't," I said. "At the same time, I'll admit I wasn't really listening."

Slater laughed. "I appreciate your honesty."

"Good," I said. "Because I've got more of it for you. I want to talk to someone who works at Maple Valley. And I want to do it alone."

He frowned. "Who?"

"Friend of a friend," I said. "Tori, my associate, she's been cutting her teeth on estate planning and probate cases."

"Good strategy," he said. "She'll get experience in a little of everything that way."

"Yes. But ... she has a client she's working with who raised some questions about a family member's care out at Maple Valley."

"Is Tori here?" Slater asked.

I picked up my landline and buzzed Tori's office at the other end of the hall. A minute later, she came to join us.

"Have a seat," I said. "I was just telling Keith about your client. The one with a mother out at Maple Valley."

"Right," Tori said, seating herself beside Slater. "There was some concern that her mother's health started to deteriorate after placement there. She noticed bed sores. Her mom started refusing meals. There were other behavioral changes that seemed to begin shortly after her transfer from a facility down in Toledo."

"Wendy had signs of bed sores too," I said.

"That alone doesn't mean she got substandard care, Cass," Keith said. "I read the same report. There was no sign of infection. They were noted in her medical file. It was being addressed."

"So let Rafe argue that," I said.

"I'd like to talk to her," he said. "This client of yours. Could you arrange it?"

Tori shot me a look. "I can ask. Her mother has since passed away. She's still in pretty deep grief. I'm not sure she'll talk to you. She's afraid."

"Of what?" Keith asked.

"It's a messy probate," Tori said. "My client got a lot of heat for moving her mom out of the other facility. I think it's better if we ..."

"She won't talk to you," I said. "But she'll talk to Tori. More importantly, she'll get us in touch with a witness who might help. There's an aide who worked with her mom. She's no longer employed at Maple Valley."

"You two had this worked out between you already," he said. There was that exasperated facial expression again.

"You said you want everything run by you," I said. "Well, here's me running it by you. I'm telling you. These women will be more forthcoming if I'm the one asking the questions. They're both from the east side of the lake."

He screwed up his face. "And that means what?"

"It means they won't like your suit," I said, smiling.

"Great."

"Just let me field it first," I said. "If anything useful comes of it, I'll get them in here to talk to you. Promise."

"Thanks, Tori," Keith said, using a dismissive tone and waving her off. She looked a little shocked at his abruptness. So was I. But she rose and excused herself. As soon as she shut the door, I leveled a stare at Keith.

"Not a good look, counselor. Tori's younger than you and a woman. You just treated her like an underling."

"She is an underling," he said.

"Besides your suits, you could use a new attitude," I answered.

"Thanks for the input, I'll keep it in mind."

"Tori is better than both of us were at her stage in our careers. I guarantee it."

"Speak for yourself," he said.

"Okay ... she's better than you at that stage of your career. I was just being diplomatic. See how that works?"

"I knew this was a mistake," he said. "Look, I'm trying to keep a man out of prison for the rest of his life. You want to give me wardrobe and etiquette lessons for those with fragile egos. I don't have time for this."

"What I want to do is make sure you don't trip over your own two feet while trying to keep someone I care about more than you out of prison for the rest of his life. I need you to be perfect. Eric needs you to be perfect."

"I can't keep having this same argument with you," he said.

"Not arguing."

He grimaced and let out a low noise from the back of his throat.

"Truce," I said. "Let me make a couple of phone calls. See if I can convince Tori's client to come in for a formal interview. I'm certain the cops haven't talked to her yet. You show up on her doorstep, it'll take maybe five minutes before her neighbors notice and tell another neighbor and within an hour, Craddock will know."

"How small is this town?" he asked.

"Tiny. That's going to be your best or worst asset, depending on how you play it."

"And you're the one who can teach me the rules?"

I tapped my temple. "Exactly."

"One phone call," he said.

I saluted. Keith shook his head and went back through the conference room door. He shut it hard enough to make the frame shake. I grabbed a sticky note off the desk. Tori had given it to me an hour before I mentioned a word to Keith. Using my landline, I dialed the number.

Chapter 10

THE FOLLOWING FRIDAY, Tori and I drove to Allen Park to
meet Audra Kaminski, a former nurse's aide who had worked
at Maple Valley. We'd gotten her name from Tori's client,
Ellie Palmer. Audra waited for us in a small park near a creek.
We found her sitting on a green bench with badly chipped
paint, chain smoking. She kept a Styrofoam cup beside her
where she dropped her butts.

She was young, maybe twenty-two, twenty-three, with thin
blonde hair she pulled into a ponytail half hidden by a
baseball cap. "Audra?" Tori said. "I'm Tori. The one you
talked to on the phone. This is my boss, Cass Leary. We're
really glad you agreed to meet with us."

"My grandma lives in that neighborhood over there," she said.
"I told her I went for a walk. I can't stay out here very long.
My grandma has Alzheimer's. She's actually the reason I
became a nurse's aide."

"Thank you," I said. I sat on the opposite end of the bench.
Tori leaned against the cement garbage can frame.

"Audra, I won't take up much of your time. You know why I'm interested in talking to you?"

"Yeah," she said, snuffing out another cigarette butt. "Sorry. I can't smoke in the house. There's oxygen."

"It's fine," I said.

She exhaled and waved away a plume of smoke. "Ellie Palmer told you why I left Maple Valley?"

"Yes."

"Do you think you might be able to help me with that?" she asked. Tori and I exchanged a look.

"Do you think you were wrongfully terminated?" I asked.

"There's something called Whistleblower's Protection, isn't there? I googled a little bit."

"Yes," I said. "If you tried to report a crime and your employer fired you because of it. Is that what happened?"

"I don't know," she said. "That is, I don't know if it was a crime."

"Why don't you tell me exactly what did happen?" I asked.

"Medicare fraud," she said. "One of the nurses who trained me, she was fudging a lot of the patient records and charge notes based on what Medicare would pay out. I saw some other stuff."

"What kind of stuff?" I said. Though the allegations about insurance fraud were alarming enough, I wasn't sure what help that would be for Eric's case.

Audra got quiet.

"Audra," Tori said. "Ellie thinks you might have information about mistreatment of patients. Specifically her mom, but she said you also mentioned concerns you had with other patients."

"They were rough," she said. "A couple of male nurse's aides in particular. The way they handled some of the more disabled patients. Like they were slabs of meat, not human beings."

"Did you notice any injuries to patients as a result of this mistreatment?" I asked.

"Yeah. Ellie's mom got dropped when they were trying to transfer her onto a gurney so they could take her for some scans. They never took an official incident report. I saw it happen. I tried to say something to the head nurse, but she just kind of blew me off. After that, I got treated different. Got written up for petty stuff."

"Can you tell me the name of this nurse?" I asked.

"I don't know if I want to go that far," she said. "I'm not looking to get anyone else fired or in legal trouble. I have to work. I need to keep a good reference from Maple Valley."

If there was anything to Audra's concerns, I could see getting her to go on record would be a problem. I'd have to find another way to skin the cat.

"Audra," I said. "You might not have to talk to anyone outside of the two of us. Let me be clear. There is a man accused of killing a patient at Maple Valley. If he's convicted of it, he'll spend the rest of his life in prison. No possibility of parole. I believe he's innocent. I believe something else happened at Maple Valley, and I'm determined to find out what. You're telling me you suspect some of the staff at Maple Valley provided negligent patient care. I'd like to get to the root of that. Other than Ellie Palmer's mother, are there other patients you have suspicions about?"

"It wouldn't surprise me," she said. "Like I said, I witnessed aides making a joke out of dropping Ellie's mom. It got covered up. I was told to stay out of it."

"Do you think Ellie's mother died as a result of improper care?" Tori asked. "Ellie implied that might be the case."

Audra fumbled with her next cigarette. "I think she was in better shape before she was at Maple Valley. Ellie thinks so too. I saw a few patients go downhill after they came to Maple Valley. I think the atmosphere there was toxic. And I think that matters. That toxicity was in the air. I don't care how gone you think someone is. They're human. You have no idea what they see and hear. If you treat them like things, they know. On some level, they know. And they give up on themselves if you give up on them. I've seen it happen. Beds are dollar signs to the people that run Maple Valley. That's it."

"Did you ever provide care to Wendy Wray?" I asked.

She looked down. "Not directly, no. She was in a different wing to where I was assigned."

"But you knew of her," I asked.

"I did. She was talked about a lot by other staff members. She was one of the youngest patients we had. And everyone knew the circumstances around how she ended up like that. It was sad. Like soap opera sad. So, it got talked about. And also ..."

Audra's face went very still.

"Also what?" I asked. "Please. Any light you can shed on the kind of care Wendy Wray received."

"It was gross, okay? The way some of the male aides talked about her."

"Do you mean the same ones who you saw dropping Ellie Palmer's mother?" Tori beat me to the question.

"Yes," Audra said. "Wendy was young. That was the difference. Most of the people in that place in her condition are old. Those guys had a running joke. She was the hot girl."

I felt the bile rise in my stomach. "Audra, do you have any reason to believe Wendy Wray was at risk of sexual assault from someone at Maple Valley?"

"Look, I don't know for sure. I just know how they talked about her in the break room and stuff when they didn't think anyone else could hear. That place, Maple Valley. Everyone raves about it like it's the gold standard. The best care. The best doctors. If you're rich in Delphi or one of the nearest towns, you send your people to Maple Valley Rehab. I just didn't agree with that. I wouldn't send my grandmother there. Not after what I saw."

"Their names," I said, trying to keep my anger in check.

"I don't know."

"Audra, if you suspect there are patients at Maple Valley who are at risk of abuse or neglect, it's your duty to say something. I can help protect you. Besides, you don't work there anymore. You don't have to be afraid of anything they can do to you."

"But I can't prove it," she said. "That's the thing. Yes. I can tell you what I saw when they dropped Ellie's mom. But that happens sometimes. They'll say it was an accident."

"If there was an accident," Tori said, "there should have been an incident report filed. I've reviewed Mary Palmer's medical files in depth. There's no mention of anything like that. If the staff at Maple Valley is in the habit of covering up stuff like that, it needs to be brought to light."

"It'll be their word against mine," Audra said.

She wasn't wrong. At the same time, this way lay the path toward reasonable doubt for Eric. As disgusted as I was, I felt a familiar buzzing in my brain I only got when I felt close to making a breakthrough in a case.

"The orderlies," I repeated. "Will you give me their names? Do you know if they're still on staff at Maple Valley?"

"Hector Ruiz," she said. "The other was Wayne Warren. I don't know for sure if they're both still there. The incident I'm talking about happened over a year ago. The turnover is pretty high."

"Do you know why that is?" I asked.

"A lot of them work as temps. They get hired in on a permanent basis at other places."

I took a pad of paper out of my bag. I had a pen clipped to it and handed it to Audra.

"Please," I said. "It would help if you wrote those names down. Do you know who was assigned to Wendy Wray's wing when you worked there?"

"I know some of them," she said. "Again, I can't say for sure who still works there. It's been four months since I left."

"It's okay," I said. "It's a place for me to start. That's all I'm asking for."

"Wayne and Hector don't belong working with patients," she said. "That doesn't mean I think either one of them are capable of actually murdering someone."

"That's for me to worry about," I said. "You're doing the right thing."

"Do you think it'll help Ellie?" she asked. "Do you think she might be able to get some money from them for what they did to her mom?"

"It's hard to say," Tori answered.

"She doesn't want to go after them," Audra said. "She's afraid of the rest of her family."

Audra finished writing her list of names. She handed the pad of paper back to me. It was sparse. She'd written Wayne Warren and Hector Ruiz. She wrote down the charge nurse, Kim Crane, and three other nurse's aides she believed worked in the wing where Wendy Wray was. Gloria LaPlante, Travis Mateese, and Olivia Corey. I knew Travis Mateese had already been interviewed by Craddock. He claimed not to have been on duty the day Wendy died. The other names matched what I'd seen from Craddock's report for the most part.

"He was good to her," Audra said. "I know that much."

"Who was?" Tori asked as I slipped the notepad back into my bag.

"Her husband," Audra explained. "Wendy Wray's husband. He came to see her every week. Then it dwindled to every month. That's another thing that used to make the gossip table in the break room. We thought it was cool that he hadn't given up on her. It was so sad, though. Good-looking guy like that. Not just good-looking. Like, really handsome. Rugged. A bunch of the other girls had a crush on him. He was always so nice and polite too. A wink and a smile for anybody."

"That's Eric." I smiled.

"There were two nurses in particular who used to practically throw themselves at that guy when he came around. I'll admit, it got my blood pumping a little faster when he showed up. It's just hard to believe he would do anything to Wendy. Except ... it had to be really hard on him. She was never going to wake up. It just didn't seem fair."

"No," I said. "Not fair at all."

Audra snuffed out another cigarette. This time, she picked up her Styrofoam cup, rose, and tossed it in the nearby trash.

"I've gotta get back to my grandma."

"Thank you," I said. "You've been helpful."

I handed her my card. "If you think of anything else, please give me a call. That's my private cell phone number."

"Sure," she said. Audra cocked her head to the side. "Only ... well ... never mind."

"Never mind what?" Tori asked.

Audra shrugged. "You never asked me what I think."

"What you think about what?" I took the bait.

"Whether I think Wendy Wray's husband could have been the one who offed her."

I froze, afraid to take a breath.

"No," I said. "I suppose I didn't."

"It was killing him to see her like that. She was gone, Ms. Leary. Totally gone. I hate the term, but Wendy was a vegetable. And that man of hers deserved to be able to get on with his life. Seeing her suffer like that and be in that state had to have really worn him down over the years."

Tori caught my eye. She gave me a nearly imperceptible head shake that told me she was thinking the same thing as I was.

Audra Kaminski might do far more harm than good if Slater ever tried to put her on the stand.

Chapter 11

"You HAVE to put her on the stand anyway," I said. A few weeks after my clandestine park meeting with Audra Kaminski, we'd hit a dead end with the staff at Maple Valley. Slater had interviewed Kim Crane, the charge nurse, and aides Gloria LaPlante and Olivia Corey. They would all make solid witnesses for the prosecution so far. The two male aides Audra mentioned were proving more difficult to pin down. Neither of them worked for Maple Valley anymore. One of them, Hector Ruiz, worked his last day two weeks before Wendy's death. I had Jeanie working on tracking him down, anyway.

The other, Wayne Warren, had my warning bells going off. He'd worked the day of Wendy's death, though in an entirely separate wing. There was no record of him in any of her chart notes that day. When questioned by Craddock, he claimed he saw nothing and heard nothing. None of that was remarkable except for one thing.

"Wayne Warren quit Maple Valley the week after Wendy died," I said. "Why?"

Slater shrugged. "Turnover can be high in those places. Nobody claims to have seen Wayne anywhere near Wendy."

"I still think you should talk to him," I said. "It's just odd. Audra says he and Ruiz have an unhealthy obsession with Wendy. Then he just up and quits within a few days of her mysterious death? At the very least, you put him on the stand and let the jury ponder it."

"Audra's a problem. She thinks Eric's guilty," Slater said. He'd made himself comfortable at the conference table with his hands behind his head and his feet up. I considered it a marked improvement over the constant stick up his rear he'd walked around with since moving to Delphi.

"Technically, she didn't say she thinks he killed Wendy. She hinted she would understand if he did. There's a difference."

Slater had a tablet sitting next to him. He slid it across the table toward me.

"It's more than that," he said. "Rafe Johnson will tear her a new one in about ten seconds. She's got a history of being a troublemaker. I had my investigator do some deep background work on her."

I picked up the tablet. He had it opened to a PDF file. The document bore the letterhead of the one of the lower Michigan Big Boy franchises. I quickly scanned the scrawling cursive writing written in various blanks on the document.

"Are you serious about this? She was written up when she was a busser at sixteen years old?"

"For stealing," Slater said.

I looked back at the document. "Jelly Bellies. You have to be kidding me. She was accused of stealing candy from the counter at the hostess station."

"And fired for it," he said. "Keep reading."

I did. The next entry was another personnel record from a Sunoco gas station where Audra worked while going to community college.

"Perpetual tardiness," I said, then set the tablet down.

"There's a pattern, Cass. This woman has left every job she's ever had under bad circumstances."

"Jelly Bellies," I said. "This is a murder trial, Slater."

"If I'm Rafe Johnson, I make the case she's a disgruntled ex-employee. An immature narcissist who thinks every time life gets hard, it's someone else's fault. I can't call her if we don't get corroboration on these two orderlies and the incident with Ellie Palmer's mom. I know you know that."

I did. And I hated it.

"She can be rehabbed," I said. "And you're not trying to prove Ellie's mother was mistreated. You're only trying to raise reasonable doubt. You've got an employee who can talk about corners being cut when it came to patient care. And you've got two orderlies who were expressing pretty disturbing thoughts about Wendy Wray specifically. You have to use that. You have to get the jury to at least hear it."

"I need more," he said. "A whole lot more. As much as I hate the prospect, I need you to do something for me."

I tilted my head. "Solve your case for you?"

He lifted his feet from the table. "I need you to take that Leary brain of yours and figure out what was going on with Eric and Wendy's family."

"Your client should be telling you that," I said.

Slater pursed his lips. "He won't go there."

My heart dropped. "He's stubborn," I said. "He thinks he's still got to protect Wendy."

"He's on trial for the rest of his life. Wendy no longer needs protecting."

"It's how he's wired," I said. "As much as it frustrates things, it's one of his best qualities."

"Will you try talking some sense into him?" he asked.

I smiled. "Yes."

"And I need to take a look at Wendy's probate file."

I had my leather bag on the floor next to me. Smiling, I pulled out a thick accordion file. Tori had just secured the thing for me late yesterday afternoon from the courthouse. I hadn't yet had a chance to dig into it. I lobbed the thing on the table.

"Where did you get that?" Slater asked once he realized what it was.

"Tori ordered it from the clerk," I said.

"Some of that is supposed to be sealed," he said. "My investigator was working on getting it. I figured there was more to what Eric was saying."

I folded my hands in my lap and said nothing. Slater knew better than to ask me his next obvious question.

"Make me a copy," he said.

I reached back in my bag and pulled out a second file. I slid it across the table.

"You shouldn't have that," he said.

"And you just asked me to dig into it. I know these people. They've lived in and around my town their whole lives."

He shook his head. "It's better I don't know the details."

"Agreed. Now, I've got work to do. Why don't you make arrangements with the jail to get me in to see Eric in the next day or two? I want to know this file inside and out before I do."

"You sure about that?" he asked. "You might find some things you don't like."

"Eric didn't keep secrets from me," I said. "He didn't like to talk about Wendy, but that's not the same thing as keeping secrets. I respected his relationship with her. Always. Our situation was unique, granted, but I never begrudged him his time with her. Or their past."

"Sure," Slater said, but without a trace of sarcasm.

I picked up my copy of the file and gathered the rest of my things. "It looks like I've got my afternoon planned. If you need me, I'll be in my cave on the other side of this door."

Slater gave me a weak smile. "Thanks, Cass," he said, and it felt genuine.

When I left him, I found Jeanie walking into my office from the other door. I closed the conference room door and set the file down on the desk.

"How much of that did you hear?" I asked.

"Enough," she said. "This is hard for both of you."

"Which both of us?" I asked as I pulled up my chair and started pulling court documents from the file.

"Good point," she said. "Right now I'm talking about you and Keith. Neither of you are used to group projects. You're a couple of hopeless control freaks. I'm glad he's starting to recognize he needs you. And you need him."

She smiled at the last sentence. I gave her a growl in response. Jeanie laughed and closed the door behind her.

I started leafing through the court files and realized something else. I was wrong. Eric had been keeping secrets. Big ones.

Chapter 12

WENDY'S PROBATE file was opened two weeks after she was admitted to the hospital. Eric had requested he be appointed her legal guardian. This all went down almost a year before I came back to Delphi. I paged through the documents chronologically.

It was standard fare, though the circumstances surrounding Eric's petition were heartbreaking. As required by law, Eric had submitted affidavits from several doctors involved in Wendy's care. One by one, they painted a bleak picture of Wendy's prognosis.

Persistent vegetative state. No meaningful brain activity. Poor chance of ever regaining consciousness or the ability to make decisions for herself.

At the time Wendy Wray hit that telephone pole going nearly eighty miles an hour, she had been just thirty-seven years old.

Eric and Wendy had done no estate planning prior to the accident. He was her next of kin, but had no advanced directives appointing him as her patient advocate when she was still healthy. It wasn't uncommon in people that young. We put off the things we don't want to think about. Everyone thinks these are things you should worry about when you're old. And we shouldn't.

I'd advised hundreds of clients over the years, warning them not to put these things off because you just never know. I had a spiel I knew by heart.

"Think of it as a gift you can give to your loved ones, rather than something negative. If you plan properly, if you make your wishes known now, then the people who love you will have one less thing to worry about in what may be a very difficult time."

Family Court Judge Moira Pierce had granted Eric's petition and made him Wendy's legal guardian and conservator. It gave him the authority to make decisions on her medical care as well as handle all of her finances.

It went well. Nothing of note for over two years. Eric filed all of his annual accountings on time. I saw no attorney of record. He had represented himself. There was just a stamp on the bottom of all of his documents showing he'd procured the forms from a local pro bono legal clinic.

The trouble started eight months ago. Cam and Dar Maloney filed a petition objecting to Eric's last final accounting.

Tori walked into my office and shut the door.

"Slater asked me to see how your progress was going."

"Have a seat," I said. I handed her the Maloneys' petition. Tori looked it over.

"This looks frivolous," she said. "Eric wasn't even asking for reasonable compensation for managing the estate."

A few weeks later, the Maloneys filed a second petition. My stomach churned as I read the factual background their lawyer had submitted.

"Eric wanted to move Wendy out of Maple Valley and into hospice care," I said. "He'd consented to the removal of her feeding tube."

Tori took the file from me and read. "Geez," she said. "How awful. There's a report from a Dr. Wilkins recommending it. He was her treating doctor. Cass, I know him. He's got a stellar reputation."

"Two more reports from neurologists," I said, sliding those reports to Tori.

"They recommended palliative care," she said. "She was starting to decompensate."

"Cam and Dar wanted Eric removed as her legal guardian," I said. "They got a second opinion from a Dr. McNulty. I've never heard of him. Looks like he practices in Cleveland."

Tori picked up her phone and did a quick browser search. "Lyman McNulty. He's another neurologist. Has privileges at the Cleveland Clinic, among others. Oh ..."

"What?" I asked.

"He routinely testifies in right-to-life cases," she said. "Cass, there's a reference here to a video McNulty took during one of the Maloneys' visits with their daughter. Is that in the file?"

I thumbed through more pages. Sure enough, stapled to the exhibits was a DVD.

"Oh boy," Tori said. She extended her hand. I put the DVD in it. She walked over to the side table against the wall. I kept a small player there for things like this.

Tori popped the DVD in. After a few moments of static, the video started in Wendy's hospital room. She sat up in bed, leaning heavily to the right. My eyes stung with tears as I watched.

I hadn't seen Wendy since she'd been admitted to Maple Valley. I hadn't seen her since I was maybe seventeen years old. She was beautiful still. Thick dark hair pulled into a loose ponytail. Someone had braided a pink ribbon through it.

"Hi, baby," a female voice said. Then Dar Maloney stepped into the camera frame. She had her phone in her hand.

"This one's your favorite," Dar said. She placed earbuds in Wendy's ears. Wendy stared up at the ceiling, her lips slightly parted. Her blue eyes darted back and forth but didn't seem to focus on any one thing.

Dar showed her phone to the camera and selected a song from her playlist. Moonlight Sonata. She hit play.

It took about thirty seconds, then Wendy began to coo. Her eyes flicked back and forth.

"It certainly *looks* like she's responding," Tori said.

I looked back at the probate filings. Eric had filed a response to the petition. Again, no lawyer of record. He'd written the thing himself. He referred heavily to Dr. Wilkins's report. The doctor insisted that despite the heavily edited video filed in support of the Maloneys' petition, Wendy Wray's diagnosis and prognosis, in his opinion, remained unchanged.

"Was there a final ruling?" Tori asked.

I kept reading.

"A second evidentiary hearing was held a few months ago. Basically, both parties reiterated their same arguments. At one point, it looks like Judge Pierce advised Eric to get a lawyer. Doesn't look like he did."

"He didn't tell you any of this was going on?" Tori asked. "Don't you think that's odd? He knows what I've been working on. Why wouldn't he at least make a phone call and ask for my opinion?"

"I don't know," I said.

I reached the final page in the file. Judge Pierce issued a ruling on the Maloneys' petition.

Tori waited, then stepped to the side of my desk and read over my shoulder.

"Petitioner's request is granted in part, denied in part," she said. "Pierce kept Eric on as Wendy's guardian."

I looked up. "But she also blocked Eric's request to have her moved into hospice and remove her feeding tube," I said.

Tori sucked her breath in. "Ugh. That doesn't look good. When did Pierce make that ruling?"

I closed my eyes and gripped the arms of my chair. "Two weeks before Wendy died."

I hadn't heard the door open to the conference room. I hadn't realized Keith Slater stood behind me until he spoke.

"Dammit," he said. "That looks awful."

"You didn't know?" I asked. "He didn't tell you?"

"It's becoming pretty clear that my client is keeping too many things from the both of us. If you can't talk some sense into him, consider me off this case."

Chapter 13

A week later, I had permission to visit Eric at the Woodbridge County Jail. A frequent flyer as a defense lawyer, most of the C.O.s knew me. I expected to meet him in one of the rooms reserved for lawyer/client meetings. Instead, they brought me into the common room.

A dozen cubicles separated the center of the wall. Inmates on one side of the glass, visitors on the other.

"Third one down from the wall," the officer told me. "You'll have ten minutes."

"I was under the impression ..."

"You'll have ten minutes," he abruptly repeated.

Despite the glass partition, I'd left my messenger bag, purse, and phone in a locker outside. Straightening my back, I went down the row past the other visitors and inmates. When I got to the third seat from the wall, I saw no one on the other side of the glass.

Would he blow me off?

I took a seat and waited. Then waited some more.

Finally, the steel door opened on the other side of the room and Eric walked in. My throat went dry, and I focused on finding a smile.

He'd lost weight. Dark shadows framed his eyes. He shuffled forward, casting a mean glance back at the C.O. who ushered him in. He set his jaw into a hard line as he made eye contact with me, then lowered himself into the chair.

Something was wrong. His movements were stiff and awkward as he sat down. He favored his left side.

I picked up the phone and waited for him to do the same.

"Hey," I said.

He lifted his chin. "Hey."

"I won't ask you if you're okay. I can see that you're not. Tell me what happened."

Eric shrugged. At least he tried to. The motion caused him to wince.

"You're hurt," I whispered, leaning far forward in my seat. "Eric, what happened?"

"I fell," he said. "Nothing to worry about. Bunk's not very comfortable. I'll get used to it."

It was a lie. Alarm bells went off inside my whole body. Other than the outcome of his case, this was the thing I feared the most.

Eric Wray was a career detective. It made him a prime target inside.

"Eric, you have to level with me. Or at least with Slater. If you're in trouble, we can work on getting you moved."

Eric gave me a sad look that tore at me. "Cass, I'm handling it. There's nothing you and Slater could do that won't make it worse. You're going to have to trust me on this one."

"Eric ..."

He put a hand up. "Please. Tell me what's going on with you. It's good to see you."

"Good to ... what's going on ..." I took a breath. "You're the only thing that's going on with me. And I'm worried sick about you."

He smiled. "I miss you."

"I miss you too."

"But you've got that look in your eye," he said. "You're holding back a rant. So let's have it. Hit me with both barrels."

There was mirth in his eyes. This man made me want to laugh and scream all at the same time. I centered myself, gripping the phone tighter.

"Why didn't you tell me what was going on with Wendy's family? They took you to probate court. I would have helped you."

The weary lines in Eric's face seemed to deepen. "And that's exactly why I didn't tell you. Because you would have wanted to help me."

"Is that so bad?" I asked. "I do happen to know what I'm doing."

"I know. But I've been dealing with Dar and Cam for years. None of this was new. The only thing new was that they filed court documents."

"You didn't talk to Slater about it either," I said.

"Yes, I did."

"He said you told him there was some tension with the Maloneys, not a court action. It was stupid, Eric. Did you expect it wouldn't come out? That Rafe Johnson wasn't going to make it a centerpiece of his case against you?"

"It was nothing," Eric said. "They got bad advice from some shyster out of Cleveland who makes his living going on televangelist shows. It's not the first time. It's partly my fault. I've indulged it over the years. She's ... she was their daughter. Every other month, Dar had some new-age remedy she wanted to try to cure Wendy."

"It wasn't nothing," I said. "They accused you of breaching your fiduciary duties. They were trying to have you removed as her guardian."

He squeezed the bridge of his nose. "It's complicated, all right? My relationship with the Maloneys wasn't great even before Wendy's accident. I loved them. Don't get me wrong. And they were good in-laws. Always supportive of both of us. But Wendy was their angel. I don't begrudge them that. They just didn't know how to tell her no when she was healthy. That didn't change after Wendy's accident. I had to be the one grounded in reality. That's the source of the tension. That's it."

"I'm sorry," I said. "That must have been very hard for you. And you were going through all of that and never talked about it."

"It's not your fault," he said. "And it wasn't a problem you had to fix, Cass."

There was that word again. The Fixer. It must have made me smile. Eric touched his hand to the glass.

"What's funny?" he asked.

"You sound like Jeanie," I admitted. "She says that's my fatal flaw. Always trying to fix everything."

He laughed and gave me the first easy smile since we sat down. "She knows you pretty well, I'd say."

We got quiet. The seconds ticked by. I didn't know how much time we had left. Not enough. Not nearly enough.

"I wish you hadn't come," he said. "I don't like seeing you sad."

"Tough," I said. "I get to be sad. I get to care about you. And I get to be mad at you that you keep doing things that don't help. You want to call me out for trying to fix everything; it goes both ways. Quit trying to protect Wendy. And quit trying to protect me. It's going to get in the way of your defense."

My words hurt him. I hated that. But he had to hear it.

"So that's why Slater let you come here," he said.

"And when have you known me to wait for people to let me do something I want to do?"

Eric shook his head. I missed him. I missed that frustrated look he'd get when I was winning an argument.

"Eric," I said. "You've hired Keith Slater to help you. As much as it pains me to admit it, he might possibly be in the realm of as good at this as I am. On my bad day."

I winked. Eric's smile broadened.

"You can't keep things from him," I said. "I get it. Talking to me about a lot of this is awkward. We never came out and laid ground rules where Wendy was concerned ..."

"Haven't we?" he asked. "Cass, whether we talked openly about it or not, Wendy's existence has framed our entire relationship."

"You weren't cheating on her," I said. "You would have had every right. Even before her accident, she was planning to divorce you. She was openly seeing Owen Corbett. And he allied himself with the Maloneys. It's going to get very ugly if this goes to trial."

"If?" he asked.

"If," I said. "Craddock has made too many mistakes, as far as I'm concerned. The last thing Rafe Johnson wants to do is take this thing to a jury if it's weak. He's still building his reputation in this town."

Eric snorted. "Seems like there are a lot of people willing to use Wendy's death to build their reputation."

"Walden," I said. "He's a weasel. Slater's not done working your appeal on the bail issue. It's ludicrous. And it's also why you have to level with us about what's going on with you in here."

"Leave it," he snapped.

"No," I said. "I will not. You want to try to convince me if you lifted your shirt right now, I wouldn't find you black and blue? You got jumped, didn't you?"

"Cass," he said through tight lips. "I'm telling you. Leave it. I know you think you're helping, but you're not. You have to let me take care of things my way."

My fear bubbled to anger. I wanted to bash him in the head with the phone receiver, hoping it might knock some sense into him.

"Your way," I said. "Eric, your way is what probably got you into this mess. You cannot keep any more secrets. You cannot think you know better than the rest of us. On this point, you don't."

"They're going to put you on the stand," he said. "You get that, right?"

I expected him to argue with me in a different way. I searched his face. Slowly, finally, the root of his fear dawned on me.

"Eric," I said. "You think I'm going to hurt your case."

He slowly closed his eyes. When he opened them, his face was softer. "No. Not on purpose. No."

We grew silent. I jumped when I felt a tap on my shoulder.

"Two minutes," the guard said. "Wrap it up."

I waited for him to move down the row. "They can't," I said. "If it comes down to it, they can't make me testify. We have a personal relationship, yes. But we also have a professional one." In my mind, I saw the dollar bill I kept taped to the side of my refrigerator. My retainer. I made Eric pay me years ago when I pieced together the biggest secret he kept.

Three years ago, when he found out another man had hurt Wendy and other victims in unspeakable ways, he had ended his life. He had kept that man from hurting anyone else. He had killed before.

"Cass," he said.

"I mean it," I said. "I can refuse to testify. I have grounds. I can claim privilege."

"And then what?" he asked. "Because Johnson will put you on the stand. Slater can't prevent that. Rafe will use that crap as theatre. He'll ask you a question and let the jury hear you evade it. We both know how that will go over."

He was right. The only saving grace was that no one, not another living soul, knew for sure what I knew about Eric. And no one ever would. I'd taken an oath. I meant to keep it.

"Cass," he said. "You do what you have to do. Promise me that much."

"What do you mean?"

"If ... when Rafe Johnson puts you on the stand, tell the truth. Tell them everything if you have to. Don't lie for me. Don't do anything that would come back to haunt you. I'd rather spend the rest of my life in here than bring anyone else I cared about down with me. Do you understand me?"

I shivered, though not from the cold.

"I've never lied in court before," I said. "I don't plan to start now. But there are things Johnson can't ask me about. You're close to me. He knows that. Nobody will think twice about the fact that you've asked me for legal help before. There's nothing wrong with that. You keep saying you want me to trust that you can handle things your way. That's a two-way street. I can handle Rafe Johnson."

"That's my point, Cass; I don't want you to try handling him for me."

I slapped a hand on the table in frustration. "You sound like you're giving up."

His nostrils flared as he let out a sigh. "No. I'm being pragmatic. And I'm done watching other people suffer for my mistakes. That's all."

"Eric ..."

"Time's up!" the guard called out.

"See ya later, Cass," Eric said, smiling.

"Eric," I whispered as he started to shift in his seat. He leaned forward and put his hand flat on the glass. My heart twisted as I touched mine to it. Fingertip to fingertip, with an inch-thick wall between us.

"Don't come back here," he said. "I don't want you to see me in this place again."

Before I could protest, Eric put his phone back on the hook. He knocked his knuckles once on the table and another guard came to take him away.

I waited, unable to make my feet move. I was still holding my own phone receiver as they led Eric out of my view.

I knew what he thought. I'd been avoiding it in my head the whole time. Despite everything I might try or do, Rafe Johnson was about to use me as a weapon against Eric. And he might just draw blood.

Chapter 14

NINETY DAYS Judge Castor had scheduled Eric's trial to begin on March 2nd of next year. Ninety days from now. Keith Slater marked the occasion by installing a deadbolt on my conference room door, keeping me out.

"You're lucky I'm letting you work from your office at all," he said when I pounded on the door, demanding his attention.

"I pay your rent," I said. "I own the building."

"And if I'd have known that when I set up shop here, I never would have," he said, hands on hips, staring me down. "I can't risk you accidentally walking in here and having a look at my work product, Cass."

"So you're building a literal wall?" I asked. "I spent over a decade in corporate law, Slater, I know my ethical boundaries."

He eyed me with suspicion, but apparently thought the better of challenging my statement.

"Your testimony is going to be problematic enough. I'm not giving Rafe Johnson more ammo to impeach you on the stand. When he asks, and he will, you'll be able to say you have been figuratively and literally barred from anything to do with Eric's actual case file. I can't stop you from rooting around in public records at the probate court, or helping one of your associates on whatever cases she's got, but I can damn well keep you out of my office."

I was in a mood to argue more. But we both knew I lacked the grounds. His next point would likely be that I'd do the same if our roles were reversed. And he would be right.

"My testimony isn't going to be problematic," I said, maybe trying to convince myself more than him.

"Great," he said. "Glad you feel that way. I was just about to ask you to clear your schedule for the rest of the afternoon. We need to go over it. Jeanie's letting me use her office. She's handling a real estate closing for one of her divorce clients."

"You're taking over her space too?" I asked. "How'd you talk her into that?"

"I can be very persuasive." Slater smiled. "You ready?"

"Let me talk to Miranda about the rest of my afternoon," I said.

"No need," Slater said, closing the door behind him, using his shoulder to block my view.

"You already talked to my secretary?" I asked.

"Yep," he said. Slater looked at his watch. Below us, I heard the lobby door open and a booming male voice greet Miranda.

"Punctual as always," Slater said. "I've brought someone in to consult. Can't wait for you to meet him."

Intrigued, if not still a little miffed, I followed Slater downstairs. Miranda sat at her desk facing me. She peered up, moony-eyed, at a tall figure standing in front of her. He wore a well-fitted black suit. I could only see the back of his head, but he had thick, wavy salt-and-pepper hair. Whoever he was, he was working on charming the pants off of Miranda Sulier.

"Norm Slater," Slater said. "Allow me to introduce you to Cassiopeia Leary. Cass, this is my father."

The elder Slater turned. I'd seen him in pictures before, of course, but Norman Slater cut a more dynamic figure in person. Evenly suntanned skin, he had a devilish gleam in his green eyes. He smiled, showing a perfectly straight set of capped teeth.

"Great to finally meet you," Norm said. "I've been hearing about you for years. Feel like we've already met."

"Likewise," I said. Behind Norm's shoulder, I caught a glimpse of Miranda. The woman had her hands folded beneath her chin. If she were a cartoon, I swear her pupils would be in the shape of hearts.

"I've been watching your career," Norm said. "I'm a little in awe."

"Of me?" I asked. "Didn't know the goings-on of the Woodbridge County Bar went much further than Woodbridge County."

"You're being modest," he said. "And I don't just mean your latest iteration. You were starting to make a few people in the

Justice Department quake in their boots with the work you did on behalf of the Thorne Law Group."

I stiffened. I couldn't tell if that was genuine professional adoration or judgment. I knew what a lot of people thought of my past career. Mob lawyer. Compromised.

"Why don't we get settled in this office?" Slater said, putting a hand on his father's upper arm. He took command of the space and led his father toward Jeanie's office door.

"Can I bring you anything, Mr. Slater?" Miranda asked.

"Please," he said. "I mean it. Call me Norm. And if I need anything, my son here will point me in the direction of the break room. You've got far better things to do than play server to me."

I glared at Miranda and made a motion with my fingers under my chin, gesturing for her to pick her jaw up off the floor. She cleared her throat and went back to her computer screen.

"Cass?" Slater said. "I want my father's input on this, if you don't mind. I always like a fresh set of ears after I've been elbow deep in something for as long as I have with Eric's case."

"Sure," I said. "Be right there."

When Slater disappeared behind Jeanie's door, I turned to Miranda. "Does Jeanie know he's here?"

Miranda threw her hands up. "Not from me. I don't expect her back for at least an hour. I know Keith asked if he could borrow her office because he didn't want you near the conference room. He said he had a colleague come in. He didn't say it was his father. Should I tell her not to come in? Should I tell her *to* come in?"

"She's not going to burst into flames if she's in the same room with the guy," I said. "You, on the other hand …"

Miranda blushed. "Pipe down, you."

"Cass?" Slater called out.

"Better hop to," Miranda said, rolling her eyes. "I, for one, will be glad when the Slater show rolls out of town."

I was about to concur. Then a whole fleet of butterflies flipped in my stomach. The Slater show wouldn't be leaving until after Eric's fate was decided.

I found a smile, tapped Miranda's desk, then went to join the Slater father-and-son road show.

"This can't be easy for you," Norm said. "Never mind having someone you care about facing trial for murder. But having your workspace invaded."

"We're making do," I said.

"Sure. Sure."

"I think there's a strong likelihood Rafe Johnson is going to put you on the stand sooner rather than later once trial starts," Keith said.

"It's what I'd do," his father agreed.

"I'm his motive," I said bitterly. "That's what everyone wants to think."

"You're one of them," Norm said. "A darn pretty one, I might add. How long have you and the detective been a couple?"

I opened my mouth to answer and realized what they were doing. My mock cross-examination had already begun. They were testing me.

"I don't know if I'd describe us as a couple," I said. "Eric and I are close. But ..."

"You're romantically involved," Keith said. "Are you going to deny that?"

"No," I said. "I won't deny that. But it's a platonic relationship."

Keith's father leaned casually against Jeanie's desk. He chewed his bottom lip, considering my statement.

"He's had trouble with her family. Campbell and Darleen Maloney have money?"

"They're affluent, yes," I said.

"Son, you told me the parents have pushed pretty hard to get the husband removed as her guardian and conservator?"

"That's true, yes," I answered for him.

"You sure you haven't been followed?" Norm asked.

"What do you mean?" I asked. "Like by a private investigator?"

"That's exactly what I mean. There's no telling how far they were willing to go in probate court. I understand they had Lyman McNulty in their corner firing off his so-called expert opinions." Norm used air quotes around expert opinions.

"The substance of their complaint was that Eric wanted to follow the advice of Wendy's treating doctors and move her into hospice care."

"Yank her feeding tube," Norm said. I winced at the inelegance of the description.

"More or less, yes," Keith answered.

"Dr. McNulty plays dirty," Norm said. "Or rather, the people who fund him play dirty. I know of a few cases where they've resorted to blackmail to get one side to back off. So, I think you have to be prepared for the distinct possibility that Rafe Johnson by way of the Maloneys has access to photographs of you and Eric Wray together that you might not want made public."

"There are no photographs like that," I said. "Because we've done nothing that would contradict what I just told you."

"You sure?" Norm asked. His folksy charm was gone. His narrowed eyes raked over me. Pure scorn. Pure judgment. I rose to it.

"I am one hundred percent sure," I said. "I wasn't sleeping with Eric Wray."

"Might there be pictures of you doing something just short of that?"

I felt the tips of my ears burn hot. My own defense lawyer instincts flared. If Rafe Johnson asked me anything of the sort, Keith needed to shut it down.

"That's irrelevant," I said. "I answered your question."

Norm slapped his knees. "Fine. So tell me about August 17th."

It was then I knew Norman Slater knew the facts of this case as intimately as his son or I did.

"On August 17ᵗʰ, I met Eric Wray for lunch at Linda's Diner on the northeast end of town," I said.

Keith picked up a stack of papers from Jeanie's desk. I could see from where I sat they contained screenshots of my text exchanges with Eric that day.

"You texted him at twelve twenty, telling him you'd already arrived. How long before he got there?"

I knew my statement to Craddock the morning after Wendy died. I couldn't veer from it.

"So," Keith said. "What time did Eric arrive at the restaurant?"

"I didn't note the exact time," I answered.

The elder Slater looked over his son's shoulder at the text printout. "You texted him at just after twelve. Nothing after that. You *wouldn't* have needed to text him if he were already at the restaurant by then. What's the tower hit for Eric's phone between twelve and one?"

"Inconclusive," Slater said. "The phone's shut off from ten o'clock on."

"He would have done that if he were at Maple Valley," I said. "Eric was pretty circumspect when he visited Wendy. No calls. No distractions."

"He's off the grid," Norman said. "So, what time did he arrive at Linda's Diner again?"

My blood thickened. The implication in Norm's eyes was clear.

The tracking data from my phone and Eric's phone was inconclusive. The waiter who served us at Linda's had already gone on record with a fuzzy memory of the time frame. If I said Eric arrived sooner than he had, no one would be able to refute it but the two of us.

They wouldn't outright ask me to lie. But the implication was clear. I could muddy the timeline. I could raise the question.

"Norman!" Behind us, the door swung open and Jeanie walked in. She'd gone bone white. Keith's father's face split into a devastating smile at the sight of her.

For my part, my pulse thundered inside of me. I could be Eric's alibi. With a single word. A faulty memory, perhaps; I might have the power to blow open the entire case against him.

Only if I was willing to lie.

Chapter 15

THE SLATERS, father and son, didn't press me further on how I would testify about my memories the day Wendy died. But it was there, playing at the corners of my mind. A last resort maybe, but could I muddy the waters just a bit from the witness stand? Say Eric arrived sooner than he had? Was I willing to go that far?

I had never lied under oath. But I had lied before to protect the men I loved. Soon, I knew I'd have a choice to make. How far was I willing to go to try to fix this?

A week before Christmas, though, I got an unexpected gift. A call came in while Slater was out interviewing a medical expert who might refute the ME's homicide ruling in Wendy's case. I just happened to be standing over Miranda's shoulder when she wrote down the message. Slater's investigator had tracked down Hector Ruiz, one of the two male orderlies Audra Kaminsky claimed had mishandled another patient. He'd been spotted visiting an aunt on the other side of town. The message was curt. "If you want to talk to the guy, come in the next hour."

"Cass," Miranda warned. "Slater's left pretty strict rules. You leave the witness interviews to him."

"Well, he's not here," I said. "Who knows when we'll get another chance?"

I grabbed my coat. Miranda knew better than to try to stop me. I took the pink message from her hand and blew her a kiss.

"If he asks," she started.

"You had nothing to do with it," I finished for her. She tossed me my keys, and I hustled out the door.

Slater had hired a P.I. Someone local. He'd worked a few cases for us and I found him reliable, if not socially awkward. His name was Pete.

Pete sat in a gray Suburban down the street from the address Miranda gave me. He got out as he saw me approach.

"He's waiting inside," Pete said, his voice a monotone. Pete was retired FBI. He walked with a military bearing and kept his gray hair buzzed short.

"He knows I'm coming?" I asked.

"Yep. He said you get ten minutes."

"Do I want to know how you persuaded him to give me that much?"

"You do not," Pete said.

As we approached the tan and two-story, I saw Hector sitting on a wicker chair in the enclosed porch. An older woman with steel-gray hair wiped her hands on her apron and promptly smacked Hector in the back of the head. If I had to guess, Pete didn't need to persuade Hector of anything. His aunt took care of it.

"Hi," I said to both of them. Hector leaned forward, clasping his hands between his knees. He tapped the heel of his left foot, impatient.

"You be nice to the lady," the woman said. "You tell me if he gives you any trouble."

"I'm sure he won't." I smiled. When offered a seat, I decided to stand. Pete kept a watchful eye from the yard and the woman went back in the house.

"I take it you know why I'm here," I said.

"I told your guy ten minutes," Hector said. "I already gave a statement to the cops. I already went through the review board at Maple Valley. That crazy bitch tried to get my certification taken away."

"Who are we talking about, Hector? I'm here to ask you a few questions about Wendy Wray's case."

"Yeah," Hector spat. "I know that. And I'm tellin' you. I already said all I gotta say to the review board."

"What review board?"

"To do with Maple Valley. They sent someone out here asking me a bunch of questions."

"When was this?" I asked.

"A few weeks ago. Somebody filed an anonymous complaint against me at Maple Valley." He emphasized the word anonymous as if he knew full well who was behind it. My sense of unease grew. I knew nothing about any formal complaint filed at Maple Valley. Tori's client Ellie wasn't behind it. Had Audra Kaminsky finally gotten the courage to follow through on her concerns?

"Well, I don't have access to those records," I said. "I'm interested in what you know about Wendy Wray's care and the days leading up to her death. I wasn't aware that Maple Valley looked into anything regarding you."

"Well, they did," he said. "And I didn't do anything wrong. I was cleared."

"I'm sorry," I said. "You understand there's a man awaiting trial for murdering Wendy Wray?"

Hector gave me a sideways glance. "I got nothing to do with that. Just like I got nothing to do with anything that happened to Mary Palmer."

Mary Palmer. There was no longer any doubt in my mind that Hector's anonymous complainant was, in fact, Audra Kaminsky.

"For now, why don't you tell me what you did when you worked at Maple Valley?"

"Transported patients," he said. "When they had to go down for P.T. or labs or something, I'd move them."

"And you're telling me you were investigated for negligent treatment of Mary Palmer?"

"It was nothing!" he said. "Like I said, they tried to tell me it was an anonymous complaint. I'm not stupid. This was Audra. I told you. She's crazy. I didn't drop that Palmer woman."

"You're saying Audra was lying about you dropping Mary Palmer and injuring her?" I asked.

Hector pulled a cell phone out of his pocket. He tapped the screen and pulled something up. Then he turned the phone and shoved it at me.

"I told you," he said. "She's nuts. I got the receipts. Same thing I showed the board."

I took his phone from him. He'd pulled up a text exchange. It took me a second to orient myself, but these were presumably messages from Audra to Hector. They started last spring and ended about a month before Wendy died.

I swiped with my thumb.

"See?" he said.

I did.

"You were dating," I said, my stomach dropping. Audra hadn't said a word about it.

"Wouldn't call it dating," he said. "We hooked up. She instigated it. You can see that. Then, she started acting all crazy. Why wasn't I calling her back? Was it true I was back with my ex? On and on."

He was right. If these texts really were from Audra Kaminsky, they painted a damning picture. The tone of them became increasingly hostile. She called him a creep. And worse. Text after unanswered text from Audra to Hector.

"You're saying you think Audra reported you for misconduct with a patient to get back at you?" I asked. "Why would she wait this long to do it?"

"You catch on," he said. "And I don't know why that chick does anything she does."

"Maple Valley questioned you about it," I said.

"Yeah. They cleared me of that."

"So why did you leave Maple Valley? Was it because of Audra?"

Hector shook his head. "Cuz I was a temp. I got a better, more permanent gig. But I had nothing to do with whatever you think happened to Wendy Wray."

"What do you think happened to her?" I asked.

Hector finally met my eyes. "None of my business."

I gave him his phone back. "Hector," I said. "Audra told me about another aide who you worked with. Wayne Warren. She said he had some pretty sick fantasies about Wendy. Do you know anything about that?"

Hector pocketed his phone. "We weren't friends."

"Okay. But did you ever hear Wayne Warren say anything inappropriate about a patient?"

"It was just talk," he said.

"What was?"

"Wayne was a bullshitter. Liked to say crap just to get a rise out of me. Let's just say he had a sick sense of humor."

"Did you ever see Wayne do anything he shouldn't? I mean, with a patient?"

"You'd have to ask him about that," Hector said.

"I would," I said. "We're having some trouble finding him. Were you aware Wayne quit working at Maple Valley within a few days after Wendy Wray died? Last I heard, he never picked up his final paycheck. He never gave a forwarding address. I'd like to find him. I'd like to talk to him."

Hector started to chew his thumbnail. The subject of Wayne Warren seemed to make him uncomfortable.

"Hector," I said, more forcefully. "If you know something ..."

"I don't know crap," he said, starting to rise. "I told them. I told the cops. You got a beef with Wayne Warren, you take it up with him yourself."

"Are you scared of Warren?" I said, rising to meet him.

Hector shook his head. "Not scared of anybody."

"Was he your friend?"

"Nah. Screw that guy."

"Did you ever hang out after work?" I asked.

"Maybe once or twice," he said. "There's a bar not far from Maple Valley. We grabbed a beer a time or two. Played pool. I wouldn't say we were friends. And I haven't seen him or talked to him since I left Maple Valley. I don't know what else to tell you, lady."

He got up and made for the front door. I pulled out a business card. "Hector, I need to find Wayne Warren."

"I can't help you with that," he said. "We done here?"

I handed him my card. "We're done if you can at least promise to call me if you think of anything."

"Like what?"

"Like where Wayne might be staying. Do you remember anyone else he hung around with? I find it odd he just disappeared off the face of the earth."

Something went through Hector Ruiz's eyes. Was it fear? He snatched the card from me. His aunt stood behind the screen door, staring hard at him. I wondered if he would have taken the card if she hadn't been.

"Sure," he said. Then he opened the door and disappeared into the house. His aunt came out, dusting her hands off on the apron she wore.

"He's a good boy," she said. She extended her hand to shake mine.

"I'm sure," I said, smiling. I took out another business card and handed it to her. "In case Hector loses the other one. He's not in trouble. I just need a little help finding someone Hector worked with."

"I know what you want," she said. "I hope you find it. I follow the news. Detective Wray helped me one time. My daughter, Hector's cousin, got into some trouble a long time ago. An ex-boyfriend didn't treat her so nice. That detective got her to file a report. He arrested that piece of ... well ... you know. I hope you find what you're looking for."

"Thank you," I said as I turned to go. But if Hector's story checked out, as I suspected it would, I'd just hit another dead end.

Chapter 16

I HADN'T WANTED to celebrate Christmas. The state of
Michigan conspired against me. Starting at two o'clock in the
afternoon, Christmas Eve, fat, fluffy snowflakes began to fall.
By early evening, the town turned into a winter wonderland
postcard. All the drab, brown grass and sludge lining the roads
disappeared. A solid, packable four inches of snow fell evenly.
It clung to the barren branches of the trees framing my lawn.
The lake had frozen for good a week before. It happened
overnight during a quiet stillness that would make for perfect
ice skating once my brothers cleared a makeshift rink.

Vangie came first. "I know you don't feel like cooking. I picked
up a spiral honey-baked ham a couple of days ago. The one
with the seasoning packets."

Jessa, her almost-ten-year-old daughter, burst through the
back door like a thunderclap. She kicked her boots off and
collapsed in a fit of laughter as Marby and Maddie, my two
mutts, tackled her with kisses.

"We made cookies," Jessa managed through the hilarity. "The big ones."

She meant my grandmother's recipe. I'd always joked the things could double as door stoppers. But they were good. Cream cheese was the secret ingredient.

"Hope you brought your stocking," I said. The snow showed no signs of letting up. Vangie lived on the other end of the lake. We'd have a rough time keeping up with the driveway.

Jessa pulled her green-and-red knit stocking out of her jacket and waved it in front of me. I leaned down to give a tug on her left boot. It popped off, and she fell backward as Marbury climbed on her chest.

Tires crunched on the gravel. Matty came in his black pickup truck with the plow attachment. Behind him, Joe drove in. From the laundry room window, I could see his wife Katie in the passenger seat.

"Where's Emma?" I said to Vangie.

"Apparently spending the holiday with a friend she met in school. Her family rented a place in Vermont. Katie and Joe thought it would be good for her to have a change of scenery for a bit."

Emma had had a rough year. A traumatic break-up that bordered on epic. She'd taken the semester off school. She, Joe, and Katie were all getting family counseling.

I hugged my younger brother as he came through the mud room door. He was healthy, strong. He'd put on some weight, which I knew he didn't like. I did. My baby brother's struggle against his addictions had nearly taken him from me in the not-too-distant past. For the first time in his adult life, he had his feet firmly on a better path.

"Just came in to grab some water," he said. "Then I'll start getting that driveway plowed."

"It'll snow over again in an hour," I said.

"It'll be easier if I do it a couple of times through the night."

I smiled. It seemed like I'd have a full house on Christmas morning after all. "Oh, Vangie told me to bring these."

He heaved a sack of potatoes onto the top of my dryer.

"Jessa's going to help me peel them," Vangie said. "Then we'll mash them."

I laughed. "No fuss, huh?"

Vangie ignored me. She threw the sack of potatoes over her shoulder and started singing "Santa Claus Is Coming to Town."

As Matty went back out, Joe and Katie came in. Katie barely stopped to say hello. She gave me a quick hug, then hustled after Vangie to help with the potatoes. It left me for a brief moment with my older brother.

He looked weary. The last year had aged him. I knew kids could do that to you. Emma had put us through enough to last a lifetime.

I stepped into Joe's arms. He felt solid and warm.

"Sorry," he said. "This wasn't my idea. Vangie and Katie cooked the whole thing up. They said you didn't have a choice. You don't get to be alone on Christmas. Nobody does."

I laughed. "It's okay. I'm glad. Come on. Help me get a fire going."

Within a half hour, my house smelled like heaven. Katie, Vangie, and Jessa shooed me out of my own kitchen at every turn. Matty shoveled a path for the dogs after he finished the driveway. Joe and I sat together, bundled up on the porch as we watched the snow fall and the stars come out.

It was good to have them here. It occurred to me it had been months since we'd all been in one place at one time.

"I'm glad you built this place," Joe said.

"Me too," I said. I'd done it after our grandfather's old lake cottage burned down. Now, I had my own private peninsula in a protected cove on the southeast end of the lake.

"How's Emma?" I asked. "Have you talked to her today?"

"I did," Joe said, sipping a Heineken. "Another friend of hers from her waitressing days tagged along to Vermont. It's doing her good. They're keeping busy."

"I'm glad," I said. "How's therapy going?"

Joe shrugged. It had been no small feat getting him to go. My brother liked to carry on the long-standing Leary tradition of cramming our problems deep down until it was time for an old-fashioned, take-no-prisoners, epic meltdown.

"We talk," Joe said. "When you walk away from me, I feel frustrated. I can see that my smashing my fist into the garage wall is perhaps not the most constructive way to express my frustration."

He grew silent for a moment. I lifted my glass of wine to my lips but couldn't pull it off. I did a spit take.

"Don't laugh," he said. "Katie thinks you should come to one of our sessions. She thinks our codependent family dynamic needs to be addressed."

"Ah," I said. "Noted."

"She's trying," he said. "I get it. And I'll keep going for her."

"Sometimes that's all we can do," I said. "And it'll get better. You guys just need some time. Emma's strong. She'll pull through this."

"Yeah. Though I think I'd be a lot happier if she'd just chuck it all and become a nun."

I clinked my glass with his beer bottle.

"So," he said after a few quiet minutes. "You gonna tell me what's going on with Eric?"

"Nothing you don't already know. I got locked out of my own conference room. And I'm officially on forced vacation until the second week of January. They're worried my continued nearness to Keith Slater's trial prep could compromise my testimony."

"Yikes," Joe said. "You really have to testify against Eric?"

"Not against him," I said. "Not if I can help it."

The sliding door opened and Vangie came out. "Aunt Katie is helping Jessa frost more cookies," she said. "We'll have to save that batch for Matty. There's some double dipping going on."

"Thanks for the warning," Joe said. Vangie had the open wine bottle. She refilled my glass and poured one for herself. She sat in the chair beside me.

"Sorry if we're overstepping," she said.

"Our family dynamic of codependency." I parroted Joe's phrasing from a few minutes ago.

"And a partridge in a pear tree," Vangie sang back.

"When's the trial start?" Joe asked.

"Little over two months," I said.

"Have you seen Eric?" Vangie asked.

"Once," I said. I refrained from telling them my concerns about Eric's physical condition. "He's doing about as well as can be expected."

"I wanted to tell you," Vangie said. "I ran into Owen Corbett at the grocery store the other day. He's gossiping about the case to anyone who will listen. You'd think Wendy Maloney was a saint, the way he tells it."

"No one's a saint," I said. "But I know it's been terribly difficult for her family. I'm trying very hard to keep all of that in perspective."

Vangie got quiet. "What's wrong?" I asked her. I knew her moods. There was something else she wasn't telling me. "Did Owen say something to you? Did he give you a hard time?"

"No," she said. "It's just ... Cass, Rafe Johnson showed up at my house a couple of days ago. He served me with a subpoena."

I took a breath, then another sip of wine. "That's not totally out of left field," I said. "You know both Eric and me. He's going to make an issue out of my relationship with him. Just tell him the truth, as you know it. Joe, don't be surprised if you or Matty get one. He's put half the people in town on his witness list."

Vangie nodded, but her troubled expression didn't ease.

"Cass," Joe said. "Do you think there's any chance that ... I hate to even say it. It's just, if that were Katie. If she were in the hospital like that. To see her like that week in and week out. With no hope of ever getting better."

"No," I said quickly. "There's no chance. None at all. And not that I need to tell you, but yes, I asked him point blank. Eric said he didn't murder Wendy."

"Hmm," Vangie said. "Didn't murder her? Were those his exact words?"

I tilted my head. "What?"

"Well, did he say he didn't murder her? Or he didn't kill her?"

I wanted to snap back that it was the same thing. I stopped myself.

"Enough," I said. "It's almost Christmas ..."

Behind us, the dogs started barking to wake the dead.

"Someone's here," Vangie said. Headlights flooded the yard.

"Aunt Jeanie!" Jessa squealed.

"Now it's a party." Joe laughed. "I hope she brought something stronger than beer. Your bar's empty and it's going to be a long night."

"She's not alone," Vangie said, through clenched teeth.

"Oh my," I said. "That's Norman Slater. Keith's father."

Joe whistled. "Nice Beemer he's driving,"

Norm had a light hand on Jeanie's back as they walked toward us.

"Merry Christmas!" Jeanie called out. She had a gift bag in her hand. She waved it at Joe. He looked inside and smiled. Jeanie didn't disappoint. Whatever was in that bag qualified as something stronger than Heineken. Joe leaned down and kissed her on the cheek.

Jeanie made quick introductions of Norm Slater.

"Didn't mean to crash your family get-together," Norm said.

"Nah," Joe said. "Jeanie's more family than family half the time."

Matty slugged him. Jeanie reached up and pulled my little brother into a hug. She'd always had a soft spot for him in particular.

"We've got plenty!" Katie called from the house. "The more the merrier."

I laughed to myself. It seemed the holiday coup of my house was complete.

Jessa came forward and took Jeanie and Norm's coat. I walked in from the porch last. The others filtered in and started setting my dining room table. Dinner was almost done.

Norm hung back, waiting for me. As the rest of the party moved toward the front of the house, he caught my eye. My heart twisted.

"Let me guess," I said when I knew the rest of my guests' attention was firmly elsewhere. "You weren't just in the mood to crash my family Christmas party. Where's Keith?"

"He went back to Bloomfield Hills for the weekend. He's got a girl he's seeing."

"Wow," I said. "I didn't know he still had a social life outside of Delphi. Why don't you?"

Norm blanched. I opened my mouth to apologize. It wasn't a fair thing to say with regard to Jeanie.

"He took a meeting with Rafe Johnson this morning," Norm said. He took my elbow and gently guided me back into the garage. I closed the door behind us.

"He sent you here to handle me," I said. "That's what's going on."

"Keith doesn't send me to do anything," Norm said.

"No." I shook my head. "But Jeanie does."

He frowned but didn't deny it.

"What's going on?" I asked.

"All right," he said. "I'd hoped maybe we could get through dinner. But all right. Johnson's offered Wray a plea deal."

My ears started to ring. Time slowed.

"Voluntary manslaughter," Norm said. "On the theory this was a mercy kill."

Vangie's words echoed. Did he say he didn't murder her? Or did he say he didn't *kill* her?

"A mercy kill," I repeated. "You've got to be kidding."

"She was never going to wake up. The doctors were suggesting a course of action that could have taken weeks for her to die. She would have been made comfortable, yes. But how can one really know that? A quick death might have been more humane."

"I'm going to throw up," I said. "Eric would never ..."

"He's considering it," Norm quickly said.

"What? That's insane. It's impossible. Wait a minute. You mean to tell me your son is counseling him to consider it?"

"Cass, calm down. With a deal like this, Rafe would recommend leniency in sentencing. He could be out in ten years. Maybe even less."

"No," I said, backing away. "He isn't ... he's not."

"Yes. He's considering it," Norm said. "Both Keith and I think this is as good a deal as he's likely ever going to get. If you could put your emotions aside, I think you'll also see that it is."

"I need to leave," I said. "I need to talk to Eric."

The mud room door opened. Jeanie stepped out. She looked from me to Norm, her expression grim.

"You knew," I said. "You knew about this?"

"Cass," she said, coming toward me.

"You think this is a good idea? You want Eric to admit he killed Wendy?"

She didn't answer. She didn't have to. I found the answer in her eyes. The ground seemed to give way beneath me as I heard my niece begin to sing a Christmas carol in a sweet, clear voice while my heart ripped in half.

Chapter 17

THE MONDAY AFTER CHRISTMAS, Keith Slater and I
squared off. I pushed past Tori into the conference room. No
lock would keep me out.

Keith had taken over the whiteboard easel I kept. Photographs
of his key witnesses stared down at me where he had them
taped in a pyramid formation. I saw my own face at the apex.

"Cass," Slater started. "You can't be in here."

"No," I fumed. "You can't be in here. You can't be serious. I'm
going to give you the benefit of the doubt that your old man
was just too jolly and casual on Christmas wine the other day.
Because he walked around as if Eric spending ten years in
prison for something he didn't do is a win. So I told myself,
that can't be coming from Keith Slater. He can't possibly be
thinking that's something worth considering. Surely he's been
a good advocate for his client and told him he's planning to
tell Rafe Johnson exactly where he can shove his plea deal."

There was movement behind me. I looked over my shoulder.
Jeanie, Tori, and Miranda pressed into the room. With a look

from Keith, they all took seats at the conference table. Tori turned all the whiteboards around before she sat.

"You're upset," Keith said. "I understand that. This is personal. It's tragic."

"Stop," I said. "Don't try handling me, Slater. This isn't some irrational emotional outburst I'm having. What this is, is ludicrous. If you're even considering counseling Eric to take this deal ..."

"He's not counseling Eric," Jeanie broke in. "It's what Eric wants."

My ears rang. A shudder echoed through my bones.

"What?"

Jeanie and Keith passed a look. I wanted to scream.

Jeanie laid her hands flat on the table as if she needed it to brace herself for what she was about to say.

"Eric is the one who asked Keith to explore the possibility of a plea deal."

"Why?" I asked.

"Because he's got legitimate fears about the outcome of this trial," Slater answered. "And he's pragmatic."

"Pragmatic? This is absurd. I need to go talk to him. Slater, I need you to pick up that phone and arrange it. I need to see him today. Now."

"Cass," Jeanie said. "He won't see you."

I put my hands on top of my head as if it might actually pop off. "I don't believe you."

"I spoke to him," she said. "When Keith relayed Rafe's offer to him, Eric asked to talk to me. He knew you'd react this way."

"Arrange the meeting," I said to Slater.

"It won't do any good," Jeanie continued. "Eric knows you too well. Cass, he thinks this deal might be in everyone's best interests."

"Certainly not his," I said. "He's not thinking clearly. Despite everything else going on, he's grieving. If he's telling you he wants to take a deal, it's got to be part of some overblown sense of guilt he's got about how things went down with Wendy before her accident. He thinks he's doing penance for past sins. We can't let him. This is not the way."

"It may be his way," Slater said.

"Look at me," I said. I got close to him. I planted my hands on the table right beside him and peered into Keith Slater's face.

"Look me in the eye and tell me you really believe this is a just outcome."

He leveled a stare at me, but Slater's eyes were weary. For the first time, I noticed new lines in his face. He looked like someone who hadn't slept in days. I suppose if I could have detached my emotions from the moment, I might have found some empathy. I couldn't. I wouldn't. This was Eric's life he was playing with.

"I think sometimes the best outcome isn't what we want for our clients. It's what they want. It can't always be about the win."

"Yes," I said. "It is. In this case, it is. He didn't kill Wendy. You seem to be forgetting the central point here. Eric ... seems to be forgetting the central point. He didn't kill her. Assuming the ME's conclusions are correct, someone did. Someone else. So, if Eric's willing to take the fall for this, he lets a real killer walk. And everyone in this room who gets behind him is complicit in that. You want that on your head?"

"Cass," Jeanie said. "Let's take a walk."

I reared up. Miranda and Tori had been conspicuously silent through all of this. I wondered how much convincing it had taken to get them to line up against me.

"I don't need a walk," I said.

"Yes," she said. "You do."

Jeanie rose. She came around the table and gently took my arm. For all her four feet eleven inches, Jeanie seemed to tower over me. She gave me her sternest, maternal look. If she wanted me to feel guilty, I wouldn't. But I loved her. She banked on it.

"Fine," I said. I walked with her out of the conference room and down the stairs.

We went to her office, and she locked the door behind her. I paced in front of the fireplace as Jeanie kept her back to the door.

"I need you to consider something for a moment," she said.

"All I'm doing is considering things," I said.

"Cass. Think. Are you certain? One hundred percent certain that you can't think of another reason why Eric's amenable to a plea deal?"

I stopped pacing. "You want me to say I think he actually killed her?"

"You've asked him," she said. "Point blank."

"Yes," I hissed. "I've asked him. I asked him the very first moment I heard. He told me he didn't kill Wendy."

"Didn't kill, or didn't murder?" she asked.

I shook my head. "Vangie said the same thing. You telling me you put her up to that?"

"It's a question, that's all."

"You said you talked to him. So you tell me, did *you* ask Eric if he killed her?"

She looked down. "No. I didn't ask. I just listened. I love you, honey. But right now, that's something you need to start doing. Listening. That man is trying to tell you something. It's his life. Not yours. I told you, you can't fix this one. So maybe you need to let Eric do just that."

"Fix? Nothing about this fixes anything. I know Eric didn't kill Wendy. I know it in my soul."

"Cass, you know exactly what's going to happen when Rafe Johnson puts you on the stand."

"I don't want to hear this anymore. I mean it, Jeanie. I am not ashamed of my relationship with Eric. He didn't cheat on his wife with me. He's never cheated on her. What this is, is Eric's stubborn need to protect her. He thinks he failed her when she was alive."

"We both know that's not true. Honey, you weren't in Delphi when the worst of their troubles happened. Wendy was ... she needed help of a different kind. I see that now. But at the time, she was making it her mission in life to make that man miserable. Her affairs were an open secret. She flaunted them. And it seemed like she chose her men specifically to hurt Eric."

"I've heard the rumors," I said.

"They weren't rumors," she said. "That woman was going through something. It was like she was trying to get him to hate her. Only he never did. He never lost his temper with her. One night, he went to Mickey's bar after work. It was a retirement party for one of his lieutenants, I think. Pretty much the whole Delphi P.D. was there. I was there. Wendy knew it. She was there with some accountant she was sleeping with. Draped herself all over him. It was painful to watch. Eric didn't lose his cool. He just sat at the bar like he was made of stone as Wendy ranted and screamed at him. Even her date was embarrassed. When Eric got up to leave, she slapped him and threw a drink in his face. I'll never forget that. He just squared his shoulders and walked past her with bourbon dripping off his nose."

"Right," I said. "He didn't do anything. He took it. You didn't see him lose his temper. You didn't see him lash out at her. And for the last four years since her accident, he hasn't abandoned her. So now you can stand there and tell me you think he actually killed her?"

"I don't know. That's the God's honest truth. I think if he did, it was out of some sense of trying to protect her even now. Because he didn't want to see her suffer anymore. But what I'm trying to tell you is this. The whole town knows how Wendy treated him. Rafe Johnson is skilled enough to use it. It won't be hard for him to sell a story that Eric finally snapped. That after all those years of mental cruelty on her part, Eric just finally had enough. He saw a moment, and he seized it. Put Wendy out of her misery, sure. But put him out of his own, too. The jury might even sympathize with him. But they're still going to believe he killed her."

"I don't buy it. I'm telling you I know he didn't," I said.

"Cass." Jeanie sighed. "He lied to you. He showed up for that lunch almost an hour late. And I know you can't lie about that. But you're ignoring the bigger problem. You refuse to admit even to yourself why Eric was late. He was at Maple Valley. He admits it. The visitor logs confirm it. He was there. And he didn't tell you. He kept it from you. That is going to kill the both of you at trial. If he were anyone else, you'd see this deal for what it is."

"Bull," I said.

"Cass ..."

"Enough," I said. "I'm done. You tried. You can tell Slater and Eric and anyone else. Check off the box that you tried to talk some sense into Cass. I'm going to talk to Eric and put an end to this."

I left my phone in my office, so I stormed out of Jeanie's office and over to Miranda's desk. Jeanie followed but didn't try to stop me.

I grabbed the address book Miranda kept in her top drawer and thumbed through it. Then, I punched in the number to the Woodbridge County Jail. It took a few tries to get to the right person, but I finally did.

"I need to arrange for a meeting with an inmate as soon as possible. Today, if there's any chance of that. I need to see Eric Wray."

Astoundingly, I got transferred yet again. Another deputy came on the line.

"This is Cass Leary," I said. "Who am I speaking with?"

"This is Deputy Hertz," he said. I knew him. He knew me.

"Fred," I started.

"Cass," he said. "You're not next of kin."

"No," I said. "But I'm one of Detective Wray's attorneys. This is urgent. If you could see clear to bend the rules just a little. I'd like to see him this afternoon. Come on, Hertz, Eric is one of your own."

I heard a heavy sigh. "Cass, we've been trying to reach someone from Wray's family."

"He doesn't have anyone local," I said. "His sister and parents are all in North Carolina now. I told you. I'm his attorney. What's going on?"

"Cass, there's been some trouble."

I felt the blood drain from my head. Jeanie must have seen something in my face. She rushed out of the room and ran upstairs.

"What trouble?" I somehow found the words.

"Cass, Eric's been stabbed. I don't know all the details but ..."

"Where is he?" I shouted.

"They've taken him to Windham Hospital by ambulance," Hertz answered.

"How bad?"

No answer.

"Hertz? How bad?" By now, Slater, Jeanie and Tori all gathered outside Miranda's office.

"It's bad, Cass. Real bad. He ... Cass, he coded in the ambulance."

I dropped the receiver. Going on autopilot, I pushed past the others. Slater grabbed the phone.

"Hello?" I heard him say. "This is Keith Slater. Eric Wray is my client ..."

I grabbed my keys and was already out the door as Slater took the news, then told the others what happened to Eric.

Chapter 18

I BARELY MADE it past the parking lot at Windham Hospital. Squad cars lined the ambulance bay. Press started to gather. Someone had leaked the news.

"No," I whispered. I saw several uniformed members of the Delphi P.D. wandering near the emergency room doors with somber faces, embracing.

"No," I shouted. I parked in a restricted area. Let them tow me. I heard voices shouting my name but didn't care. Racing through the lobby doors, I went to the first familiar face I saw. Former Detective Megan Lewis. She wore a patrolman's uniform now. All black, her shiny new badge gleaming.

"Megan," I said, my voice breaking. Her lips were pursed in a colorless line. She stood with two other patrol officers. Hatred filled their eyes when they saw me. I knew what they thought. If it weren't for me, Megan wouldn't have been bounced back to the street.

"Megan!" I raised my voice. She put up a hand and said something to the other officers. They shot extra glares my way but moved off.

"He's alive," she said. "Barely."

"What happened?" I asked, feeling my knees shake. I gripped the back of a nearby chair.

"Deputies aren't saying much," she answered. "The warden's got everybody's lips locked tight. Near as we can figure, someone jumped Eric coming out of the commons. They found him in a broom closet. Wouldn't have found him at all if it weren't for the blood."

My stomach rolled as she continued.

"Some of it seeped out under the door," she said. "Another inmate found it."

"Where were the C.O.s? What about the security cameras?"

Megan looked over her shoulder. She grabbed my elbow and leaned in to whisper. "Not here. Not now. I'll find out what I can. But I'm worried he's not safe. Not even in here. If he even makes it out of surgery."

Megan's voice caught. Eric had been a mentor to her. She was a good cop. Or could be. If she could learn to check her ego and ambitions and focus on the work. I hoped when the dust of her career settled, she could work her way back into the detective bureau.

"I'm going up there," I said. "He's in general surgery?"

"Yeah," she said. "But they won't let you. Admin and the sheriff's office have things blocked off. Family only."

"They can try to stop me," I said. I turned toward the elevators.

"Cass!" Keith Slater had just arrived.

"Good," I said. "I may need you. We're going up to the sixth floor. Be prepared to raise hell if anyone tries to get in our way."

"Lead the way," he said.

I grabbed Megan's hand and squeezed it. "Thank you. Do what you can down here. I'll do what I have to for him up there."

She nodded. "Let me know. If he ... if there's a change. If you find out before I do."

"I will," I promised. Then Slater and I made our way toward the elevators.

Five minutes later, Keith Slater earned his salary at the nurse's station.

"That man's next of kin is in North Carolina. He's my client. Nobody goes in or out of that waiting room that I don't know about. You know who he is and you know who she is." He pointed to me.

Though Slater could be intimidating, I didn't have the heart to tell him his bluster was only part of the reason we were finally let through to the surgical waiting room. The head nurse was one of Vangie's best friends.

We settled ourselves in chairs and Keith went to find some coffee. Jeanie appeared. I hadn't realized how much I needed her until she wrapped her arms around me.

"He's gonna make it," she said. "He's too stubborn to die, Cass. Plus, you didn't give him permission. The man knows better than to cross you."

This got a laugh out of me that ended in a strangled sob. I allowed myself a minute to cry. By the time Slater came back with the coffee, he would see no trace of it on my face.

Seven hours. We waited seven hours. Slater and Jeanie offered me dinner, donuts, vending machine snacks. I turned it all down except for more cups of coffee. I stopped after four.

Finally, two scrub-clad figures walked down the long hallway toward us. I'd been here before. For Eric. He'd taken a bullet meant for me years ago. My brain locked the memory into place. Was I dreaming? Had all of this really happened? Had it only been borrowed time?

"He's alive," the surgeon said. He was young, with a clean-shaven face and wide, brown eyes. I knew him from somewhere but couldn't place it. He pulled his scrub cap off and gestured toward the chairs.

"All right," he said as I lowered myself and sat across from him. Slater stood behind me, Jeanie stayed at my side with her hand on my knee.

"We found three distinct stab wounds. Two weren't life-threatening, they cut him just under the rib cage. The third punctured his spleen. He lost a lot of blood. From what I understand of the circumstances, that might have oddly saved his life at the same time it almost ... didn't."

Jeanie looked confused. I hadn't told her or Slater what Megan Lewis said about how Eric was found.

"The blood trail is what led him to be found when he was," I said. Jeanie put a hand over her mouth.

"Right," the surgeon said. Kellogg. Dr. Morrell Kellogg. "We had to remove the spleen, but we managed to stop the bleeding. He's stable for now. The risk of infection is high, though. You need to be prepared for that. He's on massive amounts of IV antibiotics. If we can keep sepsis at bay, he's got a good chance of pulling out of this."

"Is he awake?" I asked.

"In and out," Kellogg said. "I'll have a nurse come down and tell you when he's ready for visitors. But only one of you to start with. I understand his family isn't local."

"We're his family," I said, taking Jeanie's hand.

"All right," Kellogg said. "I understand you're his patient advocate?" The intern standing behind Kellogg held a clipboard. He handed it to Kellogg, who handed it to me.

I took the form and held my breath. It was a copy of Eric's latest advanced directive for health care. By the date on the bottom, he'd signed it while he was in jail, just two months ago. He designated me as the person authorized to make medical decisions on his behalf.

"He didn't mention it to you?" I said to Slater.

Slater shook his head. "No."

The stamp on the bottom of the form identified a local legal clinic that did basic work for prisoners.

"Thank you," I said, handing it back to Kellogg.

"Okay. We're sorted for now then. Hang in there. Detective Wray is made of strong stuff. If I'm a betting man, I'd say the odds are in his favor. A lot of times in cases like this, it's up to the patient's will more than anything I can do. So, when you see him, do what you can to keep his spirits up."

Kellogg slapped his knee and rose. He was off to his next surgery before he even made it to the nurse's station.

I sank into the chair, gripping the arms. "We have to do something," I said.

"We're doing everything we can," Jeanie said.

"They're not protecting him in there," I said, careful not to raise my voice. Besides the hospital staff, we had plenty of ear witnesses in the form of sheriff's deputies milling around. Eric Wray was still in custody, after all.

"Slater, how's the interlocutory appeal coming on Eric's bail? I'd say the last twelve hours should be considered as extenuating circumstances."

"I've got one of my clerks writing up an emergency motion," he said. "But Cass, I gotta be honest. I'm not optimistic about our chances. Absent an abuse of discretion, the higher court isn't likely to overturn the trial judge."

"Don't spout legal standards of review at me," I said. "I know them."

Slater gritted his teeth. "Then you know the kind of battle we're facing. I am doing everything within my power from a legal standpoint. That's my job."

"Ms. Leary?" A nurse came around the corner. "Dr. Kellogg said we can take you back. Your friend is just waking up."

I shot to my feet, adrenaline pumping through me. Blood rushed to my head as I found my feet and followed the nurse down the hallway.

Chapter 19

THE NURSE LED me into the recovery room. It wasn't private. She led me past rows of curtained off cubicles and blinking machines. The rhythmic sound of ventilators nearly deafened me.

"He's still intubated," the nurse said. "We'll try getting him off the vent in about twelve hours. He should be able to breathe on his own. The doctor just wants to take the burden off his body for a little while longer. He can see you. He can hear you. He just can't talk. If he tries to fight it, do your best to calm him down. He's feisty, this one."

She pulled back the curtain and my heart left my body.

Tubes, wires, and machines: I'd seen them all before. Everything around Eric worked to keep him imprisoned on that bed. I heard a minor commotion on the other side of the curtain.

"They're going to assign two deputies to him," the nurse whispered. "Don't worry. No cuffs until we get him moved out of recovery. I'll make sure they give you some privacy. Five minutes, though. And try not to upset him."

"Thank you," I said, grabbing her hand with both of mine. It was then I recognized the name on her ID badge.

Chaney. "Your brother," I said. "He's with Delphi P.D.?"

"Yeah," she said. "Works the east side of the lake."

"Thank you," I said again, then turned to Eric. His lids began to flutter. I took his hand.

"Don't try to move too much," I said. "And don't try to talk or they'll put you under again. You're okay. You're safe for now. I plan to make sure you stay that way."

Slowly, sleepily, Eric's eyes focused on mine. I tried to keep the tears out of my eyes. It seemed important not to let on how worried I was.

"Did you see who did this to you?" I asked. "Slater's working on fast-tracking your bail appeal. I have to get you out of there, Eric."

He squeezed his eyes shut and slowly shook his head. I wasn't sure if it was in answer to my question about his attacker, or his bail hearing.

"You didn't see them?" I asked. "Blink once for yes, twice for no."

He blinked twice.

"Failing that, I'm going to make sure you stay in the hospital as long as possible. You're safer here."

One blink.

"I love you," I said.

One blink.

"I'm going to get you out. But dammit, Eric, I need you to join the fight. I don't want to hear any more about you taking a plea deal. Are we clear?"

He froze. Then slowly blinked once. His clear blue eyes misted.

"Good. Why do you have to be so stubborn? Huh? You gotta get nearly gored before you realize I'm right."

His body racked with spasms. My pulse jumped until I realized he was trying to laugh. If it was possible to smile through a vent tube, Eric did. Then he gave me another solid blink.

"We'll arrange for better guards for you if and when you go back," I said.

Quickly, he blinked twice.

"No?" I whispered. I grabbed his hand. He squeezed it. The strength of his grip made my heart soar.

"Eric," I leaned in close. "Are you telling me you think one of the C.O.s had something to do with what happened to you?"

His nostrils flared. He blinked once. It turned my insides to stone.

Slowly, achingly, it dawned on me. Nothing Slater did with the appeal or anything Megan Lewis tried to do through channels would help.

Eric was a marked man. He was a cop. He'd only gotten lucky enough to nearly bleed to death today. I knew in my soul that he wouldn't be so lucky again.

There would be no next time. I'd been angry. I'd been sad. I'd been heartbroken. At that moment, it all just washed away with a new clarity that strengthened my heart.

"Eric," I whispered. "I'm going to ask you this again. One more time. The truth. Did you murder Wendy?"

He fixed his eyes hard on me. A beat passed. Another.

"Tell me the truth," I said. "If you did this ... if you thought it was the only way to protect her, I'll understand. But I need to know. I'm your lawyer too. Consider this a consultation. Anything you tell me doesn't go any further. Did you do this? Did you murder Wendy?"

He made a sound. A small struggle against the tubing. I put a hand on his arm to help quiet him. He was trapped. Frozen. In every way a person could be.

Tears filled the corners of his eyes. I held his hand in mine. His grip went firm. For as much as he'd endured, he still had strength.

"Eric?"

Slowly, with a deliberate pause, Eric blinked twice.

No. He had not done this. It was all that mattered.

"Has it occurred to you that whoever hurt you in jail is connected to what happened to Wendy?" I asked.

One blink.

"No more half-truths," I said. "No more trying to protect me. When you get that tube out of you. When you can talk. You tell me what you know. All of it. I need a list of every faction in there that has a reason to want you dead. If there's a connection, I'll find it. No matter what it takes."

One blink. He squeezed my hand.

"I'll find a way," I said. "I swear to God, I'll find a way. Do you hear me? Promise me one thing. You'll stay alive. You'll fight. You know now you won't survive in prison. No deal. Are we clear?"

He fixed a laser stare at me and gave me a single blink.

To save this man from hell, I'd have to go to the devil himself.

Chapter 20

A WEEK LATER, the devil met me halfway at a rest stop off I-90 just a few miles outside of South Bend, Indiana. He'd flown in his private jet to a small airstrip just outside of town. But I wouldn't go there. I knew he'd try talking me into climbing into that jet, citing some business meeting or other. It would just be a quick trip. Then I'd find myself in L.A. or Toronto or who knew where. No. I'd played this game before. Today, I would play it from a crappy little greasy spoon right next to the on-ramp. No matter what else happened, I'd leave here of my own accord.

"You sure you don't want to order some lunch?" the waitress asked me. "Our turkey club is on special. The curly fries are homemade. We don't use anything frozen."

"Sounds good," I said.

"Do you want me to put in an order for your friend whenever he gets here?" She eyed the extra menu lying face down across from me. I picked a booth in the back so I could see when he walked in. Though the man knew how to make an entrance regardless of the little chime above the door.

"He can take care of himself," I smiled, sipping my lemonade. That was homemade too. Nothing frozen or from a can.

"No doubt," the waitress said. Her eyes went to the door and her face fell a bit. She straightened and immediately found a bright smile.

Oh yes. Killian Thorne knew how to make an entrance.

His jet-black wool coat swept around him. He called out a greeting to the hostess standing nearest to him. She asked him where he'd like to sit. By then, he'd scanned the diner and found me.

"I've got this," he said, earning a gasp from the hostess when she heard his thick, Irish brogue. Then he strode past the other tables and stood next to me. We stared at each other for a moment. He blinked first, letting his grin shine through as he pulled off his wool trinity cap and ran a hand through his hair.

Killian leaned down and planted a kiss on my cheek. I gave a polite smile to the waitress.

"Would you like to look at the menu, sir?" she asked.

"Just bring me whatever Cass ordered," he said. "She has good taste."

Killian sat. He tossed his hat and gloves on the seat beside him and folded his hands on the table.

"Thanks for coming," I said. "I know it was short notice."

He eyed me in that critical, calculating way he always did. For ten years at the Thorne Law Group owned by his brother, Killian Thorne was my biggest client. My only client. I didn't ask too many questions back then. I did my job. More than once, I'd kept the feds off his tail. They'd been trying to pin a racketeering charge on Killian for going on twenty years. I was good at what I did. Until finally, I found a line I wouldn't cross and almost got myself killed.

"Oh," he said. "You knew I'd come. Haven't I promised you that enough times? And I know you wouldn't call unless you had no choice."

I sipped my lemonade. The waitress came and brought Killian one. He gave it a dubious glance, then took a sip

"Agh," he said, pursing his lips. "Too sweet."

"Would you like something else?" the waitress asked.

"I'll suffer in silence, darlin'," he said, charming her. "You've already gone to the trouble."

"Your food will be out in just a few minutes," she said, lingering a bit longer than she needed to. Killian had that effect on people too. There was no middle ground with him. He was either charming the pants off you or scaring the crap out of you. It was the latter side I needed today.

"So," he said, once the girl left again. "Lay it out for me. How big a mess are you in?"

I leaned back, draping my arm over the back of the booth. "Right," I said. "As if you don't already know exactly what I called you for. The Killian Thorne I know has never taken a meeting blind, no matter who's asking."

His smile widened. So it was charm I'd get for a little while longer. This was a look he'd once saved only for me. But that was a lifetime ago. I'd loved him once until I finally realized I couldn't give him my heart without losing my soul.

"So there's trouble in little Delphi again," he said. "And you or someone you love is at the center of it."

"Not just someone," I said. "I'm talking about Detective Wray."

Killian kept his face even. He and Eric had had their run-ins once upon a time.

"You almost lost him," he said. "Is he going to make it?"

There it was. Of course, Kilian knew every detail about my life in Delphi. It would do me no good to ask, but he likely kept tabs on me through professional means. He'd use someone at the top of the field. I'd never know they were there.

"He's recovering," I said. "They tore some pieces off him, but Eric's going to live. He's being transferred back to the jail infirmary the day after tomorrow. The doctors say he'll be healthy enough to attend his own trial in six weeks."

"Glad to hear it," he said. "I won't pretend I like the man. But I respect him. Now, why don't you tell me what you really want from me, Cass?"

"Protection," I said. It was nearly imperceptible. But I knew Killian's face better than anyone. He blanched.

"For Eric," I said. "He was denied bail. We appealed. It went nowhere. Best-case scenario, Eric stays in jail for weeks until his trial. Worst case ..."

"Worst case," Killian picked up my thought. "He stays there for the rest of his life. Which, under the circumstances, might be a very short sentence."

"He's a target," I said. "He's surrounded by people he's either directly put behind bars or their affiliates."

"There's a price on his head," Killian said.

"It could be anyone," I said. "Never mind the decade or more he's spent putting killers away. Before that he worked undercover in vice. Pick your gang. Crips. Bloods. Aryan Brotherhood. The cartels. Eric's got blood on his hands as far as they're concerned from all factions. This latest attack? There was help from the inside. The closest security cameras were disabled."

"No one saw anything, no one knows anything," Kilian said.

"That's about the size of it. So, whatever it takes, I need to secure protection for him on the inside. I'm asking you to pull whatever strings you have to make sure he gets it. For me."

He raised a brow. We went silent as the waitress brought our food. Killian took a hundred-dollar bill out of his pocket and politely told her to keep it but not come back. His hand lingered over hers as he put the bill in her hand. Just long enough to make her blush. Then she disappeared.

"You think my influence reaches all the way to the Woodbridge County Jail?" he asked, popping a curly fry into his mouth.

"I know it does," I said. "It reaches everywhere there are men who can be bought."

"You sure I owe you that much?" he said, eyes sparkling.

"You owe me that and more, but this will be enough. For now."

He laughed, a deep, broad bellow. He knew I was right.

"I need the word to go out. Today. Eric Wray isn't to be touched."

"A big ask," he said. "There are consequences for that sort of thing. You sure Wray's willing to live with them?"

"The key word is live," I said. "He won't survive without help. He understands that now. A shank to the spleen has a very persuasive impact."

We ate in silence for a while. Killian wouldn't come out and say yes. But he stayed. It gave me all the answers I needed.

"So," Killian finally said, wiping his hand with his napkin then tossing it over his plate. "What are his chances at trial, do you think?"

To anyone else, this might have seemed like small talk. I knew Killian was gauging how deep he'd have to go to deliver on the promise he was about to make me.

"I don't know," I said. For him, I would have to give complete honesty. "I haven't turned up any solid, alternative leads to give the jury."

"You haven't?" Killian asked. "What about Eric's actual lawyer?"

"Do you know him?" I asked. "Keith Slater?"

Killian nodded. "A big gun. Good choice. Though, if it were me, I'd still rather have you fighting in my corner over anyone else."

"I'm flattered. And I am fighting in Eric's corner."

Killian nodded. "Tragic circumstances, though. Cass, if it were me ... I'd want you to do the same thing. Don't ever let me live like that."

"Eric didn't kill Wendy," I said. "Of that, I'm sure."

He stared at me. His eyes held the question I'd answered at least a hundred times, both for myself and others.

"Eric didn't kill Wendy," I said.

Killian exhaled. "Fair enough. But my answer is the same. If the time ever comes, you'll know what to do."

"If the time ..." I stopped myself. "Killian, I shouldn't still be the one making that decision for you. We're no longer engaged. I'm not your lawyer anymore."

"But there's still no one else I'd trust to do what needs to be done," Killian said.

I finished my food and folded my napkin. There was no arguing with him. I just hoped that someday, Killian would move on and find someone else to trust with his life besides me. Right now, I needed him for Eric's.

"I'll do what I can for your ... friend," Killian said.

I felt a weight lift from me even as a different one settled in.

"Thank you," I said simply.

Killian paused. He had something else to say. "Did you think I wouldn't remember?" He had a twinkle in his eye that still carried the faint echo of the power he used to have over me.

"Remember what?"

"Happy birthday, a rúnsearc," he said, using a Gaelic nickname he saved only for me.

I blinked. I'd been so focused on this meeting and everything going on with Eric, I marked days as a countdown to the trial. Nothing more. But he was right. I was thirty-nine years old today.

"You did forget." He chuckled softly. "Don't forget to take care of yourself too. I would have brought you a gift. But I know you won't accept them from me anymore. So consider this as part of my gift."

"Thank you," I said one more time as Killian rose to leave.

"Be careful, Cass," he said. "This thing with Eric. Whatever he's done or hasn't done. It might not end how you think."

"I know," I said. "But it won't be for my lack of trying."

"That's exactly what the rest of us are afraid of." Killian smiled. He called out a goodbye and compliments to the cook behind the counter as he made as grand an exit as he had an entrance.

Chapter 21

KILLIAN DIDN'T TELL me when it happened. Or how. But two weeks later, a small white card showed up on my doorstep. I didn't see who left it. The drop hadn't even been picked up by my home security cameras. That fact alone sent a chill down my spine as I opened the card and read the two simple words.

"It's done."

I pressed the card to my breast. I walked into my home office and sent the card through the shredder.

I had a meeting today. Another diner. Another person who wouldn't meet me inside the boundaries of Delphi. Instead, he picked a park bench one town over. A light snow fell. The latest models showed this one would gather strength, but might be the last significant storm we'd see of the season.

I hoped so. But this was Michigan.

"Can we at least sit in the car?" I asked. He sat with his hands stuffed in the deep pockets of a tan Carhartt jacket. He'd pulled his knit cap so far down I don't know how he could even see.

"This will be a short enough conversation," Detective George Knapp said. George was now the most senior detective with the Delphi P.D. He'd already tried to retire twice.

I sat down beside him. "Well, thanks for whatever you can share with me."

"I'm doing this because Eric asked me," Knapp said. "Not because I think it's a good idea."

"We want the same thing, don't we?" I asked. "Eric's sitting in jail for something he didn't do. If he stays there, something worse could happen to him. I know you don't want that."

Knapp turned at the waist and peered at me under his hat. "I don't know how much I can tell you."

"Look, George," I said. "You don't have to like me. I get it. It comes with the territory. Defense lawyer and all. For right now, that's not who I am. Right now, I might be the best chance Eric has of clearing his name."

George laughed, a deep guffaw. It unsettled me. Why was he fighting me so hard?

"I need names," I said. "I'm working a theory that maybe somebody framed Eric for killing Wendy. Someone who had a vested interest in getting him behind bars. Whoever that is already tried and almost succeeded in gutting him, Knapp. I'd like to make sure that doesn't happen again."

"Rumor I heard is that you've already worked your magic on that," he said.

I went silent. I stared straight ahead. After a moment passed, I heard Knapp's breathing change. A sigh of defeat, perhaps. Detente.

"You said you're here because Eric asked you to be," I said. "So then he also would have asked you to give me what I needed. For some strange reason, I'm getting no help from the department."

"Strange?" he said. "You really think that's strange?"

"Yeah. I do. Eric's one of your own. We're on the same side. How many ways do I have to say it?"

"We may both want Eric out of this mess, but that doesn't mean we're on the same side."

"Fine," I said. "So let's cut to it. You must have a theory. Eric knew it wasn't safe to get into details with ears all around. To be honest, this is a leap of faith for me talking to you like this. There's a theory that one of the C.O.s helped plan the attack on Eric, or at least looked the other way at the right time. I don't exactly know who to trust either, George."

"Eric's been a cop for a long time. He's put hundreds, maybe thousands of very bad guys away. Any one of them could have an axe to grind against him."

"Maybe," I said. "But I think it's someone with the means to pull something like this off. This was orchestrated. Lots of moving parts. So give me the big ones. Please."

George inhaled. He let it out in a whistle. "You know, he spent a few years on vice," he said.

"Yes," I said. "It's occurred to me he likely got in the way of the business of some of the major drug cartels."

"Yeah," George said. "Only he didn't act alone on that. I just don't see why he'd get singled out. Bad luck, I guess. There was a guy by the name of Frank Rossi. Maybe eight years ago, Eric busted up a pretty lucrative cartel vein into Toledo. Part of a task force he worked. Rossi got life."

I didn't want to spook Knapp by writing anything down. It was a start. I could start working Rossi's associates and any possible connections to the known players in Wendy's case.

"Who else?" I asked.

"You know about the Steel Beasts M.C.?" he asked.

"Sure," I said.

"Well, Eric made a pretty big notch on his belt when he helped send Ansel Jameson away on murder charges. The feds had been trying to get him for years. Jameson got sloppy and murdered his brother-in-law."

"Who was Jameson to the Steel Beasts?" I asked.

"He was club president," George said, apparently exasperated that I didn't already know it.

"Thing was, Ansel's brother-in-law, Snake Watson, had it coming. Snake beat the crap out of Ansel's sister. Kicked her in the head with a steel-tipped boot until there was nothing left of her. She was six months pregnant at the time."

"How awful," I said.

"Eric broke the case," Knapp said. "Putting Ansel behind bars almost broke the back of the club for a while. And he paid for it."

"Who paid for it?"

Knapp pulled a photograph out of his jacket pocket. He showed it to me. I gasped, not expecting the image. It was a man, strapped to a gurney. Blood poured from a horrific wound in his mouth, his eyes were swollen shut.

"That's what happened to Ansel inside," Knapp said.

"That happened in jail?" I asked, incredulous.

"Yeah," he answered. "Somebody got scared he was going to start ratting on the club, or maybe a rival gang to shorten his time. They cut out his tongue but left him alive to send a message."

"Put it away," I said. "I get the picture."

"I don't think you do," he said. "The Beasts have deep connections into organized crime. Rumor is they run guns for a ring through Detroit. These are seriously bad men, Cass."

"You think it's possible someone from the Steel Beasts called in a favor once Eric got locked up?"

"I think any of it's possible," Knapp said.

"Okay," I said. "Who else do I need to know about?"

"Those are the biggest busts Eric has on his resume. The ones that might fit your theory. The rest? Who knows? You might be looking for a needle in a haystack. And it might just be somebody unconnected to Eric, looking to score points by killing a cop."

"Well, thank you," I said.

"Let me make one thing clear," he said, raising his voice to a shout. "I'm not doing this for you. If it were up to me, I wouldn't be here."

"You can lay down your sword, Knapp," I said. "I told you. I have one goal. Helping Eric."

"You ever think the best way you could help him is by staying the hell away from him?"

"What?"

"You're bad luck, Leary."

I blinked. George Knapp rose to his feet and pulled his coat tighter around him.

"You leave a trail of bodies and careers in your wake," he said.

It was my turn to rise. "That's ridiculous. You're talking about Megan Lewis? She's responsible for her own sloppy detective work."

"Lewis is just the latest," he said. "I told you. There's a trail of bodies behind you. Lewis, Tim Bowman, Rick Runyon. Now Eric. It seems like anyone who crosses your path either ends up in Internal Affairs hell, jail, or the morgue. I'm six months from retirement and a full pension. Consider this our last conversation. I've told Eric the same."

My jaw literally dropped. "You can't be serious. You think I'm cursed. That sounds like kooky Louise, the courthouse psychic, talking."

He stayed stock still. His eyes said it all. "You gotta be kidding me," I said. "That *was* kooky Louise talking. She told you I'm actually cursed?"

Knapp didn't answer. He just shoved his hands in his pockets and turned his back. As his footsteps crunched through the snow, he took the last bit of help I'd get from anyone in law enforcement on this one.

Chapter 22

March 2ⁿᵈ. 9:45 a.m.

I WASN'T ALLOWED in the courtroom. Slater would have kept
me out of the courthouse altogether if I didn't have a
legitimate reason to be there. That reason was a pre-trial
conference on one of Jeanie's domestic cases. She was my eyes
and ears on the third floor while I covered her in Family
Court today.

When Judge Moira Pierce finalized Jeanie's scheduling order
and dismissed the parties, she motioned for me to approach
the bench. Her clerk and bailiff had already left. It was just
the two of us in her empty courtroom.

"You sure you need to be here today?" she asked. I liked
Moira. She'd held her own against the good old boys' network
in this town like I did. Though she did excellent work in
Family Court, I hoped she had greater ambitions. I'd love to
see her handling felony cases upstairs. Eric's case would be in
good hands if she presided. As it stood, we drew a visiting
judge when the rest of the Woodbridge County Circuit

judges recused themselves for conflicts of interest. While I wanted to believe it was a show of support, I knew it cut off one path to appeal if the verdict didn't go his way.

"I'm just doing my job," I told the judge.

"Well, hang in there, Cass. I know it's got to be killing you not sitting at the defense table today."

"I appreciate that," I said. "Can I ask you a question though? Off the record?"

She unzipped her robe and hung it on the hook behind her chair.

"Shoot," she said.

"What's your read on this Judge Mitchell?"

She smiled. "They sure went far enough north to find him. You ever been up to Helene County?"

"I haven't. I've been to Charlevoix and Petoskey, never in between."

"I've met Bart Mitchell at a couple of conferences. Kind of quiet. Didn't belong to any of the judge cliques."

"There are judge cliques?" I asked.

"Definitely. I wish I could give you a better read. But as far as I know, he's a good judge. Not flashy. Happy where he's at and not looking to advance. Though, I'm not sure what opportunity one would have out of Helene. If I had to wager, I'd say Mitchell came here to do a job, not make the papers."

There was a touch of sarcasm in her voice. Though I wouldn't ask her point blank, I took it as a swipe against Bill Walden. Two seconds later, I didn't have to.

"That bail decision horrified me," she said. "And I'm not the only one. I'm sorry about that. I hope Detective Wray is recovering."

"He is," I said. "And thank you. When I get the opportunity to tell him, I'll let him know you're thinking of him. He could use as many friends as he can get."

Moira reached out and took my hand. It startled me. I blinked back tears, not realizing how close my emotions were to the surface.

"Do what you have to for that man," she said. "If he's got you in his corner, I think he's got a fighting chance."

The door to her courtroom opened. Moira gave me a quick smile, grabbed her robe off the hook, then exited through the side door to her chambers. Though I wanted to ask her what she meant by my doing "anything" for Eric, I didn't get the chance.

"Cass?"

I turned. Jeanie walked toward me. She wore her best suit, transforming into the courtroom bulldog she was. This was the woman who made me want to be a lawyer in the first place.

We still had Moira Pierce's courtroom to ourselves. It occurred to me that was her doing. She probably told her bailiff not to shoo us out just yet.

"Jury's seated," Jeanie said. "Pretty good mix. But the usual. Four retired teachers. Two under-twenty-five-year-olds. We got a first responder, a thirty-seven-year-old E.M.T. Six men. Six women. They seem serious."

"I need to be down there, Jeanie," I said, my voice breaking.

"You will be," she said. "Judge won't put up a stink after you testify. Slater got the ruling from him. You can sit in the courtroom after you're off the stand. Johnson was none too happy about it. So you'll have to be on your absolute best behavior."

"How's Eric?" I asked. I hadn't seen him face to face in weeks. We'd had a few brief phone calls after his transfer out of the hospital. He knew I met with Knapp, but it wasn't safe for me to talk about it with him. I was working deep background but making slower progress than I liked. There had been no further security incidents. I hadn't heard from Killian or his people, but knew his influence was already at work.

"He's present," she said. "I won't lie. I'm a little worried. He's his usual, stoic self, but I can see he's in some pain. Sitting for long periods might be a problem for him, so Slater might ask for more frequent breaks."

"Okay," I said. "What about opening statements? Am I allowed in for those?"

"No can do," she said, then her face spread into a sneaky smile. "But there's nothing stopping you from parking yourself out in the hallway. Soundproofing in this building is for crap. Also, I don't know if you've noticed, but Castor's door doesn't shut all the way. If a person sat on a certain bench at a certain angle, you could practically see right through it."

She got a laugh out of me. The first genuine one in months. "I love you, you crotchety old nut bird."

"Yeah. I'll try not to let it go to my head," she said. I put an arm around her as we left Pierce's courtroom and headed upstairs to Judge Castor's. While visiting Judge Mitchell took over his courtroom, I'd heard Castor headed down to Florida.

Jeanie and I took the stairs. When we emerged on the third floor, a lump settled in my throat at what I saw. Matty, Joe, and Vangie sat on the bench along the wall. They'd saved a place in the middle for me.

"We figured you'd need your own cheering section," Jeanie said, squeezing my hand. "Now behave or you'll get us all in trouble."

As Jeanie opened the courtroom door, I lingered, catching a glimpse inside. Rafe Johnson had just strode up to the lectern to face the jury. My eyes tracked to the defense table. Eric sat tall and straight but gripped the side of the table. Jeanie was right. He was hurting. He wore a crisp blue suit. One of my favorites. I'd told him he looked handsome in it once.

"Ladies and gentlemen of the jury," Rafe started. "Allow me to introduce you to Wendy Maloney Wray."

Chapter 23

THE COURTROOM LIGHTS DIMMED, and Wendy's beautiful, smiling face appeared on the overhead at the front of the courtroom. I stood frozen for a moment as the door slowly began to close. The screen changed. Johnson played a video of Wendy's last birthday party before her accident. She was laughing, dancing, sticking her tongue out at the camera. A second later, the video cut to Wendy in her hospital bed last year. Her mother sang to her. Her mouth hung open, but she seemed to be trying to smile as her mother showed her a pink mylar balloon.

The courtroom door shut. Jeanie was right. It didn't quite close all the way. The door on the right stuck out, leaving maybe a two-inch gap which allowed me to hear everything going on and see the back of the lectern where Rafe stood.

Arms came around me. "Come on, Cass," Joe said. "Sit with us. It's going to be a long day."

I hugged him. "I'm glad you're here. If you'd have told me beforehand, I would have told you to stay away."

He laughed and whispered, "We know. Why do you think we kept our mouths shut? You're the one who always says it's better to apologize instead of ask for permission."

"We're not sorry though." Matty smiled. Vangie playfully punched him in the arm.

I went with Joe and sat between them. From here, I had a clear view into that small gap in the door.

Rafe's video ended. "Wendy Wray was everything you see in that video. Young. Beautiful. Fun-loving. She volunteered at the local animal shelter in her spare time. She loved her job. Her co-workers. Nothing gave her greater pleasure than helping other people build their dreams. That's what she strove to do as one of the top real estate agents in the county. Her clients became more than that. They became her friends. One night, four years ago, that light got snuffed out. You'll hear how one instant on a winding stretch of road changed everything. How the light in Wendy's eyes went out. But it didn't go out completely. Even in her convalescence, Wendy brought joy to those who loved her. Her mother and father. Her closest friends. She was a human being. She could still feel. Still smile. Still bring joy and experience joy. She had purpose. She had a future.

"But to that man sitting before you, Wendy became a burden. A chain around his neck. He'd moved on. Found someone new. Eric Wray was done with Wendy. So he tried to throw her out like yesterday's garbage."

I went rigid. Joe tightened his grip around me.

"You'll hear how Eric Wray bided his time," Rafe continued. "How he connived and manipulated doctors and the court system to try to get them to give up on Wendy so he could move on to his new life. How he lied to Wendy's family and tried to drive a wedge between them even before Wendy's accident. How his anger and need for revenge against her drove every action he took. Until one day, he seized the opportunity to end her life for good.

"Wendy's death wasn't peaceful. She was aware of everything going on around her. She trusted Eric Wray. She believed he would protect her. He didn't though. He played God. Or maybe he played the devil. That will be up for you to decide. And when you do, the evidence will show, through incontrovertible proof, that Eric Wray, Wendy's protector, instead became her executioner. Thank you."

Slater waited a moment. He rose; buttoning his jacket, he stepped up to the lectern.

"Ladies and gentlemen," he started. "Thank you for your time. A tragedy occurred last August. But it was the end of another tragedy that began over four years ago. The state is going to tell you one heck of a story. Part romance novel. Part suspense thriller. But in the end, I know you'll see it for what it was. Just a story. A work of fiction. Wendy Wray's tragedy was of her own making. A horrible accident to an imperfect woman who didn't deserve it. And in the four years since, Eric … her husband … kept every vow he ever made to her. No matter the personal cost to him and the other people he loved. He is also a victim of Wendy's accident in many ways. And of her choices. But at all times, Eric Wray acted in his wife's best interests. He committed no murder. No crime at all. He is an innocent man, but not a perfect one. None of us are, after all."

Slater paused. He looked back at Eric. I wished I could see his face. Slater would have instructed him not to show any sign of anger during Rafe's opening.

"Eric Wray did nothing wrong," Slater said. "In the end, all the prosecution has is an epic, tragic story without a happy ending. Not for anyone involved. But what they don't have is evidence of murder. Thank you."

"Mr. Johnson?" the judge said. He had a strong, gravelly voice. I'd only seen the man from the picture he had taken for the State Bar. "You ready to call your first witness?"

"Yes, Your Honor," Rafe said. "If you'll permit me just a moment for the bailiff to secure the witness, the state calls Cassiopeia Leary to the stand."

Chapter 24

I KEPT my gaze straight ahead as I walked through the gallery toward the witness stand. As I turned, I caught my first glimpse of Eric's support section. His sister, Monica, and her husband sat directly behind him. I hadn't seen Monica since we were in high school. With fair hair and freckles, she looked nothing like her brother. She shared Eric's pale-blue eyes, though. Hers were red-rimmed, and she dabbed at them with a tissue. Her husband, Greg, leaned in close and whispered to her. She nodded her head and took a deep breath.

I raised my hand and swore my oath. I shot a quick look at Eric. He stared at me tight-jawed, giving nothing away. Behind him, Monica gave away plenty. She stared at me with white-hot hate that startled me.

Rafe came to the lectern. He started with the basic, foundational questions required of any witness. Over the course of twenty minutes or so, I explained my basic background to the jury. I was Delphi, born and bred. Most of them likely already knew of me, so Rafe ran quickly to the meat of his direct.

"Ms. Leary," he said. "How would you describe your relationship with the defendant?"

"He is a close friend," I said. "On occasion, he is also my client. We've also shared a professional relationship as he is a homicide detective and I do criminal defense work. I would also characterize our personal relationship as romantic."

No point in skirting the obvious.

"Romantic," Rafe said.

"Yes."

"You've dated."

"Yes."

"For how long?" he asked.

"On and off for about two years," I said. "It didn't start out that way, mind you. But Eric and I have come to rely on each other over the years."

"Do you currently date anyone else?" he asked.

"No."

"So you're exclusive? Is it fair to say that Eric Wray is your significant other?"

I paused. We knew this was coming.

"Yes," I said. I waited, expecting Rafe to ask me about our sex life.

"All right," he said. "I'd like to bring your attention to last summer. Your relationship with Eric was as you described at that time? You were dating?"

"Yes."

"And he wasn't dating anyone else, was he?"

"No," I said.

"That would have upset you if you found out he was, wouldn't it?" Rafe asked.

"Objection," Slater said, not rising from his seat. "Calls for speculation and counsel is leading the witness."

"Sustained, Mr. Johnson, try again," Judge Mitchell said.

"I'm trying to understand the ground rules of your relationship with Eric Wray," Johnson said.

"I didn't write a rule book," I said.

"Did you assume that you had an exclusive dating relationship, though?" Rafe asked.

I considered the question. "To be honest, it wasn't something I thought about. Not in the way you describe."

"You're not aware of any other dates the defendant went on besides with you?" Rafe asked.

"No."

"How often did you and the defendant go out together?"

"I couldn't give you an exact number," I said.

"Well, was it every week?"

"It was our regular routine, yes," I said. "But you have to understand, Eric and I both have demanding jobs. We don't always get weekends off. We made time for each other when we could. Sometimes we were able to plan things once or twice a week. Sometimes weeks would go by."

"Did you speak to Eric every day?" Rafe asked.

"Probably," I said. "Most days, anyway. If either of us were working on a case, that might interfere. Certainly if I was preparing for a trial, I might not come up for air for days, even weeks."

"I see," he said. "Did you ever spend the night at the defendant's house?"

"Yes," I said. "A few times, I believe. Once before we became romantic. There was a safety concern that related to a case I was working on. Eric offered me his guest room."

"Did Eric make a habit of spending the night at your house?" he asked.

"I don't know if I'd use the word habit. But yes, Eric would on occasion stay at my house on the lake depending on how late it was. Or if we'd been drinking."

Rafe rifled through some of his notes. I knew it was for show. He knew exactly where he was going with his questioning. I think the jury did too.

"Ms. Leary," he said. "Did your relationship with Eric Wray become sexual in nature?"

I leaned forward. "No," I said.

"No?"

"No."

"And why is that?"

"Objection!" Slater said. "This is irrelevant."

"Your Honor," Rafe said. "The sexual dynamic of the defendant and his girlfriend while he was married to the victim is at the core of this case. If you'll allow me some latitude, I'll make a showing."

Mitchell put his pen down. He folded his hands on the bench. "The witness may answer," he said. "But let's not veer to tabloid fodder, Mr. Johnson."

"Of course not, Your Honor. Would you like me to repeat the question, Ms. Leary?"

"You asked me why my relationship with Eric Wray hadn't become sexual, I believe," I said, meeting Johnson's stare.

"I did," he said. "Please answer."

"We hadn't reached that point in the relationship," I said.

"You'd been dating for two years. He made a habit out of spending the night at your place. You're both consenting adults. Now you're telling me it hadn't reached that point in the relationship. Were you waiting for a ring, Ms. Leary?"

"Objection!" Slater said. "Counsel is badgering this witness. The question's been asked and answered."

"Sustained, Mr. Johnson. Rephrase," Mitchell said.

"Ms. Leary, why hadn't your relationship reached that level yet?" Rafe asked. Eric clenched his fists on the table. Slater put a light hand on his arm. The jury, for their part, kept their eyes on me.

"It just hadn't," I said, hating myself for it a little. I expected Rafe to challenge me on this point. I thought he would accuse me of lying about it.

"Because you don't sleep with married men, do you, Ms. Leary?" Rafe said. My blood froze. He set the trap, and I'd walked straight into it.

"Objection!" Slater stood. "This is improper character evidence. This witness's character is not at issue."

"Your Honor," Rafe said. "I'm not attacking this witness's character in any way. Furthermore, as I've stated in response to defense counsel's last objection, the relationship dynamic between this witness and the defendant forms the core of what happened to the victim."

"Overruled, you may answer, Ms. Leary," Mitchell said.

I threw my hands up and glared at the judge. "He's asking me about my sexual habits? That's okay with you?"

"I'll rephrase," Rafe said. "Ms. Leary, isn't it true that the defendant's marital status played a part in your decision not to take your romantic relationship farther?"

I shook my head and stared at the ceiling. Judge Castor never would have allowed this line of questioning. Slater was on his feet. Eric made fists again.

"We were always respectful of Wendy," I said. "So in that regard, the answer to your question is yes."

"Did you spurn the defendant's advances?" Rafe asked.

"What? Spurn? No. I wouldn't call anything a spurning. Eric and I understood each other. And what you're describing ... this wasn't something that we spoke about in detail."

"So, you believe that the defendant understood, while his wife was alive ... while she still *was* his wife ... your relationship would not become sexual," Rafe said.

"No," I said. "That is not what I believed. That was not the understanding. You're asking me to predict the future. I am telling you at a single point in time what the character of our relationship was. That's all."

"I see," Rafe said.

"Move on, Mr. Johnson," Judge Mitchell said. I had to bite my tongue not to make a sarcastic comment.

"Ms. Leary," Rafe said. "Did you and the defendant ever discuss marriage?"

"No," I said.

"He never asked you to marry him?"

"No."

"You never asked him to marry you?"

"No."

"Were you aware that he wanted to marry you?" Rafe asked.

"Objection calls for speculation," Slater said.

"Sustained," the judge said. "You'll need an offer of proof, Mr. Johnson."

"Ms. Leary," Rafe said. "What size ring do you wear?"

I reared back. He was going somewhere. Rafe Johnson didn't fish.

"An eight," I answered.

"Were you aware that one week before Wendy Wray's death, the defendant was seen shopping for a ring at Raphael Jewelers in Ann Arbor?"

"Objection," Slater said. "Counsel is testifying and assuming facts not in evidence."

"Sustained, Mr. Johnson!"

The jury started to move in their seats. I kept my face neutral. I knew Rafe wanted a reaction out of me. This was the first I was hearing of this. I couldn't let that show on my face. If Rafe asked the question, it meant he had a witness who would confirm the story. At the defense table, Eric had gone to stone as well.

"All right," Rafe said. "Let's talk about the afternoon of August 17th. Can you tell me what you did that day?"

"I worked in the morning, at my office. I had a brief evidentiary hearing in this courtroom, as a matter of fact. Nine forty-five. I was back in my office by eleven. I then went to Linda's Diner for a lunch date with Eric."

"What time did you arrive?" he asked.

"A little after noon," I answered.

"What time were you supposed to meet with the defendant?" he asked.

"Twelve thirty," I said. Just that one word. I knew it was probably the most damaging one I would say.

"You spoke to him throughout that morning?" Rafe asked.

"By text," I said. "Briefly." This was all part of the record. I'd made this statement to Deputy Craddock. Rafe had my cell phone records and Eric's as well as the time-stamped receipt from Linda's Diner.

"Whose idea was it to meet at Linda's?" Rafe asked.

"Eric's," I said. "He asked me to go to lunch with him the night before. He texted me a little after eight in the morning the day of and suggested Linda's at twelve thirty."

"He said, 'How about Linda's at twelve thirty?'" Rafe asked, reading from the text transcript.

"That's correct," I said.

"He didn't show up at twelve thirty, though, did he?"

Here it was. A small gap in time that could make a huge difference. I took a breath. I resisted the urge to look at Eric. Then, I raised my chin and told the truth.

"No," I said.

"He didn't show up at one either, did he?"

"No," I said.

"And that bothered you enough to send him a text, isn't that right?"

"Yes," I said. I knew Slater had already stipulated to entry of the text transcripts.

"You were worried, weren't you?" he asked.

"I wasn't worried, no," I said.

"He left you hanging," Rafe said. "In fact, you knew Linda's kitchen closes to new orders at one thirty. You were holding up the kitchen."

"It was a concern," I said. "But you asked me if I was worried about Eric. I was not. It's not uncommon for either of us to have unexpected delays on things like that. It's the nature of our careers. You can read the texts. I merely asked if he wanted me to order us food to go."

"But it wasn't like Eric to stand you up, was it?" he said.

"I just told you, it wasn't unusual at all to have job-related delays," I said. "For either one of us."

"So you assumed work was keeping Eric?" he asked.

"I assumed that, yes," I said.

"But Eric was on vacation the week of the 17th, wasn't he?"

"That doesn't mean he couldn't have been called in to work. Things happen."

"But you found out later that wasn't the problem at all, didn't you?" he asked.

"Eric came to the restaurant," I said. "A bit after one. I'd already ordered sandwiches for us."

"Did Eric tell you why he was late?" Rafe asked.

"I didn't ask," I said.

"You didn't ask him why he didn't answer your repeated texts?" he asked.

"I didn't," I said. "And I wouldn't describe them as repeated. I texted him once. He showed up."

"Almost an hour late," Rafe said. "Did Eric tell you he was at Maple Valley ahead of your lunch date?"

"No," I said. "But I didn't ask."

"Did Eric ever tell you when he was going to visit Wendy?" he asked.

"Tell me ahead of time? No. I knew he visited her on a regular basis. Once every couple of weeks."

"You never went with him," he said.

"No."

"And you're aware the defendant used to visit his wife every single week, isn't that true?"

"I was aware of that, yes," I said.

"He stopped going that often, though," Rafe said.

"I just told you, I wasn't in the habit of asking him how often he went to Maple Valley. He didn't owe me explanations on that," I said.

"Fair enough," he said. "How would you describe Eric's demeanor when he arrived at Linda's?"

"His demeanor? I wouldn't describe it one way or another," I said.

"If the waiter who served you told the police the defendant seemed flustered, would you challenge that?" he asked.

"I have no idea what the waiter observed," I said. "I can only answer what I observed. And I have."

"Let's move on," Rafe said. "Ms. Leary, have you ever lied to the police?"

"What?" I asked.

"Have you ever filed a false police report?" Rafe asked.

The courtroom went deadly silent. I kept my focus on Rafe Johnson. Every part of me wanted to turn my attention to Eric.

"Ms. Leary, do you need me to repeat the question?" he asked.

"No," I said.

"No, you don't need me to repeat the question, or no, you've never filed a false police report?"

"Both," I said. I could not panic. At the same time, I couldn't shake the truth. Rafe Johnson didn't fish.

"Ms. Leary," he said. "This isn't the first time you've been questioned as a witness in a homicide investigation, is it?"

"It is not," I said. My entire family sat on benches in the hallway. I knew they could hear every word.

"In fact, your brother was involved in a fatal shooting last year, isn't that right?" Rafe asked.

"Your Honor," Slater said. "This line of questioning has no bearing on the facts of this case."

"Of course it does," Rafe said. "Credibility is at issue for every witness called, including this one."

"Overruled," Mitchell said. "But get to it."

"Yes," I said. "My brother Joe was involved in a fatal shooting last year."

"A shooting that was later ruled a justifiable homicide, isn't that correct?" Rafe asked.

I glared at him. He'd already trapped me. I knew in my bones he had no idea. He couldn't. It seemed I was wrong; Rafe Johnson threw a line in the water after all.

"A shooting that was ruled in self-defense," I said. "By your office, I might add."

"Who were the principal witnesses to that shooting?" Rafe asked.

The color had drained from Eric's face. Slater had his shoulder in a vice grip.

"My brother and me," I said. "Detective Wray responded to the scene along with a few other officers whose names I can't recall off the top of my head."

"Your Honor," Slater said. "This line of questioning is inappropriate, irrelevant, and damn near grounds for a mistrial. This witness was asked a question. She answered. Now unless counsel has some outside offer of proof or wants to call into question the integrity of his own office, I'd ask this little farce be stricken from the record and the jury be admonished to disregard it."

Mitchell sat back in his chair. He crossed his arms under his robe and glared at Rafe Johnson.

"Sustained, Mr. Johnson. I don't know what you're working on here, but not in my courtroom. I gave you more leeway than I should. You're done. Members of the jury, you're to disregard all questioning after Ms. Leary's answer to whether she's ever filed a false police report. She answered in the negative. Mr. Johnson?"

Rafe was back behind the lectern. He chewed his cheek, then picked up his papers. "I have nothing further for this witness."

"Good," Mitchell said. "Mr. Slater?"

Keith rose and adjusted his tie. "I have no questions for this witness at all," he said. "You may step down."

"Mr. Johnson?" the judge asked.

"The state calls Evangeline Leary to the stand."

My step faltered as I left the witness stand. In the back of the courtroom, my sister stepped forward, her face white as snow.

Chapter 25

"Ms. LEARY," Rafe said. "Can you describe your relationship to the previous witness?"

"Cass Leary is my older sister," Vangie said. She adjusted the microphone, bringing it closer to her face. I sank to an empty spot on the bench at the back of the courtroom.

"What about your relationship with the defendant?" he asked. "How would you characterize it?"

"Eric is my sister's ... um ... they were ... they are ... um ... dating."

Lord. She was already cracking under pressure.

"Ms. Leary," Rafe said. "Do you know whether Eric Wray was planning on asking your sister to marry him?"

"I don't know what he planned," she said.

"You're sure? The defendant never discussed his plans to propose?"

Vangie looked positively ill. Johnson had questioned her. She'd told both me and Slater he'd focused on how frequently we dated. What was this?

"Isn't it true, Ms. Leary, that the defendant in fact showed you a picture of a ring that he wanted to purchase for your sister?"

She looked down. "Yes," she said. "He showed me a ring."

"When?"

"I don't know for sure," she said. "I didn't write the date down."

"Isn't it also true that he asked your opinion as to whether you thought your sister would say yes?"

"Yes," she said quietly. I tried to keep my face neutral. Vangie had never told me any of this. Eric had never told me any of this. Had neither of them told Slater either? I wanted to scream.

"I'm sorry? Could you speak a little louder?"

"Yes," she said, tears filling her eyes.

"So we're clear. The defendant asked you whether you thought Cass Leary would accept his proposal?"

"Yes," she said.

"What did you tell him?"

"Objection," Slater said, barely rising. "Calls for hearsay."

"Sustained," the judge said.

"All right. Isn't it true that the defendant expressed concerns that your sister wouldn't accept a marriage proposal while he was still legally married to Wendy Wray?"

"Well, yes. Of course they couldn't get married while he was still married to Wendy," Vangie said. She looked like she wanted the floor to open up and swallow her. I wanted to kill Keith Slater. He should have prepared her for this. He should have prepared *me* for this.

"Isn't it also true that the defendant told you he knew your sister wouldn't even entertain the idea of sleeping with him while he was still technically married to Wendy?" Rafe asked.

"He said they were keeping things light," she said. "You know. Because of Wendy. He never got specific, and I didn't ask. That's personal."

"Light," Rafe repeated. "And your sister told you the same thing, didn't she?"

He was bold. Taking chances. He had something. Vangie must have confided all of this in someone else. A friend. A coworker. Someone had given Rafe Johnson an earful and broken my sister's confidence. By the look in her eyes, she realized it at the same time I did.

Tell the truth, I whispered under my breath. Just tell the truth. It's not worth a lie. Something else pricked the corners of my mind. Vangie had called me while I waited for Eric at Linda's that day. She seemed especially concerned about our lunch date. Good lord. Had he planned to propose? Was this conversation about Eric's intentions near the time of our lunch date and Wendy's death? He'd said nothing about it. Vangie had said nothing about it.

"Yes," Vangie answered. "I knew my sister was taking things slow with Eric out of respect for Wendy."

"Respect," Rafe repeated, his tone dripping with contempt. "Thank you. I have no further questions."

Keith rose. Rafe had taken him off guard with Vangie's testimony. I saw it in the subtle way he opened and then refastened the button on his jacket. He stepped to the lectern. He gave my sister a smile. Then, he told the judge he had no questions for her either.

"All right," the judge said. "Then we're adjourned for the day. The jury is dismissed until tomorrow at eight. You're not to discuss this case with anyone in the meantime."

Mitchell banged the gavel as Vangie rose to leave the stand.

Chapter 26

VANGIE RAN TO ME AFTERWARD, once the jury was safely out of earshot. Eric gave me a pained look as they led him out of the courtroom. I met his eyes, but said nothing, mindful of any other ears that might be listening.

"I'm so sorry," Vangie whispered. "I didn't know he would ask me that. I promised Eric I wouldn't say anything. About the ring. It was nothing. Just a casual conversation. I was the one who brought it up. Then after Wendy died and everything that happened, I didn't think it was important. I didn't know Johnson knew anything about it. How?"

I smoothed her hair back. "It's all right. It is what it is. We knew Rafe was going to use me as a motive."

"But how did he know?"

"Honey." Jeanie came to us. "Did you tell a friend, maybe? About the ring he showed you or that conversation?"

Vangie bit her lip. I gave Jeanie a look that said "don't." There was no point in it.

"I'm so sorry." Vangie was crying. "I was talking to a friend of mine at work. It was just gossip. It was harmless. I didn't know she'd tell anyone. I didn't tell her *not* to tell anyone. It was nothing. I thought it was nothing!"

As I tried to console my sister, Eric's sister barreled down on us.

"I hope you're happy," Monica hissed.

"Monica," I started.

"Don't," she said. "You've both done enough."

Joe and Matty made their way inside. As Vangie kept crying, I turned her out of my arm and into Joe's. "Take care of her," I said to him over Vangie's head. He nodded. I left my brothers and sister there. There was someone else I needed to talk to now.

By the time I reached my office, my rage hadn't cooled, it hardened. Not even Miranda could talk me down.

I barely let Keith walk through my office door before I laid into him.

"What the hell was that?" I asked. "Are you trying to lose this case?"

No reaction. Keith set his briefcase down on the floor and casually helped himself to one of my office chairs. He lit a cigarette, not even bothering to ask if I minded.

I paced behind my desk. "You leave it like that? That was a bullshit cheap shot and you let Rafe Johnson land it? You left my sister to the wolves!"

Slater puffed out a ring of smoke, then took another drag. He leaned forward, grabbed a business card off my desk and used it to snuff out his cigarette.

"Which one?" he asked as he wadded up his trash and threw it in the can against the wall.

"Which what?" I asked, flabbergasted.

"Which cheap shot? Your sex life, your unscrupulous past, or your sister's screw-up?"

"I'm going to kill you myself," I said.

"I'm serious," he said. "Which one? You knew your relationship with Eric is part of Johnson's theory of the case. I would have liked it if your sister had been more forthcoming about her conversations with you and Eric. But you handled it."

"Handled it," I said. "No thanks to you. The jury thinks I'm a liar. And pretty much a criminal. Why didn't you cross-examine me?"

He rested his ankle on the opposite knee.

"Do you think you needed rehabilitating?" Slater asked.

"What?"

"Did you want me to probe more deeply into what does or doesn't happen in your bedroom? Did you want me to spin some alternate version of your life? Are you ashamed of it in some way?"

"No," I yelled. "I'm not ashamed of anything. It's just ..."

"Just what? You think I needed to have the last word? Or more to the point, you did?"

I sat down hard in my chair.

"You let him get away with whatever he wanted," I said.

"I don't see it that way," he said.

"Eric's paying you to do a job, not sit there as a spectator!"

He raised an amused brow. "You have your style, I have mine."

"I actually show up!" I said.

"Right," he said. "The great Cass Leary. No problem she can't fix. No injustice she can't right."

"Screw you, Slater," I said.

He sat up straight, intensifying his stare. "You want to know why I did what I did?" he asked.

"Enlighten me," I said.

"Because you're a problem. One of my biggest," he said. "And you think you're my ally, which makes it even worse."

"What?"

"There's a lot of trial left. I needed you and your sister off the stand as quickly as possible. You're Eric's damn motive, Cass. I told you that from the beginning."

"Eric didn't kill Wendy!" I shouted.

"I don't care!" he shouted back. "Just like I don't care if he did. That's never been the point. You're a defense lawyer. You know how this works. The fact that *you* care is part of the problem. So, now you're done. Off the hook. Instead of thanking me, you're trying to rip my face off."

"Thanking you?" I asked.

"I cross-examine you, Johnson gets to redirect. I cross-examine Vangie. He gets to tear into *her* on redirect. And he's going to come back even harder because now he knows he drew blood."

"I'm not bleeding," I said.

"Really?" he said, rising. Slater leaned against my desk, meeting me almost nose to nose.

"Back off," I said, not breaking his stare.

"Really?" he said again. "You perjured yourself today, Cass."

The air went out of me. Slater's eyes flicked over mine.

"Be very, very careful what you say to me," I said.

"I don't think I will," Slater said. "You want to tell me what really happened last year when your brother shot that scumbag who tried to hurt his daughter?"

I wouldn't. He knew I wouldn't. I'd made a pact with Joe that we'd never speak of it again.

"In case you're wondering," Slater said. "I don't judge you for it. And they should pin a medal on him. But Rafe Johnson didn't pursue charges against Joe because he couldn't. It was because he wouldn't. He knew he wouldn't get a conviction. But he also knew it really was murder".

Slowly, Slater sank back into the chair opposite me. I wanted to argue. I wanted to ... well ... rip his face off. The worst part about it was we both knew he was right.

I let things go quiet for a few minutes. Little by little, my pulse steadied. Finally, I broke the silence.

"You know," I said. "I'm really beginning to hate you."

"Likewise," he said. "But you did good today. Or at least, you didn't completely torpedo my case. So that's a pleasant surprise."

"Get out," I said, but the fight had left me.

Slater chuckled as he rose to his feet. "Get some rest. You'll need it. You're going to have to figure out a way to cork that Irish temper of yours. Johnson's putting Wendy's family on the stand tomorrow. It'll be rough for you to hear."

"I can take it," I said.

"Good," Slater said as he picked up his briefcase and left. He passed Jeanie coming in.

"Don't start," I warned her. She put her hands up in surrender. A moony expression came into her eyes as Slater made his way down the stairs.

"He reminds me of his father," she said, wistfully. "Irresistible like that."

I cocked my head like a confused dog. "You gotta be kidding me."

She laughed, then went to the credenza behind me. She knew where I kept my secret stash of whisky. Pouring us two glasses, she sat down in the chair Slater had just vacated.

I took the drink, knowing I'd likely need many more if I were going to make it through the next few days intact.

Chapter 27

THE NEXT MORNING, Rafe Johnson began to call Wendy's family to the stand. The jury heard from her parents, Campbell and Darleen, as well as her only brother, Jeff. Dar started the day. I took my seat right behind Eric's sister. She had yet to acknowledge me again, and I wondered if that was Slater's design. Monica made her sentiments quite clear yesterday. I shook it off as the intense fear of an overprotective sibling. In her place, I couldn't say I might not feel the same if it were Matty or Joe on trial.

"Mrs. Maloney," Rafe started. "Thank you so much for coming in today. I know how difficult this must be for you."

Dar Maloney looked like she'd lost forty pounds since I last saw her at Wendy's funeral six months ago. Her hands worried at a lace handkerchief. Rafe had to repeatedly tell her to speak up and into the microphone.

"Tell me about Wendy," Rafe said.

"She was everything you'd ever want in a daughter. She got straight As in school. Beautiful. Popular. Kind. I know people always say girls are so much harder. Teenage girls, especially. My sisters, my friends who had daughters, the stories they would tell. We never had any issues like that with our baby girl. I was so proud of her."

Dar's voice caught.

"How long had she been dating the defendant?" Rafe asked.

"Forever," Dar answered. "High school sweethearts. It was like a storybook. Oh, he was so handsome too. Everyone in town looked up to Eric and Wendy."

When Cam Maloney took the stand, Rafe asked him the same question. Cam's face darkened before he answered.

"I had concerns," Cam said.

"About what?" Rafe asked.

"It's not that I wanted my daughter to date around. As fathers, we'd rather not think about that. It all just seemed too intense, too fast. Whatever Eric wanted, Wendy went along with it. She was worried about him becoming a cop. We all were. But once Eric decided, that was that. He was very dominant in that relationship. Wendy seemed happy enough, though. So I kept my mouth shut."

"What about during their marriage?" Rafe asked. "Did you have those same concerns?"

Cam scratched his cheek and squirmed in his seat.

"My brother was a cop," he said. "Detroit Police. I saw what it did to him. In fact, Johnny, my brother, tried to talk Eric out of becoming a cop back when he was taking the test to get into the academy. I watched it age Johnny before his time. People don't know. They see the worst in people every single day. It ate Johnny from the inside out. He retired at forty-nine and died of lung cancer two years later. Never smoked a day in his life. It was that job. I know it. And it was hard on my sister-in-law, too. Sleepless nights. The constant worry. I didn't want that for Wendy, but I knew it wasn't my place to say it. So I tried to be as supportive as I could until ..."

Cam broke. His lower lip quivered. He gripped the side of the witness box.

"Until what, Mr. Maloney?" Rafe asked.

"They fought a lot. Wendy was headstrong in her own way. She'd come over to the house and cry in her mother's arms. She said Eric wouldn't talk. She knew the job was getting to him, but he wouldn't let her in. She was fed up. She wanted out."

"Did she say what specifically she was worried about?" Rafe asked.

"I don't know. He wasn't there for her. She felt like she was holding everything together. Like she was the only one trying. Dar and I thought maybe she should see a priest. You know, for counseling. We don't believe in divorce. You take a vow, you stick to it."

Cam raised his head and threw a pointed stare at Eric. I desperately wanted to write a note and pass it to Jeanie for Slater. She sat behind him, taking notes of her own. But the jury was watching me. Whether I liked it or not, every move I made, the very expression on my face could have an impact.

"What do you know about Wendy's accident?" Rafe asked. He'd asked the question of both Dar, Cam, and her brother, Jeff. Dar had given the most detailed answer on direct.

"We'd spoken on the phone about an hour before," Dar said through tears. "Wendy and Eric had had a fight that morning."

"Do you know what it was about?" Rafe asked.

"What it was always about. She wanted out by then. She'd tried everything to get Eric's attention. I don't condone all of her choices. But she felt like she was married to a robot. He didn't care. If he would have shown her just the slightest bit of attention or affection, she would have done anything for Eric."

"Objection," Slater said. "The witness is speculating and testifying about hypotheticals."

"Please stick to the facts, Mrs. Maloney," Mitchell said, taking a tender tone with her.

"I didn't know she was driving," Dar said. "She knew not to text and drive. I didn't even like it when she used that hands-free feature. I felt like it was my fault. I was worried about her after our conversation. So I texted her to ask her if she was home yet. She just said, 'I'll call you later, Mom, I love you.' That was the last text she sent. The police think it was a factor in the crash."

Dar became unintelligible then. A few members of the jury had tears in their eyes. My own heart broke for her. No matter what else happened, this woman would always blame herself for her daughter's car accident.

"She ... she always said that," Dar continued. "She said, Mom, if you're worried about me driving, don't text me if you think I'm driving. I never thought ... I didn't ..."

"It's okay, Mrs. Maloney," Rafe said. "I have no further questions."

Lord, I didn't envy Slater. Rafe teed him up perfectly. It was almost as if he could turn around and say, "Have fun with that!"

"Don't come at her hard," I whispered to myself. "Whatever you do."

"Mrs. Maloney," Slater started. "Do you need a few minutes? I cannot possibly imagine what you're going through. Your Honor, could we take a recess, perhaps?"

"No," Dar shouted. "I don't want that. I want to keep going."

Slater was gentle. He established Eric's care for Wendy in the years that followed. He got her to admit she had no concerns about the medical decisions he made up until the last few weeks of her life. He'd consulted with the family every step of the way.

Cam Maloney had harsher words. "She was an inconvenience to him," he said. "That was plain."

"How so?" Rafe asked on direct.

"Because he wanted to kill her, that's why!" Cam said, his voice booming.

"Objection!" Slater shouted. "This witness is assuming facts not in evidence."

"Sustained, Mr. Johnson," Mitchell ruled.

"Why do you think Eric thought Wendy was a burden?" Rafe asked.

"Because he'd moved on," Cam answered. "He spent less and less time out at Maple Valley. He had a new girlfriend. Not long after that, he came to us and said ... he said ... he was ready to pull the plug on Wendy."

"He used those exact words?" Rafe asked; even he was incredulous.

"No," he said. "He used all the fancy ones the doctors say. But that was the gist of it. Wendy was alive. She was in there somewhere. You've seen the videos. I know my daughter. I know she knew we were there when we came to visit. We asked Eric. My wife begged him to just turn the medical decision-making over to us. We would have even supported it if he wanted to divorce her then. We told him that."

It was then I did pass a note to Jeanie. She took it discreetly and read it. She tapped Slater on the shoulder and handed it to him. I saw a slight perceptible nod as he folded the paper and put it down next to him. He began his cross of Cam Maloney with the question I'd written down.

"Mr. Maloney," he said. "What reason did your son-in-law give you for not wanting to divorce Wendy?"

"I don't know what you mean."

"Well, you indicated on direct that you told Eric you wanted to have her medical decision-making transferred to you. You and your wife filed a petition in probate court to have him removed, right?"

"We did," he said.

"But you had no concerns about how Wendy's money was managed, did you?"

"No."

"And you weren't asking that she be removed from Maple Valley. In fact, you knew it was through Eric's connections that she was able to get admitted there, right?"

"I think that's right," he said.

"And you've told friends and family that you believe Maple Valley was the gold standard of care for your daughter. In fact, you said that as early as last year, correct?"

"That's what I thought," he said. "And I have no problem with Maple Valley. It's Eric."

"But it was the doctors at Maple Valley who recommended end-of-life measures be taken. You didn't initially disagree with their assessment, did you?"

"No," he said. "I mean, I didn't know."

"Isn't it true that Eric Wray dismissed any thought of divorce because he wanted Wendy to continue to be eligible for coverage under his medical insurance?"

"He said that, yeah," Cam said.

"Isn't it also true that your opinion changed only after you were approached by a Dr. Lyman McNulty? Correct?"

"We consulted with him, yes," Cam admitted.

"But you didn't seek him out. Instead, he came to you."

"He came to my son, Jeff," Cam said. "We met through him."

"Dr. McNulty never treated Wendy, isn't that right? In fact, he never even saw her before he counseled you to resist the advice of the medical staff at Maple Valley, isn't that true?"

"I don't know the timeline," he said. "You'd have to ask him."

"How much did you pay Dr. McNulty?"

"I don't ... I don't know the full amount," he said.

"He charged you fifty thousand dollars over the course of the last year, isn't that right?" Slater asked.

"Could be."

"He asked you to mortgage your house when you couldn't afford it, isn't that right?"

"We'd have done anything to fight for Wendy!" Cam yelled.

"Would it surprise you to learn that Dr. McNulty has made more than four million dollars in the last two years counseling families such as yours? Those with loved ones with terminal conditions receiving end-of-life care."

"We were desperate!" Cam yelled. "I told you, we'd do anything to save our baby!"

Slater knew to quit while he was ahead. He let the question lie.

Jeff Maloney's testimony followed the trajectory of his parents'.

"Wendy was no saint," Jeff said. "But Eric wanted her dead."

"How do you know that?" Rafe asked.

"Because he told me," Jeff answered. I saw Eric's head snap back. Slater put a hand on his sleeve.

"What did Eric Wray say to you specifically?" Rafe asked.

"One afternoon, I went with him to see Wendy at Maple Valley. He was beaten down that day. Wendy had just had physical therapy, and it was tough to watch. Her legs looked like sticks. All her muscle tone was gone. Eric said, Wendy wouldn't want this. Sometimes I think I should just make it easier for her and put a pillow over her face. She'd beg me to if she could."

"Thank you," Rafe said. "I have no further questions for this witness."

Chapter 28

SLATER practically vaulted to the lectern. Jeanie had a hand on Eric's shoulder, as if he might do the same. Directly in front of me, his sister Monica started to cry.

"Mr. Maloney," Slater said. "You were questioned by the police after your sister died, isn't that right?"

"I was," he said.

"You gave a statement. A formal statement, didn't you?"

"I don't know what you call it. They asked me questions. They wrote down what I said," he answered.

"Do you remember what you told the police when you spoke to them?"

Jeff flapped a hand as if he were annoyed by the question. "My sister had just died. I don't know exactly what I said."

"Would it help refresh your recollection if I showed you your statement?" Slater said, grabbing a single piece of paper off the table behind him.

"Sure," Jeff answered. Slater approached and handed Jeff his statement. He quietly read it, then set it down in front of him.

"You never mentioned this alleged statement made by Eric Wray to the police, did you? You never told them you heard Eric say anything about wanting to smother his wife, did you?"

"I didn't tell them that at that time, no," Jeff said. "I was upset. More than that, my parents were upset. They were right there when the cops came. I was trying really hard to manage their emotions along with my own. So no, I didn't mention the fact that Wendy's own husband said he wanted to kill her."

"Who else was in the room with you when you claim to have heard this statement?" Slater asked.

"I don't remember. Well, Wendy, obviously."

"Wendy wasn't in a private room, was she?" Slater asked.

"She had a room to herself at the time," Jeff answered.

"Isn't it true though, that Wendy's room was actually nearest a nurse's hub?"

"Sure," Jeff said.

"In fact, Wendy Maloney had no door on her room, did she?"

"There was a curtain they'd pull if they were changing her sheets or something. For dignity's sake," he answered.

"But you claim nobody else heard this so-called statement?" Slater said.

"I don't know what anybody else heard," Jeff answered. "She had a nurse and a ... like a nurse's aide that were always in and out."

"Who were they?" Slater asked.

I reached into my messenger bag and pulled out Slater's witness lists. I'd annotated and highlighted it.

"Kim Crane was her nurse," Jeff said. "During weekdays, anyway. I think she was there that day. I don't know the aide's name. They were different."

I put new stars next to the aides I knew were assigned to Wendy's care the week before she died. Wayne Warren, Gloria LaPlante, Travis Mateese, and Olivia Corey .

"One was a big guy ... I wanna say Wayne was his name," Jeff said. "Then there was a younger woman. Maybe mid-twenties. Gloria something."

"You didn't even tell your parents about this so-called conversation, did you?" Slater asked. "In fact, today's the first time anyone's hearing of it, isn't that right?"

"I told my parents a while ago," he said. "After Wendy died. And I told Mr. Johnson when he interviewed me."

"I see," Slater said. "Thank you, I have nothing further today but reserve the right to call this witness at a later time."

"All right," Judge Mitchell said. "The witness is excused. We'll stand in recess until after lunch."

He banged the gavel.

We waited until the courtroom cleared, then Slater stormed over to Rafe Johnson.

"You gave me no discovery on that bullshit statement, Rafe," Slater said.

Rafe barely reacted. He finished stuffing papers into his briefcase and turned to Slater. Two deputies assigned to Eric came forward. Rafe shooed them away.

"It wasn't exactly exculpatory, Slater. Show me where I've violated any duty I owe you. You knew I was calling Jeff Maloney. You knew he was interviewed by the cops. You questioned him yourself. And you just cross-examined him. Good job, too. I have no idea why he didn't tell the police what he'd heard. Save it for your closing argument."

"I want a meeting with the judge," Slater said.

Rafe shook his head and started to leave. Slater followed. He gave quick directions to the deputies to make Eric comfortable in the waiting room they'd set up for him on trial days during breaks.

I followed them out. Eric had yet to turn back to look at me. As he walked into the room adjacent to the courtroom, I grabbed one of the deputies by the sleeve. His name was Smith, and I knew him to be a pretty good guy.

"I need a few minutes," I said.

"Cass," Eric started.

"I'm also his lawyer," I told Deputy Smith. "You've got him back in cuffs. He's not going anywhere."

"Five minutes," Smith said. "And I'm right outside that door."

I didn't wait for further permission, not even from Eric. As the door shut behind us, I turned to him.

"Eric ..."

"Don't," he said. "I think maybe you shouldn't be in the courtroom anymore."

"Funny," I said. "I'm not leaving. Eric, think. When was the last time you were in Wendy's room with Jeff?"

"The week before she died, just like Jeff said," Eric answered, sitting down in one of the chairs along the wall.

I pulled out the witness list. "What day of the week? What time? Give me something to go on. Slater can call some of the hospital staff. We can easily cast doubt on Jeff's story."

I turned the paper toward him. "I know Travis Mateese and Wayne Warren worked on Tuesdays and Thursdays. These two nurse's aides rotated through Wendy's room on Monday, Wednesdays, and Fridays. What day of the week was it?"

Eric rubbed his forehead. "It would have been right after I got off work. Four o'clock. You know I used to go on Wednesdays."

"Okay," I said. Gloria LaPlante worked Wednesdays that month. Jeff had more or less identified her. Now that we had a date narrowed down, I could see who else was assigned to Wendy that evening.

"Good," I said. "We'll get Gloria on the stand. She's going to say she heard no such thing out of you."

Eric reached for me. "Cass, don't."

"What do you mean, don't?"

"Because Jeff wasn't lying. I said more or less what he said I did. It was a low point. I was just so worn down with everything the doctors were telling me and Wendy's parents. And just, Wendy herself. Every time I saw her, she'd wasted away even more. It was killing me to see her like that. I don't remember my exact words, but yes. I made a comment out of frustration to Jeff. I said sometimes I wondered if I'd just be doing the right thing by ending her suffering. I'd forgotten. But yes. I told Wendy's brother if killing her might be kinder."

Slater walked in just in time to hear Eric's words. His shoulders sank. His color drained. It was in that moment I knew I was the last person on earth who believed Eric was innocent.

Chapter 29

OWEN CORBETT TOOK the stand after the lunch break. I sat in the very back of the courtroom this time, scribbling furious notes. I had to find out if anyone else overheard Eric's statement to Jeff Maloney. I combed through the police report, recommitting every witness to memory as Owen Corbett tried to endear himself to the jury. Within the first fifteen minutes of his testimony, I had to wonder if Rafe Johnson realized he'd just made his first major blunder.

"How did you meet the victim?" Rafe asked.

"She sold me a house," Owen answered. "I'd seen Wendy's billboards on 127, a few commercials. I lived in Flint and was looking to move somewhere smaller, quieter. I knew Wendy Wray was the person to call if you wanted to buy in Delphi."

"I see," Rafe said. "How would you characterize your relationship with Wendy?"

"I was impressed with her. She found me a three bedroom in an older, but stable subdivision. When it came time to make an offer, she was a real shark in the negotiations. She got me a great deal. I didn't really know anyone in town, so after I moved in, I called and texted her pretty frequently. You know. To get recommendations for things. A new dentist. Someone to clean the gutters. The best places to eat, that kind of thing."

"Did your relationship ever change from a professional one?" Rafe asked.

Owen looked down. "Yeah. Um ... yes. I considered Wendy a really good friend. After I'd lived in Delphi about a year, she started to confide in me. That was mutual. She was just one of those people you could really talk to. She was having some trouble. She ... look ... I knew she was having an affair. It was ending. She was feeling really down on herself."

"You knew she was married?"

"I did. I knew she was married on paper, that is. Wendy told me fairly early on that she and her husband were separated."

"They weren't though, were they?" Rafe asked.

"I didn't know that until much, much later. Wendy always said her marriage was over. That they were just trying to work out the details. I'll admit. I didn't ask a lot of questions about that. Wendy never seemed like she wanted to talk about it. I respected that. Well, after her break-up, I started to get very worried about her."

"Why is that?" Rafe asked.

"She was depressed. I could see it. I had a sister who went through something like that, and I knew the signs. We started spending more and more time together. Then, our relationship became physical."

"When was that?" Rafe asked.

"Five years ago," he said. "Three months before her accident."

"When you say physical," Rafe said. "What do you really mean, Mr. Corbett?"

"We started an affair. I was ... I was in pretty hard love with Wendy by that time. She was too. She told me."

"But you knew she was married," Rafe said.

"Like I told you, she made it sound like they were getting a divorce. But then ... I don't know, maybe six weeks before the accident, I found out otherwise. I ran into a mutual friend, another agent at Wendy's firm. We got to talking, and I made a comment, something about how Wendy was having a rough year with the divorce or something. Well, her friend told me there was no divorce. She said Wendy had been saying she was going to get out of that marriage for years, but that it was all bull. That she was never going to leave Eric."

"What happened next?" Rafe asked.

"I confronted her about it. I was really angry. I didn't know Eric was a cop. I barely knew his name at all. That was my fault. I took a lot of what Wendy told me at face value. She was so fragile. So vulnerable."

"What happened when you confronted her?" Rafe asked.

"She ... Wendy flipped out. She was terrified. I'd never seen her like that. She burst into tears and started almost clawing at me, like she was afraid I'd disappear. It scared me."

"Why?"

"She ... she told me she was afraid of what her husband might do if she pushed the issue of divorce," Owen said.

"She was afraid?" Rafe asked. "Did she say why?"

"She showed me a scar," Owen answered while making a slash across his upper arm. "On her arm. It was healed, but it looked like it had been pretty deep. Wendy said Eric gave it to her the last time she tried to leave him the year before."

"What?" Eric yelled.

"Objection!" Slater shot up.

"That's a lie!" Monica Wray went to her feet. "He's lying! Or Wendy was!"

Mitchell banged his gavel. "Quiet down. I'll have no outbursts from spectators or we won't have any. Same goes for the defendant. Mr. Slater has made an objection. On what grounds?"

"Hearsay for one," Slater said. "Assuming facts not in evidence for another."

"Your hearsay objection is well-founded," the judge said. "The jury is instructed to disregard that last statement and everything you heard from non-witnesses. Go ahead, Mr. Johnson."

I could barely contain myself. Monica was right: either Owen Corbett was lying, or Wendy had been. Eric furiously scribbled something on the pad of paper beside him. He shoved it in front of Slater. He read it, tore it off, then handed it back to Jeanie.

"Mr. Corbett," Rafe continued. "What happened after you confronted Wendy Wray about her marital status?"

"Based on the things she told me, I backed off," he said.

"What do you mean by that?"

"I went into it thinking I was going to give her an ultimatum. Either she left her husband or I was gone. It was one thing if she were married in name only. It was quite another if she had no intention of following through with the divorce. But she seemed so broken ... I just couldn't go through with it. So, I held her. I told her everything was going to be okay, and that I wasn't going anywhere."

"What happened after that?" Rafe asked.

"Things calmed down for a bit. Wendy seemed happier. I let it go."

"For how long?" Rafe asked.

"Another couple of weeks. She made me some promises. She said she was starting to put things in place to divorce her husband."

"To your knowledge, was she?" Rafe asked.

Owen squirmed. "I found out later that she never filed," he said. "That she'd never even seen a lawyer about it."

"Did you ask her about that?" Rafe asked.

"I did," he said. "I was fed up. She kept making excuses. I told her if she was afraid, that I'd protect her. She didn't think I could because he was a cop. I was furious. So one night, I'd just had it. I worked up the courage, and I went to Wendy's house when I knew Eric would be home. I was going to have it out with him."

"What happened?" Rafe asked.

Owen squeezed his eyes shut, steeling himself before he answered.

"Nothing happened," he said. "Not with Eric, anyway. I never got past the front door. Wendy saw me in the driveway and came out."

The woman in front of me turned. She handed me a folded piece of yellow notepad paper. I took it from her and opened it. It was in Eric's handwriting, scrawled with fast fury.

"Wendy lied to him," it read. "Scar on her arm from a golf cart accident when she was sixteen."

I pulled up my phone and quickly opened my Facebook App. The Maloneys had turned Wendy's profile into a memorial page. I scrolled as fast as I could, hoping I could find what I remembered seeing there a very long time ago. Hoping it was good enough.

There. Six years ago, she'd made an anniversary post with their wedding photo. If Jeanie was right, this was during the time she started an affair with another detective with the Delphi P.D. Sure enough, she wore a sleeveless dress. It was faint, but there was a fine scar running along her left forearm. I took a quick screenshot and sent it to Jeanie five rows ahead of me.

I watched as she opened her phone. She lifted her fist up without looking backward. Then she tapped Slater on the shoulder.

This was awful. It felt like Wendy was reaching from beyond the grave to try to hurt Eric. I hated that I felt like that. She was dead. If she owed a penance, she'd paid it over and over. I did the only thing I could then; I said another prayer for Wendy Wray's soul.

"She was afraid of Eric," Owen said, finally breaking down. "She burst into tears just like the month before. Only this time, she told me if she filed for divorce, she was sure something bad would happen to her. A week later, her car went into that tree."

"Objection," Slater said. He had his phone in his hand. I could see the Facebook photo on the screen. Jeanie must have texted it. "This testimony is highly prejudicial with zero probative value. Mr. Wray is not on trial for anything in connection with Wendy Wray's accident. The cause of it is not in dispute. There has already been testimony to that fact. It was tragic. It was unfortunate, but it was an accident."

"Move on, Mr. Johnson," Judge Mitchell said.

"Thank you, Your Honor. I have nothing further."

"Do you think you can finish up by three, Mr. Slater?" asked the judge.

"I can finish up in sixty seconds, Your Honor," Slater said. He leaned over to his laptop and plugged his phone in with a USB cord. With one button, he could share the photo on the overhead for the jury to see.

"Mr. Corbett," he said. "You claim Wendy Wray said Eric cut her, is that right?"

"That's what she said, yes," he answered. "I saw the scar."

"You saw the scar," he said. "And you claim she told you he'd given it to her the year before, when she tried to file for divorce."

"Your Honor," Rafe rose. "Counsel is now interrogating the witness about testimony that he asked and succeeded in having stricken."

"Mr. Slater?"

"I'd like to withdraw that earlier objection. Also, the jury has already heard it. We all know you can't unring a bell. Some additional information has just been brought to my attention that I feel will put this issue to rest once and for all, if you'll allow me some leeway."

"Very little," Mitchell said.

Rafe looked scared. Good.

"You're certain Wendy told you she'd gotten this cut a year before?"

"That's what she said, yes," he answered.

"Can you describe that cut for us?"

"It was about two inches long, on her left arm just below her shoulder. Kind of across her bicep."

"Your Honor, I'd like to show the witness and opposing counsel a photograph."

He did. Rafe's color turned positively green. Then Owen's did when he saw the picture.

Slater put it on the screen. Blown up on the overhead, Wendy's scar was even more visible.

"Is this the scar you saw?" Slater asked.

"It ... I wasn't ... she said ..."

"Is this the scar?" Slater asked again.

"Yes," Owen said, pursing his lips in anger.

"I'd like the record to reflect we're looking at a wedding photo of Wendy Wray and Eric Wray. One that was taken almost twenty years ago. And that the witness has just confirmed the scar in question is clearly visible in it."

"So reflected," the judge said, decidedly unamused.

"Thank you," Slater said. "I'm done with this witness."

Mitchell adjourned. I sat against the wall as they led Eric out. He mouthed two words as he passed me.

"Thank you."

"Nice work," Slater said, extending his hand to shake mine.

"Johnson just made a very uncharacteristic, sloppy mistake," I said. "He won't make another."

Slater nodded in agreement. We weren't going to win this case waiting for Johnson's mistakes. We needed more. So much more. For the second time in the span of twenty minutes, I prayed. Please God, let one of my other leads pan out.

Chapter 30

Nurse Kim Crane took the stand first thing the next morning. From her posture and stony expression, I knew the jury would have a hard time reading her. Johnson took a half an hour to go through her background. At forty-five, she'd worked in elder care settings for her entire twenty-plus-year nursing career. The longest-serving staff member at Maple Valley, she pre-dated every doctor currently working there and had been there when the facility opened its doors seventeen years ago. Kim Crane fit the mold of every battle axe stereotype of a nurse. At the same time, she was exactly the one you'd want in charge of your family member's care.

"How long had you been involved in Wendy Wray's care, Nurse Crane?" Johnson asked.

"I had Wendy on my service for just over two years. She was a favorite of mine," she answered.

"Why is that?"

"She had good family support. That's not always the case. It's sad for some of our residents. They often don't get many visitors in my wing. My patient load consists of some of the more severe cases. Those who have gone beyond our capabilities for rehabilitation. My patients are generally those who will go on to need end-of-life care. At any rate, Wendy's room was always a hub of activity. Her parents came weekly. Sometimes daily. Her brother flew in when he could. Her husband. Other friends. They were all of them very respectful to me and my staff. Appreciative. Sadly, that can be rare."

"I see," Rafe said. "Nurse Crane, were you on duty the day Wendy Wray passed away?"

"I was," she said. "I worked from seven to seven. Wendy was on my service as she always was the days I worked."

"And what type of care did you render for Wendy that day?"

"I supervised the administering of her medication. Checked her vitals. She'd been recently treated for a urinary tract infection, so I checked her catheter. One of our nurse's aides, Gloria LaPlante, helped me move Wendy. She'd started to develop a very mild bed sore on her left hip. Gloria asked me for help in repositioning her pillows to alleviate pressure in that area."

"Did she have any visitors that day?"

"Yes," she said. "Wendy's husband, Eric Wray, arrived and sat with her for a while."

"Do you know whether Mr. Wray visited Wendy on a regular schedule?"

"He did," she said. "He used to come every week on Wednesdays. Over the last year, the frequency of that waned. He started coming every other week. Her parents still came twice a week, though."

"Did you ever speak to the defendant about Wendy's care?"

"Frequently," she said. "Eric was her patient advocate. He had the authority to make decisions for her. So he was always included in decisions regarding Wendy's care and treatment."

"Did you speak to the defendant about her care on that day?"

"Yes," she answered. "Wendy's condition was deteriorating. She was very prone to infection. That's why we were so concerned about this minor bedsore. There had also been some issues a few weeks before. A fungal infection around her feeding tube. It was getting to the point where she had one issue like that after another. Mr. Wray was concerned about whether she experienced any sort of pain or discomfort."

"That's what you spoke about that day?" Rafe asked.

"Yes," she said.

"Can you describe his demeanor during that conversation?"

"He was sad," Kim answered. "He was always sad. He looked haggard. I knew the doctors had begun to discuss moving Wendy into hospice care. We had really started to reach the end of what we could do for her."

"What was the plan, if you know?" Rafe asked.

"My understanding was that Wendy would perhaps be moved home or to her parents' home over the next few weeks. Eric said he wanted her to be somewhere she knew."

"I see," Rafe said. "You said you felt the defendant was distressed. Why do you think that?"

"He was a wreck," Kim said. "That morning, on the 17th, when I walked in, I found him sobbing at Wendy's bedside. He kept saying, I'm sorry, over and over."

"What did you do?"

"I left," I said. "I closed the privacy curtain and gave him a moment."

"When was that?" Rafe asked.

"I believe that was right about noon," she said.

"Nurse Crane," he said. "Who is Dr. Paul Barnes?"

"He's the medical director of Maple Valley. My boss."

"Was Dr. Barnes on the premises the morning of August 17th?"

"He was," she said.

"Did you speak to Dr. Barnes that morning?"

"Yes," she said. "In passing."

"Can you tell me if you discussed Wendy Wray's case with him at all?"

"No," she said.

"No, you don't recall, or no, you didn't discuss her?"

"No, we didn't discuss her."

"So, you were unaware of any requests Dr. Barnes might have had to meet with Eric Wray or a member of Wendy's family?"

"That's correct. He didn't run any request to meet with Mr. Wray by me that day, no."

"Would it have been normal for him to do so?"

"It would have been normal for him to let me know if he wished to speak to a visiting family member if I happened to see them, yes."

"And when did you next see either the defendant or Wendy?"

"I went back to my workstation and finished some charting. About one o'clock, I went back to Wendy's room. The privacy curtain was still pulled. I announced myself, but no one answered. So, I peeled back the curtain."

"What did you find?" Rafe asked.

"Wendy didn't look right. Her eyes were open, but she wasn't moving. She had ... there were fairly prominent red marks on her cheeks. I checked her vitals, and she had no pulse. So, I immediately called for Dr. Barnes. He was on staff at that time. He arrived within maybe sixty seconds."

"What happened then?" Rafe asked.

"Dr. Barnes examined Wendy and pronounced her dead at 1:08 p.m."

"You didn't try to revive her?"

"No, sir. Wendy Wray had a DNR order in her file. Do not resuscitate. She was terminal at that point."

"Nurse Crane, did you suspect anything amiss?"

"Well, as I said, Wendy looked as if she had an injury around her mouth."

Johnson moved for entry of a photograph. When admitted, he blew it up on the overhead. I winced. It was a photograph taken while Wendy still lay in her hospital bed. She stared sightless at the ceiling, her body turned at an odd angle with her torso flat against the bed and her lower body slightly to the left. Her lips had frozen in a pucker. Large red splotches framed her mouth, the edges started to turn blue.

"Who took that picture, Nurse Crane?" Rafe asked.

"I did. With my phone."

"Do you always take pictures of recently deceased patients?"

"No, sir. But Wendy ... something seemed off. She usually lay on her left side. The way she was lying, contorted like that, it just seemed off. Plus the bruising around her mouth. I commented on it to Dr. Barnes. He agreed that it was a good idea that I document everything. So I took the picture. Whenever we have a suspicious death, it's protocol to call the medical examiner. We did. She in turn called the Woodbridge County Sheriff's office."

"Thank you, Nurse Crane, I have nothing further."

Slater came to the lectern. Jeanie had slid into the seat beside me.

"She's neutral," Jeanie said. "Don't worry about it."

"She's not neutral," I whispered back. "She puts Eric as the last person with Wendy ... alone ... while she was still breathing."

"Nurse Crane," Slater said. "You weren't the only staff member assigned to care for Wendy Wray on August 17th, were you?"

"No, sir," she said.

"In fact, there were two nurse's aides on staff that day. Gloria LaPlante and Olivia Corey, isn't that right?"

"They were all working that day, yes."

"Wendy was scheduled for physical therapy that morning, isn't that right?"

"She was, yes. But that was for two p.m. Wendy had already passed away by then. She never saw her P.T."

I leaned over to Jeanie. "He should bring up the investigation into Hector and Wayne Warren. At least plant a seed in the jury's mind, even if it didn't go anywhere. Hector never denied the break room conversations about Wendy. And why can't anyone find Wayne Warren?"

"He knows," Jeanie answered. "Have faith."

"Nurse Crane, you're familiar with two C.N.A.s who worked at Maple Valley during August of last year. Uh. Hector Ruiz and Wayne Warren?"

"I knew them, yes," she said.

"Nurse Crane, isn't it true that you recommended Wayne and Hector be reassigned?"

"I forwarded a complaint we received to HR," she said.

"What was the nature of that complaint?" Slater asked.

"We had another staff member complain that she didn't feel safe around them," she answered.

"Not safe how?"

"I don't know," she said.

"It was pertaining to Wendy Wray specifically, wasn't it?"

"It wasn't," she said. "It was about another patient, Mary Palmer."

"But isn't it true, another nurse's aide at Maple Valley complained she overheard Hector Ruiz and Wayne Warren making lewd comments about Wendy Wray, isn't that right?"

"It was something to that effect, yes. But I don't believe it was only pertaining to Wendy Wray."

"No," Slater said. "They rated her, didn't they?"

"I'm sorry?"

"Wayne and Hector were in fact running a rating pool. On a scale of one to ten, which patient they found most desirable."

"Yes," Kim Crane said, her face registering disgust. Two of the jurors covered their mouths.

"Thank you," Slater said. "That's all I have right now."

"Nurse Crane," Rafe said. "I have one question. To your knowledge, were either Hector Ruiz or Wayne Warren assigned to Wendy Wray's care the day she died?"

Kim Crane leaned forward. "No. Hector was no longer working for Maple Valley on the day Wendy Wray died. Wayne Warren wasn't under my supervision on August 17th. In fact, neither of them currently work for Maple Valley."

"Thank you, I have nothing further."

I didn't dare breathe. Rafe had just left a huge opening for Slater. I gripped the side of the bench. Did Slater see it too?

Careful, I thought. Don't overplay your hand.

"One more question, Nurse Crane," Slater said. "You said Wayne Warren is no longer working at Maple Valley. Isn't it true that he left his employment there within days of Wendy Wray's death?"

"It was later that week, yes," she said.

"Interesting," Slater said. "I have nothing further." It was a very thin thread. But Slater had just put the onus on Rafe to explain what happened to Wayne Warren. He could make an argument on cross that Craddock's investigation was incomplete.

Chapter 31

Mitchell called a brief recess as soon as Kim Crane stepped down. We gathered in the third-floor conference room. Eric looked ragged. Bone-weary. I, on the other hand, couldn't stop moving.

"He didn't catch it," I said. "Rafe has no idea the door he just left open."

"Don't get too excited," Slater said. "Ruiz and Warren were cleared of any wrongdoing. I've seen the report. Crane was right. The complaint didn't specifically mention anything about the break room talk. We got lucky that she admitted she'd heard that rumor too. So far, nobody can prove anything about Mary Palmer's injuries. Nobody saw anything. Nobody said anything. And Audra Kaminsky isn't exactly credible. If I put her on the stand, Rafe will tear her up."

"Craddock never even tried though," Eric said. "He made up his mind I'm the one who did this. He had one five-minute conversation with Hector Ruiz and didn't go looking for Wayne Warren."

"He'll argue it doesn't matter," Jeanie said. "No one's disputing Hector had an alibi the day Wendy died. Nobody saw Wayne Warren anywhere near Wendy that day either."

"We've gotta find him," I said.

"Tori's still trying," Jeanie said. "She's running down old addresses. She's talking to the Palmer family today to see if they remember anything about Warren."

"Good. Slater, you just need the jury to raise the same questions I have," I said. "Where is Wayne? Why didn't Craddock pursue a more detailed statement from him? Why hasn't anyone been able to find him?"

"It's a risk," Slater said.

"It's reasonable doubt," I said, though no one in the room, not even Eric, looked convinced.

"Eric," Slater said. "Johnson's going to call the other nurse's aides when we go back in there. Is there any chance either of them heard you say anything incriminating?"

"They gave statements to the police," I said. "If they change their stories now ..."

"That's not what I asked," Slater said. He leveled a stare at Eric.

"I told you before," Eric said. "I don't know. You already have Wendy's brother saying I said I wanted to smother her. Do you think if I were really planning to follow through on that, I would be dumb enough to say that in front of witnesses? To her brother, for God's sake?"

Slater sighed. "So the bottom line is we don't know what they heard or what they're going to say now. I can impeach them if their statements are different from before, but it might not matter."

There was a light knock on the door. One of the deputies poked his head in. "They're ready to reconvene," he said. We rose together. I had a bad feeling about what might happen next.

As Slater predicted, Rafe called the two nurse's aides assigned to Wendy's wing in succession: Olivia Corey, then Gloria LaPlante.

Each described similar events as Kim Crane. Wendy had a wildly supportive family. They sympathized with Eric's plight. In Olivia Corey's case, it became clear she might have had a bit of a crush on him.

"He was so sweet and patient with her," Olivia said, in tears. She was a curvy girl with tightly curled hair and red glasses. "I don't know what happened. But he would have never hurt his wife. Never."

I watched the jury. The two youngest jurors, numbers seven and nine, sat in the front row. Seven was a twenty-five-year-old T.S.A. agent. He took the most notes out of the entire panel. He stopped writing and fixed hard eyes on Olivia Corey. Juror number nine was a twenty-eight-year-old kindergarten teacher. She looked straight at Eric.

Olivia Corey's statement put Rafe Johnson in the position of having to object to his own witness. Once instructed to keep her opinions to herself, Rafe asked a final question.

"Were you aware that Eric Wray had moved on romantically, Ms. Corey? That he had a serious girlfriend in Cass Leary?"

Olivia's eyes got big. Then she actually glared at me. Was this a gift? I tried to read the jury without making it obvious. Juror number seven kept on scribbling. Juror number ten, a retired postal worker, rolled her eyes. Olivia Corey hadn't impressed her.

"I wasn't in the habit of asking patients' families too many personal questions," Olivia said. "We spoke mainly about patient care."

"I see," he said. "When did you last see the patient, Wendy Wray, alive?"

"I worked day shift," she said. "I had the odd-numbered room patients. Wendy was an even. So she wasn't on my service that day, but I passed by her room plenty. I knew Mr. Wray was there visiting."

"Did you see Mr. Wray enter Mrs. Wray's room?"

"I did," she said. "It was just before noon. I was about to take my lunch break."

"Did you see him leave her room?"

"No," she said.

"Did Mrs. Wray have any other visitors that day?"

"Not that I'm aware of, no," she said.

"Thank you," Rafe said. "I have no further questions."

Slater rose. Then, he made the choice that I would have made. He let Olivia's testimony stand as is. He asked no questions of her.

Gloria LaPlante took the stand next. She had cotton-candy-pink hair with blonde roots beginning to show. She tripped on her too-high heels as she tried to climb into the witness box. The bailiff caught her elbow just in time.

She reiterated everything Kim Crane said about Wendy's care, her attentive family, the tragic figure Eric cut towards the end.

"Ms. LaPlante," Rafe asked. "Do you recall a visit the defendant made to his wife's room along with her brother, Jeff Maloney?"

"I do," she said.

"Do you recall when that was?"

"The most recent visit?" Gloria asked. A strand of her pink hair had come loose and bobbed in front of her face. She wore a plunging, V-neck top and a necklace with a pendant in the shape of a horseshoe dangled over her ample chest.

"Yes."

"He was there with Mrs. Wray's brother. I think it was the week before. I remember it because they got into an argument."

"You witnessed this argument?" I held my breath. Was she about to change her story? As it stood now, Jeff Maloney's claim of Eric's threat went uncorroborated. That and a million other reasons was why Eric could never take the stand.

Unless ...

"Part of it, yes," she answered. "I'd just finished washing Wendy's hair. They came in together. Jeff Maloney sat next to Wendy and was holding her hand. Mr. Wray stood at the end of the bed. I picked up my things and went into Wendy's bathroom."

"What did you hear?"

"The brother ... Jeff. He was telling Eric he should just let his folks handle her affairs. He said it was clear Eric didn't want to do it anymore, so quit fighting."

"What did Eric say?"

"He got really angry. He said he was doing what Wendy would have wanted. That she wouldn't want to be hooked up to machines or living like she was. I couldn't blame him. I'm sorry to say it, but Wendy was rotting from the inside out at that point. I sure wouldn't want to live like that."

"I see," Rafe said. "Can you remember exactly what Eric Wray said?"

"The police asked me that too," she said. "I really wish I could. But I try not to eavesdrop. I can just tell you that he was terribly upset. Red-faced. Crying. And Mrs. Wray's brother also looked upset."

I dropped my head. It tore at me, knowing the desperation and despair Eric was in that day. From where I sat, I saw a tremor go through him as he listened. Would she change her story? Would she now say she'd overheard Eric fantasizing about smothering Wendy?

"I can't stand this," I said.

"You have to," Jeanie said. "Keith knows what he's doing."

"You were also working the day Wendy Wray died, isn't that right?"

"Yes," Gloria said.

"Did you see the defendant in her room?"

"Um, no," she said. "I saw him later."

"Later," he said. "Did you talk to him?"

"I spoke to him, yes," she said.

"About what?"

"I saw him coming out of the stairwell. He looked upset. I asked him if everything was okay," she said.

"What do you mean, upset?" Rafe asked.

"He looked like he'd been crying. When I stopped to ask him if everything was okay, he was a little abrupt. He said everything's fine. Then he brushed past me. He was walking fast. Like in a hurry."

"Can you recall when this was?"

"It was well after twelve."

"How can you be so sure of the time?"

"Because I'd already had my lunch. I ate between 11:30 and 12:30. So it was after I got back."

"Thank you, I have nothing further."

Judge Mitchell ended for the day. It was Friday. We'd finished the whole first week of trial. Now, Eric would go back to jail. For two whole days he'd have to wait while the rest of us tried to save the rest of his life.

Eric came up behind me. My heart jumped. The two deputies assigned to transport him hung back.

"They're doing me a favor," Eric said. "Ten minutes."

"Good," Slater said. "There's just a couple of quick points I want to go over with you before ..."

"No," Eric said. "With Cass. I need to talk to Cass. Alone. Now."

Chapter 32

SLATER and the deputies cleared the courtroom for us. Eric sat back down at the defense table. I took Slater's seat beside him.

"You're doing great," I said. "Johnson will rest soon. Probably after he calls Craddock and the ME. We've seen everything he's got now. Slater has a game plan ..."

"There's something I need you to tell me. I haven't wanted to ask. I guess maybe I didn't want to know. Only I need to. What did you do for me?" he asked, his blue eyes turning stony. He clasped his hands together. The shiny metal of the handcuffs peeked out under the sleeves of his suit jacket. He'd get them off only when the jury was present.

"What do you mean?" I asked.

"You know what I mean," Eric said. "I didn't want to say this in front of the others. Word's gotten to me. Odd looks. Whispers in the yard. They've rotated in new guards."

"Eric ..."

"I'm an untouchable, all of a sudden," he said. "At first I thought it was just blowback from me getting stabbed. Too many eyes on me. Whoever it was planned to watch and wait. Bide their time. That's not it though. There's a new edict. Something big, backed by prison power brokers. I know what that means."

"I don't know what you're talking about," I said.

Eric leaned back. "So that's where we are now? Lies?"

I clenched my jaw, afraid to say more.

"You went to Killian Thorne for me," he said.

I wouldn't answer. He was right about one thing. If we started lying to each other, we were sunk.

"Cass," he said, reaching for me. "I can take care of myself."

"You can't," I snapped. "My God, Eric. The only reason you're alive now is because whoever stabbed you got you someplace where you bled enough to leave a trail. You know that, right? This time, you needed help. Help that I could broker."

"Broker," he said. "See, the thing about that is, you have to give something to get something. These people are dangerous."

"I know exactly who these people are."

"Do you? Do you really? Because I think you've had the luxury of fighting clean up until now. That was your job. Where I am ... what I've seen ... that's now how it works. The inner-city gangs, the Aryan Brotherhood, the Steel Beasts, the cartel ... these are ruthless, evil men. Time doesn't mean anything to them."

"You're right. But power does. And I used what I have to keep you from getting stabbed again. I won't apologize for it. You know me. You know exactly how far I'll go to protect the people that matter to me. So will you."

He froze. The room went deathly quiet. Finally, the air went out of him. Pain crossed his face, then left it. His eyes went blank.

"I can't live with that. I should have let you go long before this. I had no business dragging you into my life. Not when things were unresolved with Wendy."

"Stop ..."

"No," he said. "I need you to move on. Start living your life again. No matter what happens during this damn trial, it's cost you too much. What happens to me isn't your concern anymore. I don't want to be one of the people you feel you have to do anything for. I won't be the reason you get hurt. If I'd had my head on straight about Wendy, maybe none of this ..."

"You don't get to decide that," I said. "You're not responsible for my choices. You did the best you could for Wendy. You also made me a promise. Do I have to remind you?"

His eyes flicked to mine.

"You promised me that you wouldn't give up. You promised me you'd join this fight. Well, we aren't done. Not by a long shot. You want to dump me? Fine. You can do it properly when you're a free man. I'm going to make sure you get there, whether you like it or not."

"Cass ..."

"No. This is nuts. You're talking nuts. You think this is noble of you? Chivalrous? Tough. I don't need that. You didn't kill Wendy. But somebody did. Every instinct in me tells me Wayne Warren knows something. Slater can't find him. Rafe Johnson can't find him. Well, I'm going to. It might be a dead end. But I'm going to see it through. The only thing Rafe Johnson has proven so far is that you were grieving your wife's prognosis, and that you went to visit her the day she died. That's not enough. That's reasonable doubt. I could win this trial in my sleep. I plan to make damn sure Keith Slater does. After that ... well ... you can tell me to go to hell out from behind prison glass."

I rose. Eric kept his hands clenched in two tight fists. Before he could argue with me, the deputies came back in to get him with Slater following closely behind.

Eric rose. His eyes pleaded with me, but I turned away. Whatever was written on both of our faces was enough to keep Slater quiet until they led Eric out of the courtroom. As the door shut, Slater turned to me.

"Do I want to know what that was all about?" he asked.

"Probably not," I said, heaving my leather bag off the ground and sliding the strap over my shoulder.

"Why do I get the feeling you're about to lay into me again?" he asked, shaking his head. I started walking toward the courtroom doors. Slater got ahead of me and tried to open them for me.

"I've got it," I said, aware of how bitchy my tone sounded. But just then, I didn't think I could stand any more chivalry. I opened the doors for myself and walked out.

Chapter 33

AUDRA KAMINSKY DIDN'T EXPECT me as I waited outside her grandmother's house. Since our last meeting, a few months ago, she'd dodged my calls. I wasn't even sure seeing her now was a good idea. She was compromised. She'd lied to me, or at least kept a big chunk of the truth from me last time. But she still might be the best lead I had. I parked down the block and walked up to her as she tried to get in her car in the driveway. She startled as my shadow crossed in front of her.

"You," she said, putting a hand to her chest.

"We need to talk," I said. "Is there someplace private?"

Audra looked up and down the sidewalk. "I've said all I can say to you," she said. "I told you before, there's nothing I can do to help that man."

"We disagree on that," I said.

"Look, I can't be involved anymore. They opened up an investigation into Ellie Palmer's mom's death. Did you know that?"

"Yes," I said. "And all this talk about it being an anonymous complaint. We know that's not true. You initiated it. You tried to get Maple Valley to do something about what happened to Mary Palmer."

"Then you know nothing came of it. Now everyone knows I'm the one who opened her big, stupid mouth. I was in line for a job at St. Sebastian's Hospital. It's five miles away. Full benefits. Third shift. They would have paid for me to keep going to school. As soon as the word got out that I was involved with what happened at Maple Valley, the offer went away. All of a sudden, they were over-staffed. No hospital is over-staffed in nursing these days. Somebody knew somebody and poof. I'm back to doing per diem for who knows how long."

"I'm sorry about all of that," I said. "I really am. But I'm not dropping this. There's a man facing prison for the rest of his life for something he didn't do. Whether I like it or not, you might still have some use in this trial."

I handed Audra a folded piece of paper. Just this morning, Keith got Judge Mitchell's signature on a new subpoena. He'd wanted Audra to come forward willingly, but we prepared for the alternative.

Audra knew immediately what it was. Gritting her teeth, she shook her head.

"It's not going to help," she said. "Nobody believes me. They all think I'm some troublemaker looking for a pay day."

"You lied to me the last time we spoke," I said. "The reason nobody believed you in the Palmer investigation is because you weren't honest about your relationship with Hector Ruiz.

You made it sound like you barely knew him. They know you were dating. They know he broke up with you."

She crumpled the subpoena up in her hand and threw it on the ground.

"I went out with him once," she said. "We didn't hit it off."

"You acted like you barely even knew his last name, Audra. I saw the texts you sent him."

"Then why are you here?" she yelled. Further down the sidewalk, one of the neighbors had just stepped outside. She looked our way. Audra waved a hand. The neighbor gave her a sour look and hustled back inside.

"Nosy old bat," Audra muttered.

"I'm here because despite what you left out of your story, I still believe you were telling the truth about what you overheard and what you saw at Maple Valley," I said. "Do you want to convince me that you were lying before?"

"Lady," she said. "You're crazy. You and I both know exactly what's going to happen if you put me on the stand in that trial. That prosecutor is going to make me out to be some lying slut. That murder trial has been on the news. Anybody who didn't know who I was before will now. I'll have to move. Even if I do, it'll just take a google search to figure out my involvement. It's not worth it."

"Maybe not to you," I said, taking a step forward. "But it's worth it to me. And it's worth it to the families of every patient at Maple Valley or other places where vulnerable patients could be put in harm's way."

"You can't put that on me!" she shouted.

"Then why did you say anything to Ellie Palmer? Why even get involved?"

Audra leaned against her car. She held her keys between her fingers, squeezing them so hard her knuckles turned white.

"Mary Palmer was a nice lady," Audra said. "Ellie and her family were trying to make sure she was taken care of. I just couldn't stand by and let anything happen to her."

"You were right to speak up. You still saw what you saw. The jury needs to hear it."

"It didn't help!" she said. "Not one bit. Hector and Wayne didn't get in trouble. It all got covered up just like I said it would. I'm nobody. Less than nobody to them."

"You're not nobody to me. You're not nobody to the Palmer family. We can help you get your story out. I can't promise the jury will believe it. But I can promise you Eric Wray's defense lawyer will protect you on the stand. He's good at what he does. Almost as good as I am. And yes. Your relationship with Hector will come out. Your texts to him might come out. It'll look bad. It doesn't mean you're lying. Are you lying, Audra, about what you saw and what you heard?"

Audra got quiet. She hung her head low. "No," she said.

"Good."

"Do you think they did it?" she whispered. Raising her head, she asked the question.

"I'll ask you the same thing," I said. "You saw what was going on at Maple Valley. You have good instincts. Do you think Eric Wray actually killed his wife?"

She looked me dead in the eye. "No," she said. "I guess not."

"Good," I said. "Neither do I. As for Wayne or Hector? I didn't know them. You did. You saw them mistreat Mary Palmer. It was an accident. Carelessness. They had no business being involved in patient transport. So yes. I think they could have hurt Wendy Wray. Maybe they didn't mean it. Maybe they were just messing around. Hector wasn't working the day Wendy died, but Wayne was. He denied any involvement. But now? Nobody can find him. I don't think that's a coincidence."

"Neither do I," she said, her voice so soft I almost didn't hear it.

"Tell me what else you know, Audra. This isn't just about Eric and Wendy Wray. This is about making sure no other patient gets hurt. It's about holding Maple Valley accountable. I don't care if I lose my job over it."

"You don't care if I lose mine either," she said.

I took in a breath and met her eyes. "I think the truth is more important, yes."

Finally, Audra Kaminsky gave me a slow, solemn nod.

"Okay," she said. "I'll testify. I'll say what I heard and saw. But I wasn't there the day Wendy died. I can't help your friend in that way."

"You'll help him enough," I said. "And I think there's something else you might be able to do."

"What's that?"

"Hector said he and Wayne hung out sometimes after work. He said a lot of you did, that there was a bar close by everyone went to. I need you to think, Audra. We've hit a dead end as far as locating Wayne Warren. Hector claims he hasn't seen him in months. None of Wayne's last known addresses have checked out. His last paycheck from Maple Valley went undelivered and uncashed. He never even gave them a direct deposit bank account."

"Come on," Audra said, her shoulders sagging with defeat. "I don't know where Wayne is. I never saw him outside of work. I always got a bad vibe from him. I think I told you that.

"There has to be something. Can you think of anything? Was he dating any of the other staff members? Did you ever see what kind of car he drove? Did he ever talk about where he was from? Anything?"

She shrugged. "I don't know."

"Audra," I said. "I have to find him. Think."

She bit her bottom lip. A light came into her eyes. "There was someone. Maybe."

"Who?"

"I need to make a phone call."

Adrenaline pumped through me. I tried to keep it in check as I followed Audra up to the house. She keyed herself in and held the door for me.

"Is that you, Aud?" an older female voice called from further inside.

"Just me, Gran," Audra called out. "I forgot something. I've got a friend of mine with me. Do you need anything?"

"I'm good, sweetie," she said. "Maybe a fresh iced tea whenever you're done talking with your friend."

"You got it, Gran," she answered. "We'll just be a few minutes."

"I can't find the dang remote," her grandmother yelled. "I swear Grandpa keeps hiding it on me."

Audra smiled. "My grandpa passed away five years ago," she said. "She forgets."

"I understand," I said. Audra walked me into the kitchen. Her grandmother lived in a mid-century split-level house. The kitchen was up a short flight of stairs at the back.

"Have a seat," Audra said. She went to the fridge and poured a glass of iced tea from a pitcher.

"You want?" she asked.

"No, thank you," I said.

"Let me get this to her," she said. "I'll be back in a second."

Audra disappeared down a short hallway. I heard the murmur of her conversation with her grandmother. Then she came back. Audra was holding a small pink pad of sticky notes.

She sat at the kitchen table and pulled the landline off the wall. "She might not answer if she knows it's me," Audra explained.

"Who?" I asked.

"I worked with a girl, another nurse's aide. Jade Simpson. She drove this big, ugly van. People used to mooch rides off her all the time. Including me one week when my car was in the shop. Anyway, I saw her bring Wayne Warren in a few times.

Maybe she'll remember where he was staying. It's no guarantee he's still there but ..."

I put a hand over Audra's. "It's brilliant. Thank you."

Audra made the call. Jade Simpson answered pretty quickly. I only heard Audra's end of the conversation. She apologized for the out-of-the-blue call and random question. The conversation veered to some other inside baseball from working at Maple Valley. Smiling, Audra held up a finger as she nodded.

"Thanks, Jade," she said, quickly scrawling something on her sticky note. "Thanks a lot. Yeah. I know. Consider me warned. I promise, it's nothing to worry about."

The women made small talk for a few more seconds, then Audra finally hung up. She finished writing something on the note and slid it over to me.

"Jade said she picked Wayne up from this address a couple of times and dropped him off there once. The last time was maybe a week or two before Wendy Wray died in August. She said she hasn't talked to him since he stopped working there."

I picked up the note. "Audra, this is fantastic. Thank you!"

It was an address in Adrian, Michigan. About a twenty-minute drive.

"He probably doesn't live there," she said. "He ..."

"It's okay," I said. "It's a start. This address didn't show up on any of Wayne Warren's personnel records. Those might have been phony. This is real. You're sure Jade has it right?"

"Yeah," she said. "She pulled it up on her GPS app when we were talking. She plugged it in the first time Wayne called her asking for a lift."

I wanted to hug Audra. It was the first solid lead we'd had on Wayne Warren in six months. Just a glimmer, but I knew in my gut it could lead to a ray of hope.

Chapter 34

MY FIRST TRIP to Adrian produced no results. No one was home at the address Audra gave me. A "For Rent" sign was tacked to the window. As I peered in, I could see the place was vacant except for a few beat-up pieces of living room furniture.

Nothing. If Wayne had lived here, he was long gone now. His across-the-street neighbor, an older gentleman with a hopeless combover, however, was home.

He told me the man who used to live there worked nights and that he was usually home after ten in the morning. It was a promising lead. The neighbor said he thought the guy worked in health care because he'd seen him come home in scrubs.

I showed him the only photograph I had of Wayne Warren. It was a grainy copy of the ID badge he wore when he worked for Maple Valley. Slater had gotten it in discovery.

"Does he look familiar?" I asked the old man. He peered at the photo through thick glasses.

"I gotta tell you, honey," he said. "I never talked to the kid. Only saw him from across the street. Big beefy guy. Brown hair. That's all I can tell ya from this picture that looks the same. Might be him. Might not. Now I gotta get to walking Bernadine or she's gonna knock us both over."

Bernadine was an overweight French bulldog. Though I found it hard to believe she could get enough air to do anything other than bite ankles, she was solid enough to be a serious trip hazard.

"Thank you," I said. I pulled out a business card. "Can you do me a favor? If you see your neighbor come home, would you mind giving me a call? He's not in trouble or anything, but I do need to talk to him."

The old man took the card and shrugged. "Don't see the harm in it. Though we've got enough busybodies on this street. Don't like being part of the problem."

"You won't be," I said. "Nobody needs to know we even talked, Mr. ... um ..."

"Bates," he said. "Sherman Bates."

Before he could say anything else, Bernadine started to pull on her leash. I saw immediately that I'd underestimated her prowess. Sherman swore, pocketed my card, and proceeded to let Bernadine walk him down the street.

My phone buzzed with a text. It was Jeanie.

"We're back in session," she texted. "You might want to get back here."

Chapter 35

JEANIE LOOKED weary when I met her outside the courtroom. After her call, I'd driven back to Delphi as fast as I could. By the time I got there, Judge Mitchell had broken for lunch.

"ME just testified she's absolutely certain Wendy was smothered," she said. "The bruising on her face is the clincher. Slater did what he could, but I think Johnson proves murder. No doubt."

It was a long shot. We knew it. If Slater could at least raise the suspicion that Wendy died of natural causes, it would have cut Rafe Johnson's legs out from under him. Slater could still make the argument in closing, but it likely wouldn't land.

"Great," I said. "No luck in Adrian yet either."

"Who's next?" I asked her.

"Craddock," she said.

"How bad was it this morning?" I asked.

Jeanie sighed. "Amelia Trainor was on her game," she said. I'd tried dozens of cases now with Dr. Trainor on the other side. Her testimony was always laden with hard facts, but she managed to present them in an approachable way for juries. Every time I'd ever got to debrief individual jurors, they gave her rave reviews and found her credibility impeccable.

"It was rough," Jeanie said. "That picture of Wendy with the bruising on her face. Rafe was smart. Life-sized. You know he's going to lift his hand and hold it over the image of Wendy's face in closing. They'll have no trouble visualizing what happened. Jurors ten, nine and three cried. Seven looked like he wanted to kill someone."

"Damn," I said. "How'd Eric take it?"

"Not great," she said. "This is breaking him, honey. Little by little. He may not be guilty, but he feels guilty. I'm just hoping the jury is able to discern the difference."

"Me too," I said. We walked inside together and headed for the first-floor coffee shop. We grabbed a couple of sandwiches. I barely ate mine. We sat in near silence until Jeanie's phone buzzed.

"We're back," she said. "You sure you want to sit through this today? It's wearing you down as much as it is Eric. You might do more good for yourself by heading back to the office. Miranda and Tori are doing the best they can, but they're not you. None of us are. The rest of your clients are getting restless."

"There's nothing that can't wait," I said. "This is Eric's life. He needs my full attention."

"Cass ..."

"I don't care," I said, more abrupt than I meant. "I'll let the practice burn to the ground if it'll help Eric."

"Oh honey," she said.

"I'd do the same if it were you," I said. "And you'd do the same if it were me. This is Eric we're talking about."

We bussed our table and headed for the elevator, arriving at the same time as Monica Wray. Her face went white, but it was too late for any of us to avoid each other. The elevator doors opened.

"Hi, Monica," I said. They were the first words we'd spoken to each other in days. I had tried several times, but Monica always seemed to vanish before I could.

She adjusted her purse strap and stared at the elevator buttons as the door closed.

"Look," I said. "I know you're angry with me, though I'm not sure why, but ..."

She whirled on me. "You don't know why? You seriously don't know why? My God, Cass. This is your fault. Ever since you came back to town and got involved with my brother, he's had nothing but trouble. He was shot because of you. I'm the one who nursed him back to health. I begged him not to come back here. He was just starting to deal with what Wendy did to him. This town is cursed for Eric. He had a job offer in Raleigh. It would have paid him three times what he makes here, and he was eligible for his full pension on top of it. He came back here for you."

"Monica," Jeanie said. "That's not fair."

"It's okay," I said. Though it was in me to argue with her, I couldn't help seeing the situation through her eyes. And there was that word again. Cursed. Was it true?

"I have a couple of brothers of my own," I said. "If I were in your position, I might feel the same way. I would and have plowed over anyone who might hurt them. You may not be ready to believe this, but I'm not your enemy. And I'm not Eric's enemy either. I love your brother. Whether you want to hear this or not, I have his best interests in mind."

She turned back toward the elevator doors as they opened. "Do us all a favor and go back to Chicago," she said. "Let my brother go."

She stormed down the hall and into the courtroom. Eric turned the corner with the deputies just as she did. He mouthed an "I'm sorry" to me.

I had no chance to respond. The deputies led him in. I hung back with Jeanie as Deputy Craddock walked in right behind him. He looked downright fired up to take the stand.

Chapter 36

WITHIN THE FIRST few minutes of Gene Craddock's testimony, it became apparent how much he enjoyed his time in the spotlight. Craddock had a certain folksy charm that he played to the hilt. To the point he affected a slow, almost southern accent despite having lived in Southeast Michigan his entire life.

"Deputy Craddock," Rafe said after he'd established Craddock's credentials. "Do you always go out to Maple Valley when a resident passes away?"

"No, sir, I do not," he said. "My understanding was that the administration followed a certain protocol based on the suspicions of Nurse Kimberly Crane."

"What were those suspicions, to your knowledge?"

"Well, sir, Nurse Crane had just checked vitals on the patient. I believe it was an hour and a half before she was found. She was stable. When Nurse Crane found her, she noticed some bruising around her face. So, out of the abundance of caution, she alerted hospital security. They locked down the room.

Didn't let anyone in or out until the ME got there. That's Dr. Trainor. It's standard procedure for our office to be called anytime there is a suspicious death like that. So, I accompanied Dr. Trainor and secured the scene. After her preliminary examination, she suspected foul play. So, it was at that point we treated it is a crime scene and homicide investigation."

"I see," Rafe said. I was already furiously scribbling notes. Slater needed to hammer the time frame between when Wendy was found and when Trainor and Craddock arrived. Who had access to the room? He could score points either by showing there had been a lot of traffic in and out, or that the Maple Valley staff and Craddock had no control of Wendy's room for a period. I quietly tore off a sheet from my notepad and handed it up to Jeanie for Slater.

Slater made a subtle downward motion with his hand after reading it. He wanted me to stand down. He had this. I hoped like hell he did.

"Deputy Craddock," Rafe said. "What did you do next?"

"Well, I and the deputies assigned to the scene began canvassing witnesses. I wanted to establish a time frame. We were able to do that pretty quickly."

"Why is that?"

"Well, Wendy Wray's last visitor—her only visitor that day—was her husband, Eric Wray. He signed in at eleven twenty-seven that morning. The nursing staff was in and out of the room while he was there until the last staff member, Nurse Crane, left him alone with Wendy at approximately noon. Nobody saw Eric again until after twelve thirty. That was an aide, Gloria LaPlante. She provided a statement that she saw

Wray coming out of a stairwell, looking flustered. She indicated he seemed in a hurry and ran back down the stairwell and out to the parking lot."

"Were you able to establish a timeline then?"

"The victim was found just before one p.m. Dead."

"When did you arrive on scene again?"

"I was there a little after one thirty," he answered.

Slater's turn to scribble on his own notepad. It was killing me not to get to cross-examine Craddock. Killing. Me.

"At any time were you able to question Mr. Wray?"

"Yes, sir," Craddock said. "The hospital staff notified him by phone of his wife's death at one thirty, just before I arrived on scene. He was apparently at lunch and rushed over. That's when I questioned him."

"What did you learn?"

"Wray said he had a lunch date with his lawyer, Cass Leary. I found out later they were more than just a lawyer-client kind of deal. She's his girlfriend. Anyway, he couldn't give me an exact time when he arrived at the diner where he lunched. He confirmed he'd visited with Wendy from approximately eleven thirty to just after noon. That's where things got a little fuzzy."

"How so?"

"Well, Wray couldn't account for his whereabouts between five after twelve when Kim Crane saw him until twelve forty-five when Gloria LaPlante saw him when he was running away in the stairwell."

"Objection!" Slater said. I balled my fists at my side. Pretty soon I was going to need a sock in my mouth to keep from objecting for him.

"Save it," Mitchell said. "Deputy Craddock. You know better. Stick to the facts."

I swear to God, Craddock smirked.

"Did Mr. Wray give any explanation for this discrepancy?" Rafe asked.

"I didn't tell him there was a discrepancy," Craddock said. "I wouldn't be much of a detective if I had. No. I asked him to account for his time between noon and a quarter to one. He said one of the aides popped in and told him Dr. Barnes, the medical director, wanted to consult with him and he was to meet him in his third-floor office. Wray said he went up to the third floor, but Barnes was out to lunch and so apparently was his staff. I questioned the doctor. He'd never sent any message down to meet with Eric Wray. He had no cause to do so. None of the staff members had any knowledge of a meeting between the doctor and Wray. There was no corroboration. I spoke to Ms. Leary later that evening. She confirmed that Wray had been late to their lunch date. She'd texted him a couple of times asking where he was. Those went unanswered. Wray's cell phone was shut off just after he got to Maple Valley just before eleven thirty. Didn't go back on until he got to the diner. That alone seemed interesting. And Ms. Leary didn't seem to know anything about Wray being at Maple Valley that day."

"What did you do then?" Rafe asked.

"Well, over the next couple of days, I finished up talking to Wendy's family and friends and coworkers. It came to my attention that there was a pretty bitter fight going on and Wray was advocating ending Wendy's life."

"Objection!" Slater said. "The witness is speculating and adding his own spin to facts that are already undisputed."

"Overruled, the witness may continue," Mitchell said.

"Thank you, Judge," Craddock said. "Anyway, at that point, I believed we had probable cause to arrest Eric Wray for the murder of Wendy Wray. Though I took no pleasure in it, I'll tell you that. If you ask me, the man was in an impossible situation. That doesn't make it right."

"Thank you," Johnson said. "I have nothing further."

"Your witness, Mr. Slater."

Slater jumped up. I gripped the bench seat.

"Deputy," he said. "Just so I'm clear. Almost a full hour elapsed between the time Wendy Wray expired and you and Dr. Trainor were called to the scene. Is that right?"

"Yes, sir."

"So you can't say with any certainty whatsoever who might have had access to that room or Wendy Wray's body in that time frame, can you?"

"She wasn't alone, Mr. Slater," he said. "There were people all over the place. Hospital staff."

Slater was smart enough to leave that hanging right where it was.

"Deputy, isn't it true that you did virtually no investigation into other unattended deaths at Maple Valley?"

"That wasn't the focus of my investigation, no," he said.

"You didn't even question every staff member who was working the day Wendy died, did you?"

"I believe we did," he said.

"Oh, really? Did you ever question Wayne Warren?"

I pumped my fist against the bench.

"Wayne Warren didn't have anything to do with Wendy Wray's care the day she died," he said.

"But he was on the floor that day, wasn't he? You certainly reviewed timecards and staff logs, didn't you?"

"Of course," he said.

"But you just took those personnel records at face value, is that right? You never bothered to ask who else might have had access to Wendy's room?"

"I most certainly did!"

"Did Wayne Warren have access to Wendy's room?"

"I told you," he said. "Mr. Warren wasn't assigned to Wendy's wing the day she died."

"Wasn't assigned to her wing," he said. "Interesting. Were you not aware that Mr. Warren and a Hector Ruiz were later under investigation for potential misconduct involving the care of another patient who died?"

"There was a complaint filed," he said. "I knew that. But it resulted in a no cause finding. They didn't do anything wrong."

"You investigated that yourself? Or you just relied on whatever you were told by Maple Valley's HR?"

"They did an internal investigation," he said. "Hector Ruiz wasn't even working the day Wendy died. I didn't find any unfounded rumors against Wayne Warren to be relevant to my investigation."

"So you never pursued it," Slater said. "Yes, or no?"

"No," Craddock said through tight lips.

"Thank you," Slater said. "That's all I have for this witness."

"Mr. Johnson?"

Rafe barely looked up from his notes. It was an act. Craddock's testimony was a problem. But the less Rafe looked like he cared, he'd hope the jury read it as no big deal.

"Nothing from me, Your Honor," Rafe said.

"You may step down, Deputy," Mitchell said.

"Okay, gentlemen," Mitchell said. "It's three forty-five. We'll go another hour. You may call your next witness."

Rafe rose and buttoned his jacket. "Your Honor," he said. "At this time, the state rests."

Chapter 37

SLATER DIDN'T ASK for a recess. He hit the ground running with his defense and called his hired gun forensic pathologist. The guy was good, smooth. After establishing his credentials, Slater got to the meat of his testimony. He did it exactly how I would. Tee it up, hit the ball. Then walk away.

"Dr. Jasper," Keith said. "The so-called bruising on Wendy Wray's face: in your expert medical opinion, could it have occurred post-mortem?"

"It could have, yes," Dr. Jasper testified. He had a deep, gravelly voice and tanned skin. Every strand of his gray hair lay locked in place in a permanent wave.

"How certain are you of that?" Slater asked.

"Reasonably certain," he answered. "My understanding is that the victim's body was found within an hour of when she expired. It's entirely possible that pressure applied to her mouth and nose area within a few minutes after she died could have caused that discoloration. Lividity—the phenomenon by which blood pools due to the body's position and gravity—wouldn't have had a chance to set in yet."

"Thank you," Slater concluded. "No more questions from me."

Rafe Johnson only needed to ask two questions. The first was asked of every hired defense witness by competent prosecutors.

"Dr. Jasper," he started. "Can you tell the court how much you've been paid to testify here today?"

"I'm not paid to testify per se," Jasper said. "I'm paid to consult. My fee comes from the review of the medical records and time spent in court. My fee is the same regardless of the opinion I render, Mr. Johnson. I work for a living. As do you?"

"Noted," Johnson said. "But let me ask this another way. What did you bill in connection with your work on this case?"

After more dancing around on technicalities, Johnson got Dr. Jasper to admit he'd been paid close to three thousand dollars.

And one more thing ...

"Dr. Jasper," Rafe said. "Isn't it true that you never physically examined Wendy Wray's body yourself?"

"I did not," he said. "My opinion is based on the records presented by your office pursuant to the victim's official autopsy."

It was a fair cross-examination. I only hoped Slater had done enough and given those jurors inclined to acquit Eric something to hang their argument on.

Early the next morning, Slater called Audra Kaminsky. She looked so much smaller in the witness box than she had during our conversations. She wore her hair pulled back into a tight ponytail, no make-up, and a freshly pressed white blouse and dress pants that Tori had loaned her.

Slater took her through her foundational testimony. A pit formed in my stomach as she struggled through those. A young, nervous witness could engender sympathy in older jurors. At the same time, this late in the trial, it could also frustrate them. So far, our youngest jurors, seven and nine, looked irritated.

"Ms. Kaminsky," Slater said. "You filed a complaint with HR against Hector Ruiz and Wayne Warren, didn't you?"

"I went to my supervisors, yes," she said. "I had some concerns about how they were treating some of the patients. They dropped a patient by the name of Mary Palmer. I witnessed it. Nothing was ever done about it."

"Did you have concerns about the care of Wendy Wray?"

She squirmed. "I never saw them do anything to Wendy. But the way they talked about her made me uncomfortable."

"In what way?"

"Wayne said he wanted to do her. They had a rating system and Wendy Wray was a ten in his mind."

Two members of the jury, older women, covered their mouths in disgust. Slater saw it too. It could be gold.

"Ms. Kaminsky, what happened to Hector Ruiz and Wayne Warren?"

"What do you mean?"

"Are you aware if they're still employed at Maple Valley?"

"They aren't," she said. "That's what I was told."

"Do you know when they were fired?"

"Objection," Rafe said. "It hasn't been established how these two men left their employ. Or even if they have at all. Furthermore, this witness just said her knowledge on this subject comes from something she was told. As such, we're in hearsay territory."

"Sustained," Mitchell said.

Audra blinked back tears. Her emotions seemed disproportionate to the substance of her testimony. If I could, I would have transmitted a note to Keith telepathically. Get her off the stand as quickly as you can.

"Ms. Kaminsky," Keith said. "Why did you feel it necessary to come forward today?"

She looked down and pursed her lips, causing deep dimples in her cheeks.

"Because I had to do what was right. There are things going on at Maple Valley that people need to know about. I feel like what happened to Wendy Wray was inevitable."

"Objection," Rafe said. "Calls for speculation."

"Sustained, Mr. Slater," Mitchell said, losing his patience.

"Thank you, Your Honor," Slater said. "I have nothing further for Ms. Kaminsky."

Rafe stood and moved toward the lectern.

"Ms. Kaminsky, was your relationship with Hector Ruiz strictly professional?"

"No," Audra said, raising her chin. We knew this was coming. There was nothing for her to do but answer it head on.

"Why not?"

"We went out once," she said.

"Isn't it fair to say that Hector Ruiz was the one who ended the relationship?" he asked.

"He stopped calling me," she said.

"That upset you, didn't it?" he asked.

"Yes."

"Got angry enough to send him pretty scathing texts, isn't that right?"

"I told him what I thought of him, yes," she said.

"Just to be clear, you went to HR against Hector after he broke off the relationship, isn't that right?"

"We weren't in a relationship," she said. "It was just ... it was brief. I just didn't like the way he handled it."

"Handled you, you mean?"

"Whatever."

"In any case, your complaint to HR took place *after* your brief encounter with him ended in a way that made you angry."

"One had nothing to do with the other," she said. "I saw him and Wayne drop Mary Palmer *after* Hector and I were together."

"I see," Rafe said.

He took two unsure, pacing steps in front of the lectern. He shook his head. Pure theatrics. Then threw up his hand.

"I have no other questions for this witness," he said. It was a gamble on his part. But he was trying to show the jury he thought Audra was useless.

For her part, Audra nearly sprinted out of the witness box and out through the back of the courtroom.

"Call your next witness, Mr. Slater," the judge said.

"The defense calls Dr. Neil Spires to the stand."

Spires was a neurologist. He would testify that Wendy's condition was grave, irreversible, and imminently terminal. I, for one, didn't like the strategy.

Just before Spires came into the courtroom, my phone rang. I had it on vibrate. I didn't recognize the number that popped up, but instinct told me to answer it. I slipped out the back, passing Dr. Spires on the way.

"Hello!" the caller said. "Is this Ms. Leary?"

"It is," I answered.

"Hey, this is Sherman Bates. You gave me your card. You said you wanted me to call if I found out anything about that fella down the street. Well, I think there's something here you're gonna wanna see. You better get here, though."

Heart racing, I thanked Sherman Bates and clicked off the call. I sent a quick text to Jeanie, still inside the courtroom.

"Got a lead," I said. "Don't let Slater rest today, whatever he does." Then I ran for the stairwell, taking the steps two at a time.

Chapter 38

I WON'T DISCUSS how fast I drove to get to Sherman Bates's neighborhood. The whole way, I debated calling Sherman back and asking him to find a way to keep Warren in one place until I got there. I figured he and Bernadine could do a lot of good with their traveling road show. But Sherman wasn't answering his phone anymore.

With each mile I drove, my sense of dread grew. What if I was too late? What if Wayne Warren refused to talk to me?

I turned down the elm-lined street and parked my car at the end of the block. Then, I stuffed my bag far under the seat, taking only my cell phone and keys with me. If I'd had time, I would have changed into jeans. Something less "lawyerly" anyway. If Wayne Warren were the kind of guy I suspected, he'd make me a mile away.

But it wasn't Wayne I saw as I approached the address Audra Kaminsky's friend Jade gave me. Instead, Sherman Bates stood down the street. He waved me toward another house across from the Warren address.

I parked and went to him. "She's ready to talk," Sherman said.

"She?" I asked.

"My neighbor," he said. "I told her what you were looking for. You might wanna hear what she has to say."

Before I could question Sherman any further, he turned and started walking back up the street.

In the solid brick two-story just a few hundred feet from my car, another storm door swung open. An older lady with wiry silver hair held back with a blue plastic headband hustled toward me.

"You the one asking questions?" she said, pointing a gnarled finger at me. I looked back. Sherman had already reached the corner of the block, whistling as he went.

"Am I?" I set my jaw. "Yes. Yes, I am."

She looked both ways, perhaps worried her neighbors might see. "Come on in," she said. "It's time somebody did something about what's going on at that house." She pointed directly at Wayne Warren's residence.

Another dead end, perhaps. Or another wild goose chase. With nothing left to lose, I followed her inside.

She wore a blue, floral-print housecoat. I hadn't seen one quite like it since Grandma Leary passed away. We'd actually buried her in it at her request. After the formal viewing, of course. She wanted that, her favorite contour pillow, pictures of the grandkids, and a copy of her favorite book, *Outlander*.

"I'm Cass Leary," I said. The woman padded through the house, waving me forward into her kitchen. It hadn't been updated since the seventies. She had lime-green Formica countertops and a brown scalloped basket light over the kitchen table.

"I know who ya are," she said. "Sherman told me. I told him he shoulda called the cops. He told me to mind my own business. If I did that, nothing would get done around here. This neighborhood's about to go to pot. Don't plan on letting that happen while there's breath still left in these lungs, honey."

"I was looking for a man who rented a room down the street. You know who was living at 937?"

"Yeah," she said. She grabbed two cans of root beer from the fridge. She gestured for me to sit at the kitchen table, then put a can in front of me.

"You need a straw?"

"No. I'm fine. Thank you."

"You can call me Betty," she said. "Betty Schroeder. I was a Comstock before that. O'Toole before that. Started out as a Chopin. You know, like the composer? No relation though."

"I see," I said. "Betty, do you know something about this man?"

I took out my picture of Wayne Warren and slid it across to her. She glanced at it.

"Trouble," she said. "Big time. Cars in and out. Parked every which way all times of the day and night. I told that girl I wasn't going to put up with it."

"What girl?" I asked. "Betty, you definitely saw this man?"

"Sure," she said. "Wayne something."

"Wayne Warren," I said. "When was the last time you saw him at the house?"

"Been months. That girl let him in. She lets all her friends stay there. That's against the zoning. These are single-family homes. Not supposed to be renting out rooms. I don't even think she was charging him rent. All riff-raff. I know what that kind of traffic means."

"What do you think it meant?" I asked. I couldn't decide whether Betty had a screw loose or was on to something.

"Drugs," she said. "Those people would come like I said. All hours. Ride on up through the grass sometimes. Those big, loud motorcycles. They wouldn't stay but five or ten minutes, then they'd tear off again. One time, I counted a dozen of those bikes out there. Like they were having a convention. On my street. No, ma'am. Not putting up with any of that. So I called the cops. They wouldn't even come out. Said it was a public street and they can't write tickets for that. Lazy bunch of good-for-nothings."

"These were friends of Wayne Warren's?" I asked, my mind racing.

She heaved a great sigh. "Catch up, Missy," she said.

Lord, I was sure trying.

"Okay," I said. "So tell me about this girl."

"You'd think she had cotton growing out of her head. Bleached her hair all to Hades. She wore skirts so short I could see her bikini wax. Gang banger or something. Strutting around like some kind of stripper. Straddling those bikes with her knockers hanging out. If that were my granddaughter, I'd have done what my granddad would have done to me. Ought to lock her up until she grew some sense into her."

"Who was the girl?" I asked.

"Doesn't matter who she was," Betty said. "Matters what she was. Drugs and whoring. That's what's going on at that house. I got proof."

"What kind of proof?" I asked, humoring her. I could only imagine what kind of reaction Betty Chopin-like-the-composer O'Toole Comstock Schroeder would get from the Adrian police. They likely fielded calls like hers a dozen or more times a day. We did enough of our own at the office.

Betty let out a sigh. She tapped her finger to her temple. Heaving herself off her chair, she turned and went to a cupboard above her stove. Up on her tiptoes, she grunted as she tried to reach whatever was up there.

"May I help you with that?" I asked, starting to rise.

"You're three inches shorter than me, at least, honey," she said. "Irish peasant stock. Am I right?"

"More or less," I said. Kooky as she was, the old bat was starting to grow on me. She brought a brown shoe box down. She set it on the table between us and smiled with triumph.

"I'm sorry," I said. "I'm gonna need more information."

Betty rolled her eyes and opened the lid. She pulled out three small film canisters and set them in front of me.

"My hands are no good anymore," she said, as if that explained it all.

I picked up one of the black plastic canisters and popped off the top. Inside was a roll of Kodak 35mm film with its yellow-and-red label.

"Can't hardly read my own handwriting, let alone expect anyone else to," she said. "But I'm still good at this."

She'd gone back to the kitchen counter and picked up a camera. This was no point-and-shoot digital device. It was old, clunky, and she wielded it with grace. Before I could so much as blink, she brought it to her eye, dialed it in, and snapped a picture of me.

"Betty," I said, beginning to lose patience. "What do I have here?" I held up the three film containers.

"Told you," she said. "Cops won't do anything. But I've got all the license plates. I was watching that girl. Figured if I could catch her in the act, then maybe they'd have to come out and arrest her. At least scare the bejeezus out of her, or something. Sat right there and used my zoom."

She pointed to the living room. Sure enough, from the window at the side of the house, I could see clear down to Wayne Warren's old rental. Betty had a wooden stool propped beneath the ledge.

"You can take those," she said. "I trust you. Read about you in the paper."

I felt equal parts flattered and creeped out.

"You've been taking pictures of the comings and goings at 937 Ridgeway?"

"Now you're getting it," she said. "Got the girl. All her deadbeat friends. Their cars. Took a bunch the day all those biker hoodlums showed up. Not sure what all I've got. I don't drive anymore, so I have to wait for when my daughter-in-law comes over with the groceries. Every other week. She takes me to the doctor too."

"Thank you," I said, knowing Tori was going to probably kill me when I set her to the task of developing all this. I wasn't even sure where you could take stuff like this anymore. But if I could, by some sliver of a chance, track Wayne Warren through a license plate ...

"Hope it helps," she said. "If you can do anything to keep that riff-raff from tanking my property values ..."

"I don't know if I have the power to do anything like that," I said. "But I'm very interested in talking to Wayne Warren. This girl you keep mentioning. Was she someone who just visited him? A girlfriend? Do you know if he left with her?"

"Don't know. Don't care. She lived there for a while too. Lots of times. I think she owns it now. Or manages it. She's got a key. I know that."

"Do you know her name?" I asked.

"I just call her Tits Magee," Betty said. I winced.

"Got it," I said. My hopes of finding anything useful on Betty's film dwindled. The woman was nuts. For all I knew, she'd never even seen Wayne Warren at all.

"I appreciate this," I said. I refrained from giving her my business card, knowing exactly what would happen if I did. Betty would start calling our office daily to report whatever her neighbors did that made her angry.

"You'll let me know if you find anything?" she said.

"I certainly will," I answered. I should have just given her back her film. But I couldn't shake the niggling sense in the back of my brain that maybe, just maybe, this particular blind squirrel would find a nut instead of merely being one.

Chapter 39

Grim faces greeted me when I walked into the office the next morning. The air got thick as Jeanie and Miranda passed a look.

"No," I said. "What happened?" I didn't want the answer.

Jeanie's face filled with alarm. "Oh ... no ... honey. It's okay. I mean, it's not okay, but not in the way you think. Nothing happened to Eric."

I gripped the counter to keep myself from falling down with relief. "Then what?"

"You better talk to Keith," she said. "Eric's physically okay. But there's trouble."

I set my bag down for Miranda. She had a knack for making sense out of the notes I scribbled while in court to fill out my calendar.

"Am I gonna need a drink for this?" I asked.

"Just go talk to him," Jeanie urged.

I climbed the stairs and knocked softly on the conference room door. I found Slater standing at the window, hands on hips. He whirled around as I entered.

"You're late," he said.

"It's my office," I responded. "Why aren't you in court?"

"Mitchell's ruling on some final evidentiary matters. We're adjourned until after lunch. Good thing. Because I'm pretty sure I just got fired."

I grabbed the nearest chair and sat down with a thud. "What happened?"

"He won't listen to reason. Eric wants to take the stand in his own defense."

The air went out of me. "He can't."

"Try telling him that," Slater said. "I don't get it. At every turn, he's tried to shoot himself in the foot."

"Slater," I said. "You cannot put Eric on the stand."

He came away from the window. Gripping the back of another chair, he stared hard at me. "Then I think it's time you come clean about what you know. I'm tired of the riddle speak between the two of you. From the beginning, I've felt like I've had to try this case with one hand behind my back. He trusts you more than he trusts me. You need to face the fact that's going to do him in this time."

"He can't take the stand," I said.

"Tell me the truth!"

"I've told you the truth," I countered.

"Don't give me crap about attorney client privilege. I'm his lawyer too. You can tell me, Cass."

I crossed my arms in front of me. "We need to find Wayne Warren. He needs to take the stand before you rest."

"Dead end," he said. "And nobody can put him in Wendy's room the day she died. It's not enough."

"It's something!" I shouted. "Audra was shaky on the stand. I'll admit that. But she said what you needed her to say. The jury will think she was nervous, not that she was making anything up. It's a foothold. You argue from there. Ruiz and Warren had an unhealthy fascination with Wendy. They were rough with patients. Maple Valley swept it under the rug, and Gene Craddock never bothered to track any of it down. That's reasonable doubt."

"Cass ..."

"He cannot take the stand!" I shouted. "Johnson is too good. He'll ask him about the conversation with Jeff Maloney. Eric will have to admit he fantasized about putting Wendy out of her misery. He'll argue it into a confession in closing. It'll negate anything else you've done. Eric won't lie about it. He can't. He knows that."

"What else?" Slater said.

I stared at the window.

"What. Else?"

"He'll try to use me against him, okay?" I shouted. "He set a trap when he had me on the stand. That stuff about the shooting my brother was involved in."

"The justifiable homicide?" Slater said. "Cass, I think you need to tell me what really happened."

"My brother was cleared of any criminal charges," I said. "That's what happened."

"But Eric knows something," Slater said. "Christ. You're telling me he'd lie for you?"

I said nothing.

"He'd take the hit. Which means Rafe Johnson knows something you don't want him to know. He's waiting for Eric to lie so he can spring it on him. My God, Cass. All three of you will end up behind bars before this is over."

I leveled a stare at him. He shook his head. "Not if Eric doesn't take the stand. You know Johnson has combed through every internal affairs case Eric was ever involved in. Is there anything else?"

"He's a good cop, Slater," I said. "Eric's clean."

He threw up his hands. "Except when it comes to you."

"Can you get me in to see him? Today? Before you go back on the record? Maybe I can help."

"No," Slater shouted. "You don't go near him."

"You can't stop me," I said.

"The hell I can't. We're too close to the end of this. No way in hell you two are getting into a room together alone again. I'll deal with him on my own."

"You have to win," I said. "No matter what you may think, Eric didn't kill Wendy. And Wayne Warren knows something. I'm sure of it. I may have a lead on that score."

I told Slater about my conversation with Betty Schroeder, leaving out her more eccentric behavior.

"Tori's due back any time now. She found a drug store who could develop the pictures Betty took. There might be something there."

"Then what? Even if you have a picture of Wayne Warren, what exactly do you think that's going to do to help Eric? You think Warren held up a sign saying I killed Wendy and let this poor cop go up for it? Short of that, this is pointless."

"There may be a clue in there about where to find Warren. That's the least of what I'm hoping for. And it's costing you nothing."

"It's costing Eric everything!"

I rose. "If you can't raise reasonable doubt with what you have, you have no business ever stepping into a courtroom again. All Rafe has is a loose timeline. You've got plenty to stoke suspicion about misconduct at Maple Valley. That's all you need. You could rest right now. You did a good job showing the Maloney family were used by that hired gun doctor. There is no proof that Eric ever did anything but act in Wendy's best interests. This whole thing is being driven by whatever axe the Maloneys have to grind against him. Revisionist history about what kind of person Wendy was. History that is irrelevant. You even raised the question whether Amelia Trainor got the autopsy right. So do your job. Argue it. And let me get back to mine."

Just as Slater was about to lay into me again, the door opened. Tori stepped through.

"Cass," she said. "I've got the first set of Mrs. Schroeder's pictures developed. There are some things I think you might want to see."

Chapter 40

Tori pulled out a thick envelope. One by one, she spread the 3×5 pictures on the conference room table. Slater stood over my shoulder.

"Waste of time," he muttered as a pattern began to emerge.

Betty Schroeder had good technique. The pictures were clear and focused. But there was nothing there. Picture after picture of random cars parked in front of 937 Ridgeway.

In another shot, she caught the backside of a young woman, stepping up to the porch. She had damaged, white-blonde hair and wore a pink tank top and cutoff denim shorts that showed the curve of her rear end.

"That must be the girl she was talking about," I said. I picked up the picture to get a closer look. I couldn't see her face. She held the screen door partially open. I peered closer. There was someone inside talking to her. The picture was too grainy to make out his features.

Tori handed me another, taken a few seconds later. The girl had walked fully inside. The man she spoke to towered over her, but I still couldn't see his face.

"That could be Wayne Warren," Tori suggested.

"It could also be Dwyane The Rock Johnson," Slater said. "I've got Rafe's rebuttal to prep for."

I picked up another photo. More cars. Betty zoned in on license plates. Mostly Michigan. A handful from Ohio.

Three photographs at the end of the roll caught my eye. Two Harleys were parked in the driveway. There were beer cans in the yard.

"Oh, I bet Betty didn't like that," I said.

"She thinks they were dealing drugs from the house?" Tori asked.

"Among other things. I think she thinks that girl was running a brothel by the way she talked. She said she called the cops constantly."

"Oh boy," Tori said. "Let me guess, they didn't take her seriously. I've got a neighbor like that on my street. She calls anytime someone turns around in anyone's driveway."

"I know the type," I said. "But ... sometimes ..." I picked up another photograph. "Just because you're paranoid doesn't mean people aren't up to something."

"Cass," Tori said, peering at the photo I held. "That's ..."

I took out my phone and pulled up the ID badge photo I had of Wayne Warren. I laid it next to the other photograph.

"That's him!" Tori exclaimed.

Betty had snapped a shot of Warren coming out of the house. A cigarette dangled from his lower lip, but it was Wayne Warren. No question. The date on the photo read July 27th, last year. If there were any doubt, he was wearing a set of blue scrubs as if he were either coming from work or going there. He wore a lanyard around his neck. From that dangled his ID badge with the same photo I had on my phone.

"Here's the next shot," Tori said, handing me the last photo from the pack. Wayne had walked slightly out of frame. There was another man coming out behind him. I couldn't make out his face. He turned partially backward as he pulled the door closed behind him.

My pulse jumped. I flipped back a few photographs and found the one with the Harleys. Then I grabbed the last photograph.

"What is it?" Tori asked.

"The cut," I said.

"The what?" she asked.

"His cut!"

Tori gave me a blank stare. Slater's face matched hers.

"For crying out loud," I said. "Haven't you people ever watched *Sons of Anarchy*? His cut. The leather vest that guy's wearing. You can see the back of it. Look at the patch. Read it!"

I handed the picture to Tori. Her eyes got big.

"Steel Beasts M.C." she said. "You gotta be kidding me. Wayne Warren was hanging around with a member of the Steel Beasts?"

"Looks like," I said.

"I can't use any of this," Slater said. "You've got a tenuous connection between a staff member who wasn't even around the day Wendy Wray died and some biker friend?"

"It's more than that," I said. "Much, much more than that. You know full well that in his vice days, Eric was responsible for putting some seriously bad guys behind bars. He was on a gang task force. You want to tell me it's just some random coincidence that Warren works at the very facility where Eric's wife is? And that he basically disappears after she turns up dead? This is the first solid lead we've had. I'm tracking it down."

"How?" Keith said. "We're running out of time."

"That part's your problem," I said. "Make time. Call character witnesses. Call every single Maple Valley staff member you can. Find that blowhard doctor the Maloneys hired, Lyman McNulty. Let him stall for days."

"What are you planning?" Slater said. "And why am I dead certain I'm not going to like it?"

I smiled. "Now you sound like Eric," I said.

"I'm beginning to understand why he gets so exasperated with you," Slater said.

"Tori, when do you expect the rest of the pictures from Mrs. Schroeder's film rolls?"

"In a day or two," she said.

"Good," I answered. "Call me as soon as you get them."

I stuffed the photographs in my jacket pocket. "I need to get on the road," I said. I wouldn't stop for anything. I had a full tank of gas. With any luck, I could get where I needed by late afternoon.

"Cass," Tori said. "This could get dangerous. The Steel Beasts are some bad dudes. I know Wray got their president put away for murder. You can't just go traipsing into their club demanding answers."

I smiled. "I know that. Don't worry. I have a plan!"

"Don't tell me," Slater said, putting a hand up. "I have a feeling I'm better off not knowing."

I lightly tapped his cheek. "You're catching on, counselor."

Chapter 41

I HADN'T CALLED AHEAD. He had no reason to think I might walk through his door. But when I marched through the elevator on the twenty-fourth floor of the Thorne Building, Killian's receptionist calmly buzzed me through the inner bulletproof glass security door.

"Ms. Leary," she said. Her name was Lilith. She'd been with Killian for at least fifteen years longer than I had. "Can I get you some coffee? Mineral water?"

"I'm fine," I said. "I won't be staying long."

I didn't wait for further invitation. I bypassed Lilith's desk and went straight for Killian's corner office at the end of the hall. His door was open. He stood at the window overlooking the Navy Pier, cell phone in hand, his back to me.

He never said goodbye to whoever he had on the other end. He just slipped the phone into his breast pocket and turned, grinning. Maybe I should have asked how he knew I was coming. It could have been something as simple as the parking garage security cameras. I wanted to think about that. More likely, he still had eyes on me even in Delphi. It would be like him. If I questioned it, he'd tell me it was for my protection. Maybe it was. Though Killian Thorne would always protect himself above all others. He still had powerful enemies who would pay or kill for what I knew about him. I was counting on it.

"I need your help," I said, cutting to it.

He gestured toward his desk. Good. This was a business call. Nothing more. I took a seat. He didn't. He stayed at the window.

"Is your detective not doing well?" he asked.

"He's alive," I said. "No one's touched a hair on his head in jail since you intervened. But you already know that. If I asked for it, I imagine you could tell me what Eric had for breakfast this morning."

He didn't answer. It was as much as an admission.

"I believe I know who really killed Eric's wife," I said. I set my bag on the floor and pulled out a small envelope from the outer pocket.

"He was an orderly working at the nursing home where Wendy died," I said. "I believe he was a plant."

"You have proof of this?" Killian asked. He paused. "Ah. No. That's why you're here."

I laid out the two most telling photographs from Mrs. Schroeder's batch. Killian didn't move from where he stood.

"He went by Wayne Warren when he worked at Maple Valley, though that might not be his real name. Right after

Wendy died, he disappeared. I tried everything. Couldn't find him. Until now."

"What do you want, Cass?" Killian said.

"Here," I said, jamming my finger into the picture of Wayne Warren and his biker buddy. Killian finally came forward. Hands still in his jacket pockets, he peered over my shoulder. Silence. Then, he made a small noise at the back of his throat as he realized what he was looking at. He picked up the photo.

"Cass ..."

"Listen to me," I said. "This Wayne Warren was involved with the Steel Beasts M.C. I don't know how. But none of this can be a coincidence. I know it in my gut. Eric put a man named Ansel Jameson, the Beasts' former president, behind bars over a decade ago. An associate of theirs turns up at the same nursing home where his wife receives care. He was only there a few months, Killian. Wendy winds up dead and Eric is sitting in jail for it. The minute I start to dig, Wayne Warren goes to ground."

"That's not how the Beasts operate," Killian said.

"Isn't it?" I said. "I need the truth. I need to know who the Steel Beasts work for. And I think you can tell me."

"Cass, you need to be very careful what you ask of me," he said.

"I asked you to help me protect Eric. This is part of that. He's been framed. I believe I know by whom. I'm going to prove it. I have to prove it."

"You know who these men are? What they do? Because I do. But you already knew that when you walked in here. They're enforcers. Lackeys. The Beasts aren't the real power in Detroit. They never were."

"That's what I'm counting on. Whoever controls this club, that's who I need to sit down with. And I'm betting you have enough influence in Detroit to make that happen," I said.

"You're out of your mind," he said, but all traces of his cool demeanor had dropped. I was right about all of it.

"I need a meeting, Killian. I need to go over the head of the Beasts."

"What?" he yelled.

"I'm serious. I need you to set it up. Face to face. Are you going to tell me you don't have the power to make it happen?" I said.

Killian shook his head. He walked around his desk and plopped into the chair behind it. "You're not thinking clearly. You're leading with your heart. That won't end well," he said.

"I think the Steel Beasts' employer and I have a mutual goal," I said. "Wayne Warren was sloppy. He drew too much attention to himself. He was too easy for me to find. Whoever he's working for will want to know that."

"If that's all true," Killian said, "don't you think the next easiest way to handle this is to eliminate the person asking all the questions? Or this Wayne Warren? How do you know they haven't already?"

"You're not just protecting Eric," I said. "I know that. All I want is a meeting. I have a proposition ..."

Killian put up a hand. "And I don't want to know about it."

"Is this how you would have done things?" I asked. "You said it yourself. The Steel Beasts are enforcers. If one of yours got sloppy, took a risk like that over some cheap, personal vendetta, you'd open your ears to someone who could help them stop the leak."

"And you think you can?" Kilian asked.

"Again, I just want a meeting," I said.

"You've taken this too far. You've isolated yourself from friends, family, your work. Be honest. When was the last time you worked on behalf of your other clients? The rumor is, some of them are jumping ship. Your staff is good, but they're not you."

"I don't need you to check up on me," I said.

"Yes, you do!" he shouted. "You've become obsessed. You're looking for conspiracies around every corner. Has it occurred to you that you just might be wrong? That your man was just worn out. He watched this woman he used to love wither and die in front of him. Except she was still breathing. Still suffering. So he did the only humane thing he could for her?"

"Stop it," I said.

"Tell me the truth," he said. "No. Tell it to yourself. You of all people know that sometimes the simplest explanation is the right one."

I put my index finger on the photograph and slid it back in front of Killian. "A meeting. Ten minutes. I want to know who this man is. He was careless enough to be seen with Wayne Warren, wearing his cut for a nosy neighbor with a camera to spot him. If he's sloppy about one thing, he'll be sloppy about something else. Who do the Steel Beasts work for? Get me in a room with him. That's what I'm asking."

Killian let out a bitter laugh. "In all the years you worked for me, you never wanted to know. You made looking the other way into an art form. Never got your hands dirty. Plausible deniability. You do realize that digging this deep might do more harm to Eric Wray than good?"

"I'm going to find out the truth," I said.

Killian picked up the photo, stared at it, then let it fall back to the desk. "Even if you don't like it?"

"Yes."

"Once you go down this road, you might not be able to walk it back. If I do what you ask. If I arrange a meeting, they'll want something in return. What are you willing to sacrifice for Eric Wray?"

The silence between us grew thick. I knew what Killian was asking me. No ... accusing me of. During our time together, it was my ultimate inability to bend the rules which led me to leave. For Eric, I was willing to cross that line.

"The Steel Beasts work for a man named Luther Gaius. They run guns for the Russian mob. Gaius is their point person. You're right that he recognizes Eric Wray getting murdered right now wouldn't be good for business. He's made that known with the Woodbridge County Jail."

"Can you set it up?" I asked.

"Between you and Gaius? Yes," he said. "He runs a club just outside of Detroit. The Olympia."

I gathered my photos and slipped them back into my bag. "It has to be now. Tonight, preferably."

Killian smiled. "I'll arrange it. But you're not going alone."

"Killian ..."

"I'm going with you," he said. "Let's just pray to God you don't end up getting both of us killed."

Chapter 42

THREE HOURS LATER, I had my meeting.

"You get ten minutes with him," Killian said, his lips touching my ear. "I'll be at the bar ... watching. I see anything I don't like, I'm pulling you out of here. You don't get up and walk toward me after ten minutes, I'm dragging you out of here."

The strobe lights from the dance floor made my head spin. My gaze drifted upward to the mezzanine above it. My target.

Luther Gaius surveyed his kingdom as a waitress in fishnets and heels way too high for that kind of work gave him bottle service.

"Ten minutes," Killian warned again. I put a hand on his sleeve and gave him a smile meant to convey I knew what I was doing.

I hoped like hell I knew what I was doing.

When Gaius saw me mounting the stairs, he waved me forward. The higher I got, the more I could see of the crowd below me. Thirty-somethings, mostly. The Olympia was an exclusive club. You needed a key card to get in. A two-hundred-dollar cover on top of that.

Gaius wasn't handsome. He had hair plugs that might have worked if he hadn't dyed them midnight black. His face had that too-smooth look from overuse of fillers and his nose didn't at all fit his face. No doubt he'd had more than a few nose jobs that did him no favors.

"Cass Leary," he said. The padded half wall behind him did an adequate job of blocking out the sound from below. I took a seat on a swivel chair opposite him but waved off the waitress when she offered me champagne.

"Mr. Thorne says you think I can help you," he said.

"I hope you can," I said.

"You'll forgive me if I don't have time for small talk," he said.

"You're a busy man," I said. "I'm here about this man."

I handed him the photograph of the man in the Steel Beasts cut as he walked out of 937 Ridgeway with Wayne Warren. "I'm told the man in the jacket works for you."

Gaius studied the photo. "A lot of men work for me. What's he done to you?"

"I think he may have information about this other man I'd like to talk to. Someone who could help me with a case I'm working on."

We danced around it, but I had no doubt Gaius knew exactly what case I meant.

"I hope he hasn't gotten into any trouble," Gaius said.

"I think he has," I said. "I think your men have gotten sloppy in a way that could cause you some trouble. I'm this close to proving their connection to a murder that took place in Delphi. It could be a one-off. It probably was. But your continued association with the Steel Beasts could be a problem for you in the short term."

"Then why would you think I'd be eager to help you find one of them?"

I appreciated that he didn't deny the association. It would have been pretty difficult considering I could see three men wearing Steel Beasts cuts sitting four stools away from Killian at the bar. He looked casual, unconcerned. But I knew he had them on his radar too.

"Because I can help you avoid any of this blowing back on you. You didn't come this far, build this much power just to have some two-bit hood with a lack of impulse control muck up the works. You give me these men, I can promise you it'll go no further."

"And you think you have the power to make me that promise?"

"This involves a cop," I said. "You want to tell me you sanctioned a hit on a cop? Or his wife?"

For the first time since I sat down, Gaius flinched. I knew I was right. If Wayne Warren or the Steel Beasts killed Wendy or tried to kill Eric, Gaius wouldn't have wanted any part of it.

"How exactly do you plan on containing this mess, if I even knew how to put you in touch with this man?"

I looked toward the bar. Killian watched. As Gaius leaned forward, Killian raised his rocks glass.

Gaius sat back. He waved the waitress away when she came back to refill his glass.

"Or," he said. "Maybe the cleanest thing for me is to let justice play out. Maybe your man, Detective Wray, just killed his wife and needs to pay for it. Maybe you're just chasing ghosts, Ms. Leary."

"Maybe," I said. "On the other hand, maybe you've got a grenade in your backyard with the pin pulled out."

He smiled. "I'll think about it," he said. "I'll let this man know you're looking for him."

"If ..."

"I'll be in touch," Gaius cut me off. From the corner, two bouncers started moving in. I looked behind me. Killian's stool was empty.

This wasn't how I hoped this meeting would go. I wanted answers. I was out of time. But I also knew how this worked. If I pushed harder, he'd know I was desperate and that would be the ballgame.

"I'll be waiting," I said. Gathering my purse, I turned and started down the stairs. Scanning the crowd, I still couldn't lay eyes on Killian. The three Steel Beasts were also gone.

The hair went up on the back of my neck. This didn't feel right. Then, movement caught my eye toward the back of the bar. Another bouncer stood there, staring at me.

It took a few seconds for my eyes to catch up with my brain. I knew him. I'd seen him. Huge. Six three at least. Close to three hundred pounds, maybe. Cold, dark eyes. Two-day-old stubble.

Wayne Warren.

I bolted down the rest of the stairs and pushed my way past throngs of people. They were all too tall to see past. I could make out the top of Warren's head, but he was on the move.

"Watch it, lady!" An angry bar patron shoved back. I was sweating now. I saw the kitchen doors swing shut, and I launched myself through them.

"Wait!" I shouted. A few waiters and cooks in the back called after me. I ignored them and ran through the kitchen and through the service door into the alley.

Nothing met me outside but cold air and a full moon.

"Wait!" I shouted. "I just want to talk to you!"

I heard a metallic crash ahead of me. I took a step. Then, a hand clamped over my mouth and a second around my throat.

Chapter 43

My head spun. I kicked out with my feet but hit nothing but air. Wayne Warren's beefy fingers closed around my windpipe.

"Why can't you leave me alone!" he screamed in my face, spit flying.

I couldn't answer. I couldn't breathe. Somewhere, in the dark corners of my brain, I remembered something from a self-defense class I took in college.

It's good if they're strangling you. It means their hands are occupied, vulnerable, right where you can see them. Thirty seconds. Maybe less. No point kicking. No point trying to claw at your own throat.

"I didn't hurt that lady. I had nothing to do with it. Go away!" he said.

I lifted my right arm straight up above my head. Kept my eyes locked with his. I was dizzy. So dizzy. Just let me sleep.

No!

I could touch the ground on my tiptoes. I brought my right arm down over his wrists and twisted my whole body to the left as hard as I could.

He was twice my weight. A foot taller. But a person's wrist bones aren't designed to support the full weight of another human body.

You can break his grip.

Warren let go. I fell backward.

You can break his grip.

But then you better have a plan to run or fight like hell.

I kicked out for all I was worth. Warren caught my wrist and twisted it.

"You're gonna kill me?" I shrieked. "That's your plan? Convince me you didn't kill Wendy Wray by killing me instead?"

I brought my hand up hard, connecting the meat of my palm with the bottom of his chin. Warren shook his head to clear it. I'd rung his bell. But he rallied.

So much bigger. So much stronger.

You can break his grip.

But you're never going to win the hand-to-hand fight.

He grabbed me by the shoulders and shook me so hard my teeth rattled. "Stay outta my life!" he bellowed.

"Stop!" I screamed.

I curled my fist. Warren brought his hands up, going for my neck once more.

Then, a shadow blocked the moon behind his shoulder. I felt a gush of air. Then the sick crunch of metal on bone dropped three-hundred-pound Wayne Warren to the ground.

Killian stood behind him, eyes blazing. He held a sawed-off piece of rebar like a baseball bat. He raised it high, then brought it down before Warren could get back up.

"Killian!" I shouted.

He couldn't hear me. His eyes filled with crazed bloodlust as he brought the metal bar back up.

He would kill him. He would smash Wayne Warren's head like a pumpkin.

"Stop," I screamed, then brought my hands up and grabbed Killian's wrist.

"Killian," I said, lowering my voice. "You'll kill him."

"That's the plan," he said through gritted teeth. "He had his hands on you."

"I'm okay," I said. I was. Barely. "Killian, it's Wayne Warren. The guy I've spent the last six months looking for. I need him alive. I need him talking."

Killian stepped back. "Did he hit you in the head?"

"What? No. But you can't kill him. Not yet."

Killian stepped away from the lifeless lump that was Wayne Warren. I crouched down and got close to him. Blood flowed from a gash on the side of his head, but he was still breathing. Still moving. He groaned in pain and was about to come to.

"Help me," I said.

"Help you what?" Killian said.

"Help me tie him up or something. Let's get him out of here before Luther Gaius or anyone else realizes what happened."

"And then what?" Killian asked.

"Then I get him to tell me what he knows," I said.

"Cass," he said.

"You got a better idea?" I yelled. I started scanning the alley and nearby dumpster for anything I could use to tie him up with. I found some cardboard stacked and tied near the recycling bin. Quickly as I could, I untied it and brought the rope over.

"Get his arms," I said to Killian, tossing him a length of rope. "I'll get his feet."

"Oh, you'll get his feet," he said. "She'll get his feet, she says."

"Killian," I hissed through gritted teeth. "We're about to have a dozen Steel Beasts pouring through that door looking for this asshole. At the moment, he's mine. He's my best chance ... my only chance of finding out what really happened at Maple Valley. So I either need you to help me or get out of my way."

He shook his head with a fury but caught the rope I tossed. He leaned down and bound Wayne Warren's hands behind him, using a wicked set of nautical knots.

Then, he gently shoved me aside to redo the knots I'd used for Warren's ankles.

"Now what do you suggest?" Killian said, squatting beside me.

"How far away is your driver?" I asked. "We're kidnapping him."

"Connor? We're ..." Killian sputtered. Then he set his jaw into a hard, resolved line. He knew me better than to argue.

I nodded. "Have Connor bring the car around."

Killian got a devilish twinkle in his eye as he pulled out his cell phone and made the call. He could argue with me all he wanted, but the man was a brawler at his core. Twisted as it was, he was starting to enjoy himself.

Chapter 44

"In there!" I commanded. Connor, Killian's driver, barely made the turn. He went up the winding wood driveway until we came to the steel pole barn in the middle of nowhere.

"Where are we?" Killian asked. I looked back. We'd been driving for hours, all through the night. Warren was awake, but two seats behind and wearing a blindfold. I didn't want to take any chances. I mouthed the word to Killian.

"Joe's."

My brother and his wife Katie were gone for the week. They'd taken a long overdue vacation to the U.P. at my urging. He owned eight acres behind his house and had finally put up the pole barn. He meant it for his hunting and fishing equipment. Today, I planned to fish for something else.

"Help Connor get him out," I said. I slid out of the passenger seat and ran to the small keypad at the barn door. I punched in our mother's birth year and pressed the button. The large door lurched upward.

As Connor and Killian dragged Warren out of the car, I heard him groan. He was groggy but still moving under his own power. Good. I'd need him awake.

I switched on the overhead fluorescents and grabbed a folding chair from a stack on the side of the barn. I stuck it in the middle of the floor and went for more rope. Joe had loops of it on a hook nearby.

Wayne's head lolled forward, but he sat upright. He had a growing purple welt on the side of his head and it was fairly obvious Killian had given him a concussion.

"Tie him better," I said to Connor, tossing him the rope. He complied. By the time Connor finished looping the rope through Wayne Warren's ankles, the man's eyes finally came into focus.

Terror filled his eyes. "Where are we?"

I took another folding chair from the corner and put it in front of Warren. Connor and Killian stood on either side of him.

"Where have you been, Wayne?" I asked. "If you have nothing to hide, why wouldn't you answer your subpoena?"

He looked at Connor and Killian as if they might help him.

"I told you," he said, then spit blood at my feet. "I have nothing to say to you."

"You obviously know who I am. And you know what I want to know. You're not going anywhere until you tell me. I'm out of patience."

"You're crazy," he said. "You know what happens when they find out you brought me here?" He looked around, realizing he had no idea where here was.

"Nobody's looking, Wayne," I said. "Nobody cares but me. These guys? They know how not to be followed."

"You gonna let her do this?" Wayne said to Killian. "I work for Gaius. What do you think I was doing at the Olympia?"

Killian shrugged. "Wasn't my idea to bring you here, lad. Maybe you shouldn't have laid hands on the lady. She's got a temper. Besides, let's just say Gaius and I have an understanding."

I saw real fear go through Wayne Warren's eyes. Killian's bluff worked. For all Warren knew, we were acting with Luther Gaius's blessing.

"I need to know what happened at Maple Valley," I said. "What did you do to Wendy Wray?"

Warren looked back at me. "I didn't do shit to her."

"You were sent there," I said. "Don't try to tell me it was just a coincidence. I know you're affiliated with the Steel Beasts M.C. And I know they want to hurt Eric Wray. So, it seems to me you saw an opportunity. Or they did. Which is it?"

Warren clenched his jaw. He was afraid, but not enough.

Calmly, I rose. I went to the side of the barn and grabbed a hose. Joe had it hooked up to the pump outside. I cranked the nozzle and walked back over to Warren, reclaiming my seat. He looked at Killian. Killian just shrugged.

"Tell me what really happened at Maple Valley," I said.

"Kiss off," Warren said. I pressed the trigger on the hose, hitting Warren square in the face. He sputtered, choked, tried to squirm away. I let go of the trigger.

"Want to go again?" I said. "I've got all day." I didn't. He didn't need to know that. It was just past five in the morning. Slater would be back in court in three hours. Without my intervention, he would likely rest and Eric's case would be in the jury's hands by noon.

"They sent you there to kill her," I said. "The Beasts. Because Eric Wray put Ansel Jameson in prison. Payback. Tell me the truth."

"Wasn't like that," Warren said.

I hit him again with a blast of water. He got a noseful this time.

"Stop it!" he yelled. "I know who you are. Killian Thorne. I'm nobody. You really want to risk a tangle with the Beasts over this crazy chick?"

Killian turned his head away so Warren couldn't see him smile. When he turned back, his face went stone cold.

"Better tell her what she wants, lad."

"I had nothing to do with that," he said.

"You and Hector Ruiz," I said. "You were fond of Wendy Wray, weren't you? She was your favorite patient."

"You've been hearing rumors," he said, water and snot dripping from his nose. "That other crazy chick, Audra. She tried to cause me trouble. I didn't do nothing wrong. Nothing."

"You weren't at Maple Valley by accident," I said. "Admit it. You were there because Wendy Wray was."

"Wasn't like that," he said. "Somebody's been telling you stories, lady."

I had half a mind to hit him with the hose nozzle itself. Killian saw my face. Maybe read my mind. He made a gesture. Ease off.

"Listen," Killian said, stepping in front of me. "You've got two choices. Either you come clean with what you know, or you're cut loose. I either tell Gaius you cooperated, or you didn't. If you don't, do you think he'll welcome you back? Do you think anything happens at the Olympia without Gaius knowing about it?"

He was bluffing. Maybe. Or maybe this was Gaius's way of helping without letting anyone else think he was. It occurred to me I'd probably made a giant mess behind with Luther Gaius. One that might have lasting consequences for Killian's business. At the moment, I didn't care.

"You can go to hell," Warren spat. Anger boiled through me as the time ticked by. I hit the trigger and gave him a quick blast to the face.

"You want me to aim lower next time?" I threatened.

Wayne looked at Killian. "She's crazy!"

"Maybe," Killian said. "But Luther Gaius also doesn't generally like to employ bouncers who assault women on his property. How sure are you he'll be willing to take you back without my endorsement?"

Warren started to tremble. "Assault? She's the one assaulting me!"

"What happened at Maple Valley?" I said. "It's the last time I'm going to ask you nicely, Wayne."

He shook his head in defeat. "I didn't kill Wendy Wray. I had nothing to do with that. You ain't pinning that on me. I wasn't even near her that day."

"But you know something," I said, my heart sinking a bit. It wasn't that I expected him to make a full confession. But there had to be something. Anything.

"Eric Wray's a cop," he said. "The Beasts don't go after cops. They're untouchable. You should know that."

He directed the last bit at Killian.

"It's bad for business," Wayne continued.

"Someone did," I said. "Eric Wray's got a four-inch scar and relieved of his spleen, because someone decided he was touchable."

"Wasn't us," he said.

"Us," Killian said. "You're a member of the Steel Beasts?"

Wayne shook his head. "Prospect," he said.

"Prospect," I repeated. "Then it would seem like offing the man who nabbed your past club president would look pretty good on your resume when it was time to patch in."

"Beasts don't kill cops," he said through gritted teeth.

"Wendy Wray wasn't a cop," Killian said.

"Only thing more untouchable than a cop is a cop's family," he said. "That's not a road we go down. If we want to make things difficult, we got other ways. There's too much heat. Too much mess the other way. I'm telling you. I didn't touch Wendy Wray. And we had nothing to do with whatever happened to Wray inside. Sounds like he got himself mixed up with something else. Or maybe he's just clumsy."

Wayne Warren's eyes went pure evil as he looked back up at me.

"So why have you been hiding all this time?" I asked. "You were planted there. At Maple Valley. Why?"

He went silent. I'd cross-examined enough witnesses to know when I'd hit on something. My mind raced. If he was telling the truth so far. If the Steel Beasts put him in Wendy and Eric's path for some other reason other than murder ...

I rose from my chair. Something wasn't right. If Warren had gone off script. If he'd seen an opportunity to hurt Wendy and taken it without the club's sanction, why on earth would they still associate with him? They wouldn't. They would have made him disappear.

"Watch him," I said to Connor. I walked to the front of the barn and pulled open the service door. Killian followed me. I went to the edge of the woods where I knew I wouldn't be overheard.

"His story tracks," Killian said. "Sort of."

"I know," I admitted. "Only I know I'm right. It's no coincidence that a Steel Beast's probie ends up working at the same facility where Wendy Wray was. Where Eric routinely visited."

"They were watching him?" Killian offered.

"Or watching her," I said. "For what purpose? Just to keep tabs on Wendy? Where was she going to go?"

I wanted to hit something. I wanted to hit Wayne Warren.

"I need more time," I said.

"You don't have it," Killian answered.

I looked up at him. "How big of a mess did I drag you into?"

Killian smiled. He came to me and put a hand on my shoulder. "No more than usual. I can handle the likes of Luther Gaius. He's not going to upset a delicate business balance for some low-level biker wannabe. He's not worth it to them."

"So why keep him around at all then?" I asked. "I've been searching for Warren for months. They have to know. Either Gaius or the Beasts kept him hidden. What for? Wouldn't it have just been easier to make him really disappear?"

I paced. I walked a little way down one of the trails Joe had cut with his four-wheeler. It was barely six a.m., and I only had one card left to play.

I called Tori. She answered. Confused. Groggy.

"Cass?"

"Tori, did you get the rest of those pictures from Mrs. Schroeder back?"

"Uh ... yes. Last night. There's a digital file. I sent it. Didn't you get it?"

"I haven't had a chance to look," I said.

"I don't think you'll find anything useful," she said. "It was just a bunch of other cars and a few Harleys. One more picture of that biker guy with the long blond hair. And the girl he was with. There's a shot where you can see her face, kind of. Hang on a second. I'll send them again to your email. You should be able to open it from your phone."

"Thanks," I said. "Was there anything else? Did you have any luck finding the landlady? The owner of that house?"

Tori yawned. "Her name is Debbie Gainor. She owned it with her husband Paul until he died fifteen years ago. She's eighty-five and lives in Florida. I went back and talked to Betty Schroeder. She told me there's a granddaughter who comes over and mows the lawn when they're between tenants. That's her in the photos. The one you said Betty thinks is some kind of prostitute. Betty confirmed it."

"Tits Magee," I said.

"Huh?" Tori asked.

"Nothing. Thanks, Tori. I'll have a look. Keep your phone near you."

"Cass . . . is everything okay?"

I clicked off before answering so I wouldn't have to lie.

"Anything?" Killian said.

"Probably not," I answered. Tori's email just came through. I walked out of the woods to get a better signal as the digital file downloaded.

Forty-seven photos. Tori was right. Random cars. More Harleys. A picture of Wayne walking to the mailbox. One where he scowled right at the camera, aware Betty was taking his picture.

I almost blew by it. She had another shot of the back of the girl with the white-blonde hair. Wayne was with her, his hand on her elbow. He was walking her to her car. I couldn't see her face.

I flipped through the file again. There. Third picture in. I saw it.

Another shot of Wayne with the girl. Again, him walking her to her car. Chivalrous, almost. Protective. Her features were nondescript. She looked like a hundred different women. This was the most recent picture in the roll, taken just days before Wendy Wray died. In this shot, the girl had changed her hair. The white-blonde was gone, in favor of cotton-candy pink.

I felt like every drop of blood drained right out of my head.

"Cass?" Killian said. "What is it?"

"Get him in the car," I said. The sun began to peek over the horizon. "We're heading to my office."

Killian cocked his head but didn't question my demand. I picked up the phone and called Tori back.

"Hello?" she said.

"Tori," I said. "Get dressed. I need you to do me one more favor. It's kind of a big one."

Chapter 45

Jeanie met me in the courthouse parking lot. Eight a.m.

"You sure you know what you're doing, honey?" she asked.
Killian got out of the car. Jeanie's eyes went big, but she didn't
ask about him.

"Did you bring it?" I asked her, breathless.

Jeanie reached into the back seat and pulled out a garment
bag. She unzipped it. I always kept a spare suit, top, and black
heels at the office. I did not have time to go home. No time to
do anything but get here.

"Cover me," I said. We'd parked at the far end of the lot,
behind the dumpster. Nobody could see us in the shadows. At
least, I hoped. I quickly slipped out of my tee shirt and put on
the top. I could use a shower.

Killian cleared his throat and chivalrously turned his back,
blocking me from any prying eyes who happened by.

Within ten seconds, I zipped up my skirt, grabbed my jacket
and slipped into my heels.

"Time to go," I said. "Did Tori get what I asked?"

"Yes, but ..."

I didn't wait for more explanation. I sprinted as fast as I could, charging through the courthouse side entrance.

I had nothing with me. No bag. No purse. I sailed through the metal detectors as Killian and Jeanie hurried to keep up.

I didn't wait for the elevator. I took the stairs two at a time. By the time I made it to the third floor, I felt like my heart might spill out of my chest.

Sweating, I pushed through Judge Mitchell's double doors. The jury was seated. The judge had taken the bench. Slater stood at the lectern.

"If you have no more witnesses to call," the judge said.

"Wait!" I shouted, desperately scanning the gallery. For a second, I didn't see her. But she saw me. Tori waved toward me. My heart steadied as I saw the woman sitting beside her. Tori had delivered the first part of my favor. She kept her expression cool, betraying nothing to the woman she'd just dragged into court for me.

"Your Honor," I said. "Cass Leary on behalf of the defendant. We'd like to recall Gloria LaPlante to the stand."

Eric turned in his seat. Confusion lit his eyes. Dumbstruck, Slater turned.

"Uh ..." he started.

"You aren't the attorney of record in this case, Ms. Leary," Judge Mitchell said.

"Consider this my appearance, Your Honor," I said. I made eye contact with one of the deputies behind me and gestured toward Gloria. She was trying to scoot down the bench.

"Ms. LaPlante is still under a subpoena, Your Honor," I said. "We're within our rights to recall her for the defense."

"Objection," Rafe said. He looked just as confused as everyone else. I made my way up the gallery and joined Slater at the lectern.

"What's going on?" he whispered.

"Trust me," I said.

"What are the grounds of your objection, Mr. Johnson?" Judge Mitchell asked. "Ms. Leary's correct about the ability to put Ms. LaPlante back on the stand."

"Uh ..." Rafe stammered.

"Is she correct, Mr. Wray?" Judge Mitchell asked. "Does Ms. Leary represent you?"

Eric met my eyes. A beat passed. His jaw hardened, and he slowly rose to his feet.

"Yes, Your Honor," he said.

Mitchell waved a hand. "All right. This is highly unusual, but I'll allow it. Bailiff, will you show Ms. LaPlante to the stand? I see she's already in the courtroom."

Gloria came forward. She wasn't dressed for court this time. She wore a pair of floral-print scrubs. I had no idea how Tori managed to get her here, but I wanted to hug her right then and there. She'd kept her cool. Now, I could only hope my ploy would work.

"You're still under oath, Ms. LaPlante," Judge Mitchell said. "Your witness, Mr. ... er ... Ms. Leary. Let's not cover old ground, though. The rules of recross apply."

"Ms. LaPlante," I said. "Just to quickly recap, you were working on August 17th of last year, is that correct?"

"It is," she said, hesitating.

Slater was on it. Hardly missing a beat, he slipped a page of notes in front of me. They were his outline of questions for his original cross.

"Your shift started at seven a.m. and ended at seven p.m.," I said.

"Your Honor." Johnson found his footing. "This was all asked and answered days ago. You just got done admonishing the defense not to rehash old ground."

"Sustained," Judge Mitchell said. "If you have something you think this witness can add, get to it."

"Yes, Your Honor," I said. "Ms. LaPlante, your job at Maple Valley isn't your only income, is it?"

"I'm sorry?" she said.

"Isn't it true you also manage family-owned property?"

"I don't ... I don't know what you mean," she said. But some of the color had started to leave Gloria's face. Behind me, I heard Tori move into position at the defense table. I had one other favor I'd asked of her. I hoped like hell she was able to do it or I was about to crash and burn.

"Isn't it true you help manage property for your grandmother in Adrian?" I asked.

Tori was right there. She handed me a thin stack of paper with two photographs clipped to it. She'd pulled the deed to 937 Ridgeway.

"You grandmother is Debbie Gainor, isn't she?" I asked.

"Yes," Gloria said.

"And she rents out property at 937 Ridgeway in Adrian, isn't that right?"

"Objection," Johnson said. "I see no relevance here."

"Neither do I," Judge Mitchell said.

"Your Honor," I said. "If the witness will be permitted to answer, I can make a showing."

"Get to it," Mitchell said.

"Yes," Gloria said.

"Yes, your grandmother owns 937 Ridgeway?" I asked.

"Yes," she said.

"And yes, you help her manage it? Collect rent? Keep an eye on the place? Help her find new tenants?"

"Yes," Gloria said. She was nervous, but not panicked.

"Who lived at 937 Ridgeway from January last year through August of last year?" I asked.

It was then Gloria's eyes narrowed.

"What does that have to do with anything?" she said.

"Your Honor," I said. "Will you please instruct the witness to answer the question?"

"Ms. LaPlante?" Judge Mitchell said, though he rolled his eyes.

"I don't remember," she said. "I'd have to look. There's a lot of turnover on that property. It's old. My grandma doesn't have the money to really fix it up. It's not a great neighborhood. She also subleases a lot."

"So you're telling me you have no recollection as to who lived there, on your family's property, that you maintain, for a nine-month period last year?" I asked.

"I'm not sure," she said.

I pulled the photograph clipped to the pages Tori gave me.

"May I approach?" I asked the judge. Behind me, Tori went over to Rafe and handed him a copy of the picture I held. His face stayed blank as he looked at it.

"Ms. LaPlante," I said. "Can you identify this photograph?"

I showed it to her. She squirmed in her seat, then handed it back to me.

"Who is that?" I asked.

"It's me," she said, tight-lipped.

"And where are you standing?" I asked.

"On the porch at the Ridgeway house," she said.

"Objection," Rafe said. "Your Honor, counsel has offered no foundation for this photo."

"The witness just identified herself and where it was taken," I said.

"I'll allow it," Judge Mitchell said. He sat straighter in his chair.

"Do you recognize the person with you in that photo?" I asked Gloria.

"Yes," she hissed.

"Who is it?" I asked.

"I don't see how ..."

"Who is it?" I snapped.

"Wayne Warren," she said. "I was with Wayne Warren, okay?"

"Isn't it true you rented that property in Adrian to Wayne Warren for nearly eight months last year?" I asked.

"Yes," she said.

"And yet, in your cross-examination by Mr. Slater, you claimed you had no idea where Wayne Warren was, isn't that right?"

"I don't know where he is," she said.

"But you never bothered to disclose that you were his landlady. You never bothered to disclose you're the one who recommended him for his job at Maple Valley, did you?"

"No," she said quietly. My pulse skipped. That last question was a complete shot in the dark.

I picked up the second picture Tori clipped for me. She handed a copy to Rafe.

I approached the bench and showed Gloria the second photo. "Ms. LaPlante," I said. "Can you identify the people in this picture?"

"It's me," she said. "And Wayne. And ... the other guy's name is Zeke Simmons."

"Zeke Simmons," I said. "Isn't it true that Zeke Simmons is a member of the Steel Beasts M.C.?" Behind me, I heard Eric move in his chair. He muttered something low.

"So what?" Gloria said. "What does this have to do with anything?"

"You lied," I said. "Didn't you? You brought Wayne Warren into Maple Valley. You associate with the Steel Beasts M.C., an organization whose leader Detective Wray helped put behind bars. And you failed to disclose any of that."

"It's not a crime," she said.

The courtroom door opened behind me. I stayed stock still, focusing on Gloria. Heavy footsteps shuffled. I didn't need eyes in the back of my head to know what was going on.

Killian played his part. I'd asked him to wait ten minutes, then bring Wayne Warren in and sit him down against the wall.

"Ms. LaPlante," I said. "Isn't it true that you brought Wayne Warren, a prospect with the Steel Beasts M.C., into Maple Valley for the express purpose of killing Wendy Wray?"

Eric made a noise. A garbled shout. Slater cut him off. He was likely trying to sit on Eric.

"This isn't ... you can't ..." Gloria sputtered.

"You harbored Wayne Warren. You arranged for him to have access to Wendy Wray. So he could kill her for the club. And then you helped him disappear," I said.

Gloria went stone-faced.

"Liar!" Warren shouted. "I'm not taking the fall for this!"

Mitchell banged his gavel. Johnson was on his feet, objecting.

I flipped the page. Tori had written me a note. My heart fell. She hadn't been able to deliver fully on the second part of the favor I asked of her. I looked back at her. She mouthed the word "sorry."

I looked back up at Gloria.

"Gloria," I said. "You're acquainted with Ansel Jameson, isn't that right?"

"What?" she said.

"Ansel Jameson," I said. "The former leader of the Steel Beasts, isn't that right?"

She said nothing.

I picked up the piece of paper Tori left me. I had hoped for formal records. She hadn't had time to get them. It was a long shot. But what she'd written might give me just enough. I read the first three words to myself.

"She visited him."

"Ms. LaPlante," I said, making a great show of holding the piece of paper in front of me.

"Isn't it true that you in fact visited Ansel Jameson at Jackson Prison several times?"

"What?" she said.

I waved the paper. "You're aware the prison keeps a detailed visitor log, aren't you? There is security camera footage as well."

"So what if I visited him?" she said, tears beginning to roll.

Rafe Johnson made a noise. It sounded like air deflating out of a tire.

"You openly admit that you carried on a close, intimate relationship with the leader of the Steel Beasts M.C. A man who is sitting behind bars because Detective Eric Wray put him there. And you admit you harbored and arranged for Jameson's associate to have access to Eric Wray's wife?"

"Yes," she yelled.

"He put a hit out, didn't he?" I asked.

There was a commotion behind me. Wayne Warren rose to his feet.

I turned back to Gloria. "Ansel Jameson tasked you with getting close to Eric and Wendy Wray, didn't he?" I yelled.

"He did it!" she screamed, pointing a finger at Wayne.

"You lying little ..."

Wayne vaulted over the bench.

"He took Ansel away from me!" Gloria shrieked, changing the direction of where she pointed. Now, she aimed her finger straight at Eric.

Three deputies tried to tackle Wayne Warren. Mitchell's bailiff ran to the judge's side. Slater, Johnson, and Eric were all on their feet and moving.

"Wray has to pay!" Gloria yelled. "He took Ansel, so I took something from him!"

Her words hit me. It took a split second for me to process them.

I was wrong. All wrong. Wayne Warren didn't kill Wendy. Gloria did. And then she tried to frame Eric for it.

My God.

"Your Honor!" Rafe Johnson screamed it.

"I hope Wendy rots in hell!" Gloria yelled.

Time slowed. A single juror rose. One of the young ones. Juror number seven. The T.S.A. agent. He stared straight at Eric.

Juror number seven wore a bulky sweater. He pulled something from his waistband. Before I could move, I saw a flash of metal.

"Down!" The voice was Killian's.

A gun. The barrel pointed right at us.

A scream. Mine. Then my feet went out from under me as someone threw me to the ground.

Chapter 46

Deputy Smith shot to kill. I lay on the ground, but outside of my own body.

"Stay down," Eric commanded. His hand went automatically to his right hip, searching for a side arm that wasn't there anymore.

I saw juror number seven convulse backward as the round hit him square in the chest.

A gun, I thought. How in the world did he get a gun into the courtroom?

My brain exploded from the sound of screams as the courthouse deputies took control of the scene. Judge Mitchell had disappeared. They'd shoved him bodily through his side chamber door.

Another deputy had Gloria LaPlante pinned against the wall. She was yelling something incoherent, her face purple.

"You okay?" Eric asked. Slowly, achingly, the world started to slow and make sense.

"I'm okay," I said. "That wasn't ... he wasn't aiming for me. He was aiming for you."

Eric pushed himself off me and offered a hand to help me up.

"Well," Eric said. "You were in the line of fire too. Luckily, the kid had lousy aim."

"How?" I asked. As Eric and I got to our feet, I frantically searched for Jeanie. My heart flooded with relief as I spotted her on the other side of the courtroom. Killian had done for her what Eric did for me. He threw himself in front of her when the bullets started to fly. Oh, she'd regale anyone who'd listen to that story for the rest of her days.

"You okay?" I said. Tori was seated on the nearest bench, looking gray. She lifted a hand and nodded.

"This wasn't me! This wasn't the Beasts!"

Wayne Warren appeared. Two deputies had his hands behind his back and were trying to cuff him. I had no idea whether he'd broken the law yet, but the deputies were inclined to sort that out later.

"You hear me?" Warren was directing his rant toward Eric. "We don't go after cops."

"I'll keep that in mind," Eric said, wryly.

Rafe Johnson walked over. He was breathless, his face shining with sweat.

"This is ... I can't even ..."

"Just drop the charges," Slater said, straightening his tie. "And my client is walking out of this courthouse now. He can't go back into custody, even for processing. Not after this. You can't guarantee his safety."

"How the hell did he get in here with that?" Johnson yelled, directing his anger toward the nearest deputy. I had the same question, but said deputy had also just pulled Rafe out of the line of fire.

With the public cleared out, the EMTs moved in. The shooter was on his stomach, barely breathing.

"Come on," Slater said. "Time to go."

"They're going to need our statements," I said. Jeanie got to me. She was whole, but breathing hard. I put my arms around her.

"They know where to find us," Jeanie said.

"Are you okay?" I asked her.

Killian was at her side. He asked me the same question with his eyes.

"I'm fine," Jeanie said. "We're all fine."

In the corner, another deputy started reading Gloria LaPlante her rights.

"You better keep those two separate," Eric called out. Deputy Craddock had just shown up. He'd been across the hall on a different matter, but Wendy Wray's death was still his case.

Eric and Craddock exchanged a steely look. For a moment, I wondered if Eric might punch him. I knew he wanted to.

"She just confessed to killing Wendy," I said to Craddock. "Under oath. On the stand."

"Get him out of here," Eric said to the deputy holding Wayne Warren. "I mean it, Craddock, you need to keep those two separate. And lock down the courthouse. Somebody let that juror in here with a gun. You've got trouble on the inside."

Craddock squared his shoulders. He gave Eric a grim nod as his brain seemed to catch up. "Stay close," he said. "I'm going to need to talk to all of you."

"Like I said," Jeanie chimed in. "You know where to find us."

"You too," Craddock said to Killian, his tone threatening.

Killian laughed. "You think I had something to do with this?"

"Enough," I said. "Jeanie's got it right. Craddock's people know how to find us. We need to get Eric out of sight." I said the last bit under my breath.

"The office is closest," Jeanie whispered. "We'll leave out the staff exit."

With that, Eric was done waiting. He shook hands with Slater. "Thank you," he said.

Slater opened his mouth to accept it, but then clamped it shut. "I think you need to thank Cass. I'm still trying to sort out what the hell just happened."

Eric smiled. It was the first genuine one I'd seen from him since the day Wendy died. He put an arm around me. It felt good.

As the deputies hauled Gloria out of the courtroom, she resisted.

"I hope it hurt," she said to Eric. "I hope she suffered."

A sound went through me, cutting me down to the bone. Darleen Maloney stood in the back of the courtroom, her back against the wall. Eric froze. Then sprang into action. I don't know where her husband was or her son. Dar was the only member of Wendy's family in court today. But as she broke and her knees gave out, Eric was the one to catch her when she fell.

Chapter 47

"Bill Walden? Are you sure?"

We sat in the conference room. Slater was on his cell with someone from the sheriff's department. Craddock was sending two deputies here within the hour to begin taking our statements.

Jeanie had brought out the good stuff. Irish whisky in honor of Killian's contribution to the day's events. I'd already done my first shot. We'd have to get through our statements sober, but I worried we'd need another bottle before the end of this.

Slater hung up. His face looked whiter than it had after the first gunshot rang out just two hours before. He sank into the nearest chair.

"What about Walden?" Eric asked.

"They've just taken him into custody," Slater said. "Courthouse security footage has him bringing juror number seven in through a side entrance this morning. And for the last week. He waited for him in the parking lot."

"You gotta be kidding me." Jeanie said it for all of us.

"It was a setup from the beginning," Eric said, his tone bitter. "Denying my bail. Getting me in lockup. So someone could try to pick me off."

"But Wayne Warren keeps insisting the Steel Beasts had nothing to do with any of it," Tori said.

"They might not have," Killian offered. "Lad's not the sharpest knife in the drawer, but that club doesn't go after cops. Bad for business. Something tells me you've got plenty of other enemies to go around." He set his rocks glass down and slid it toward Jeanie, saloon-style. She caught it.

"How did you find out Gloria LaPlante was visiting Ansel Jameson in prison?" Slater asked.

"I didn't," I said. "It was just a hunch. Tori was working on trying to get the visitor logs, but we didn't have time."

I had the small file folder in front of me that I'd brought up to the lectern when I questioned Gloria. Tori's note was still clipped to the outside. I turned it so Slater and the others could read it.

"She visited him. C.O. I know thinks he recognized her picture."

Tori took the file from me. "I'm just sorry I didn't put that together sooner. I wasn't in court when Gloria testified the first time. I didn't really know what she looked like. Her hair was blonde in her I.D. photos," she said.

"Don't beat yourself up," I said. "I might not have recognized her either at first but for that pink hair."

"You bluffed about the prison visits," Jeanie said, laughing. "You had no idea how many times she'd been to see Jameson."

"I bluffed," I admitted.

"Damn risky," Slater said. "She could have denied it."

"I just needed Gloria to *think* I had the logs," I said, smiling.

"Well, Warren's talking," Slater said. "He claims he wasn't at Maple Valley for you or Wendy. Says the club assigned him to Gloria. She'd gone to the current president and demanded revenge for Ansel. They were afraid she was going to make trouble for the club."

"She was flying solo," Eric said. "The club wouldn't endorse a hit on me or Wendy. So Gloria decided to do it on her own. She hadn't worked there very long. Just a few months before Wendy ... before all this happened."

"You think it was just a coincidence?" Jeanie asked.

"Maybe," I said. "But Wendy's accident wasn't a secret. Gloria could have easily found out where she was and angled herself a job there."

"The club would have sent Wayne Warren to keep an eye on her. They knew she was a loose cannon, but she was Ansel Jameson's old lady. They wouldn't have made a move on her. That's as much part of their code as you being untouchable," Killian said. "I can confirm that through ... channels ... but it's what I'd do."

Dead silence. It was as close as Killian had ever come to admitting to outsiders how he operated.

"You think Wayne Warren was sent there to protect Gloria from herself?" Tori asked.

"I do," Killian said. "Only he was colossally bad at his job."

"They didn't order the hit," Eric said. "But the club stepped out of the way and let me twist for it after it was done. They don't kill cops. But there's no code against letting Ansel's crazy girlfriend frame me for murder after the fact."

"That's my bet," I said. "I wouldn't be surprised if we find out Gloria's the one who got a message to you that Dr. Barnes wanted to meet with you. So you were still in the building when she killed Wendy. And she was the one who told the cops she saw you in the stairwell looking upset just before you left. She fixed the timeline."

"I should have listened to you," Slater said. "I'm sorry, Cass. More than that, I'm sorry, Eric. I thought Wayne Warren was a wild goose chase. We would have made reasonable doubt without him."

"You sure about that?" Eric said.

"You hadn't heard my closing," Slater said, smiling.

Below us, the front door opened. A second later, Miranda buzzed up. "Sheriffs are here," she said. "I've got one set up in Jeanie's office for Eric's statement. Cass, I'm sending the other one up to your office for you. Everybody else can stay put and wait their turn, if that's okay."

"Thanks," I said. "We'll be right there."

Eric got to his feet. He locked eyes with me. I read him. We left the others, and he followed me into my office. I shut the door behind him.

"You okay?" I asked. "I mean, really. I don't want to hear whatever you think you need to tell everyone else."

He came to me. He had new lines in his face I worried might never fade.

"I'm sad," he said. "Grateful. But sad. It doesn't matter what Killian finds out. It doesn't even matter who's behind the attempted hits on me if it wasn't the Steel Beasts. In an odd way I deserve it."

"What?" I said.

"Maybe not deserve," he said. "Maybe it's more the cost of doing business in my line of work. I've made enemies. Bad ones. None of that matters now. Wendy's still gone. And I know you're not the person I should say that to."

"Yes," I said. "I am. I'd only think less of you if you didn't."

I took him by the hand. Miranda buzzed up again, and I heard footsteps coming up the stairs.

"This is almost over," I said. I went up on my tiptoes and kissed him. He kissed me back, but he was hesitant. Holding something in. It hurt a little, but I knew he needed time. For the first time in months, I knew we would have plenty, and on our terms.

Chapter 48

One Week Later

"Is this the soonest we've ever put a boat in?" Vangie asked. She carried a small cooler in one hand and used her other hand to guide my niece Jessa as she stepped from the dock to the pontoon.

"No," Joe and I answered together. He sat at the wheel while my brother Matty held the ropes at the front of the boat. Eric held the ropes at the back.

At high noon, we'd already hit seventy-eight degrees toward an expected high of eighty-five. April in Michigan was a weather roller coaster. The local news guy said we'd be down to forty and snow by mid-week. Joe, Matty, and Eric took advantage of the weekend to put in the dock and trailer my boat to the launch.

It did me good to see them together. For the last week, Eric had barely come inside at all except to sleep. He spent the first night out of jail sleeping on my front porch under the stars. It didn't matter to him how cold it got.

"Grandpa Leary put the boat in once on St. Patrick's Day," Joe said. "Did it to prove a point to Grandma, I think."

"A point he lost," I said. "I think we had a blizzard the next week, if I remember it right."

Joe smiled. "We sure did. Grandpa sat out here on his pontoon, anyway."

"He refused to concede ground in any argument," I said.

"That's silly," Jessa said. Vangie snapped her life jacket on her and she climbed into Joe's lap. He promised to teach her how to drive the boat this summer.

"We ready?" Matty asked, poised to push us off with Eric.

"I'm coming!" Jeanie said. She had a beach towel and two beers in her hand. Her flip-flops flapped as she hurried down the dock.

Behind her, a car pulled down the driveway. A sleek black SUV.

"What the ..." Joe started. Eric straightened. I shielded my eyes from the sun.

The back door of the SUV opened and Killian stepped out.

"Not exactly dressed for boating, is he?" Vangie said. Killian wore a dark-gray suit and tie. He said something to his driver and lifted his hand in a wave.

"Not exactly dressed for boating!" Jeanie yelled to him, echoing Vangie's sentiment.

"It's okay," Eric said, his tone flat. "He's here for me."

"Eric ..." I started. But Eric had already gestured to Matty. Before I could say anything else or even move, Eric and Matty gave the boat a great shove. Matty hopped on just in time as Joe revved the engine and steered us away from the dock.

I watched as Eric straightened. Killian stayed on the lawn as Eric walked up the dock to greet him.

"Did you know he was coming?" Vangie asked me as she stabbed a straw into Jessa's juice box and handed it to her.

"Uh ... no," I said. Matty and Joe looked nonplussed. Whatever was going on up at the house, I had a sneaking suspicion they were in on it.

"Make it the quick tour, Joe," I said, hardening my voice.

"Sit down," he said. "Relax."

"So," Matty said, trying to break the tension. "Jeanie, how'd your hot date with Norman Slater go last night? You leaving us?"

Jeanie blushed. "Hardly," she said. "Norman's heart couldn't take it."

Matty got a horrified expression on his face, as if he were sorry he asked. Vangie and I laughed.

"No," Jeanie continued. "Norman just came down to help his boy pack up. The Slater men are leaving Delphi behind."

"They formally dropped the charges against Eric yesterday," I said.

"What about that thug from the biker club, Wayne Warren?" Matty asked.

"No charges against him," I said. "They were dangling obstruction of justice, but he cooperated. Gloria LaPlante seemed to have been acting completely on her own. Rafe Johnson just signed off. They're going after her for first degree murder."

"You hear anything about Judge Walden?" Jeanie asked.

I looked back up toward the house. Eric and Killian had walked out of view. I really wished Joe would just turn the boat around and take me back.

"I have a feeling that might have something to do with that," I said, gesturing toward my shore.

There was only one thing I could think of that would make Eric ask Killian to stop by. Killian had connections in places I didn't even want to think about. If anyone could get a quick answer as to who Judge Walden might have been mixed up with, Killian could. It just surprised me that Eric would willingly pull at that particular thread.

Jeanie handed me a beer.

"Bottoms up," she said. "You look like you could use it."

Joe steered the boat through the cove where I couldn't see my house anymore. He took the slow, scenic route. Today, it grated my nerves. It was a good half hour before he made the final turn and my dock came back into view.

I could see Killian standing on the porch. Eric was at the end of the dock, waiting to help Joe pull the boat in.

Eric was quiet as he helped tie off the boat. He kept his head down. I paused, trying to peer into his face. He waved me off, but not soon enough for me to see. Eric was growing a very definite fat lip.

"He wants to talk to you," Eric grumbled, gesturing toward Killian. Joe was at my side. Killian started coming down the walk. In his case, he had the unmistakable makings of a shiner.

"You two have got to be kidding me," I muttered. Joe stopped me, gently grabbing my arm.

"Sis, leave it be. Trust me. Stay out of it."

"Of all the Alpha male bull ..."

"Stay out of it," Joe cautioned me again. I felt my nostrils flare. Killian got to me.

"Didn't want to leave without saying goodbye, a rúnsearc." He said the last bit loud enough for Eric to hear. It made me want to punch both of them myself.

"Thank you," I said. I grabbed Killian by the arm and practically dragged him back to his car.

"You wanna explain what that was all about?" I said, pointing to his eye.

"Just a meeting of the minds, love," he said.

"Two boneheads," I said. "What did you tell him? I know he asked you about Judge Walden. You might as well tell me too."

Killian shifted his jaw, looking down at Eric. Eric busied himself cracking open a beer and climbing back onto the boat with my brothers.

"Your Judge Walden was on the take," he said. "I expect that'll come out soon enough. Turns out he had some debts he was trying to pay off. Nasty business. Cartel had their hooks into him. Something to do with a debt someone named Frank Rossi wanted to settle against Eric for getting him locked up. As soon as Eric got arrested, Rossi's people reached out to Walden and put the screws into him. He denied Eric's bail at their demand. There's a C.O. at the county jail in Rossi's pocket too. They're working on a theory they were behind the attempted hit on Eric. And they bought that juror and had Walden smuggle him into the courthouse armed."

"That weasel," I said. "If Rossi's people bought one juror, there might have been others. But this will blow the lid off Rossi's jail organization. The Attorney General's going to get involved and launch a full-scale investigation if I have anything to say about it."

"Judge Walden's not going to do well where he's going," Killian said. "Men like him. He'll sing. He's not built for life behind bars. Trouble is, anyone with real power would know not to let the judge get too close. Whatever intel he thinks he can use to bargain with the feds won't be worth much. Almost makes you feel sorry for him."

"He's getting what he deserves," I said.

"You might get another call from the governor," Killian said. "Seems to me she's still having trouble filling that judicial seat."

"Thanks for the heads up," I said. "I still like the life I have."

Killian met my eyes. He knew what I meant.

"And thank you for ... everything else too," I said. "I couldn't have cracked this case without you."

He smiled. "Oh, I'd expect you would have. I know how you are when you've a mind to do something."

A simple statement. We both knew what it meant.

"Well, anyway. Thank you. I owe you. I know that."

He leaned in and kissed me behind the ear. "Be careful. You know I might collect."

He gave me a wink and saved a wave for my brothers on the boat. It was subtle, but I saw my brother Joe raise a quick middle finger as he returned the wave and brought his hand down. Killian had already turned.

Eric got off the boat and started up the dock as Killian slipped in the SUV and told his driver to leave.

I waited until his car disappeared up the driveway before I turned to Eric. He came to me. I ran a gentle thumb across his bottom lip.

"You want to tell me about it?" I asked.

"You should see the other guy," Eric softly teased.

"Yeah," I said. "I did. Who threw the first punch?"

"He had it coming," Eric said, but I sensed no trace of anger. Whatever had happened between the two of them, Killian and Eric seemed to have reached a tenuous detente. For now. I wondered though. Once Killian had offered Eric protection, it might be for life. I hadn't just incurred my own debt.

"You could have gotten hurt," he said. "Luther Gaius is a dangerous man. The Steel Beasts might like to pretend they don't go after cops or their families, but you're technically neither. Killian never should have agreed to let you near him. He knows who you are now. Gaius might think you owe him. I don't like it, Cass."

"I think Gaius knows I took care of a problem for him. For the Beasts too, maybe. I'm not worried about him. Besides, haven't you figured out by now? I can take care of myself."

It was an old argument and an old joke between us. He hated that there'd been so many opportunities where I had to prove it. But I had. And would again.

"What about you?" I said. "You've been pretty quiet up until now. I know there's something else on your mind. Something you want to tell me."

He chewed his bottom lip. There had been tension running through him all day that I knew had nothing to do with Killian's visit or his fears about Luther Gaius. He also knew I meant more with that question. What about you? What about us?

"I talked to the chief," he said. "He's agreed to let me take a leave of absence."

"Good," I said. "And you know ... it's not so far off for you to think about retiring. You've got over twenty years on."

He smiled. "How about I'll think about retiring when you do."

"Fair point," I said.

"I'm going to spend the summer in Raleigh," he said. "It'll be good for my folks. My dad's mind isn't what it was. And Monica ..."

"Monica isn't too big a fan of mine," I said.

Eric nodded. "She's just worried about me. Protective sister. You know the type."

I slugged him in the arm.

"The whole summer?" I asked. I hated it. Hated the idea of not getting to see him every day after everything he'd been through.

"I just need some time to sort some things out."

"To grieve," I said. "Eric, I understand." And I did.

"Yeah," he said, then again. "Yeah."

"But you'll come back?" I asked, trying to keep the pain out of my voice. Before Wendy died, he had talked to my sister about whether I would marry him. He never told me himself. I had been afraid to ask him about it. Too much had happened. It had all been ... too much. I had so many more questions. If I let it, my mind would spin. Where did we go from here? Would he decide to stay in North Carolina and take that job his sister mentioned? Was Knapp and everyone else right about me? Was I cursed? Would I have said yes?

I heard the ghost of my mother's voice from somewhere deep inside.

Be still. Be present. Because that's all there is.

I linked my hand with Eric's as we stared out at the water. Matty had put a pole in. The sun was high and hot. In a week, the frost might come. But today, the fish were biting, and that was enough.

AN UNSPEAKABLE CRIME. Everyone saw it coming. But no one stopped it. Now it's up to Cass to expose the truth and stand up to a killer. Even if it's her next client...

Don't miss Guilty Acts, the next book in the Cass Leary Legal Thriller Series. Click here or on the book cover to order https://www.robinjamesbooks.com/GA

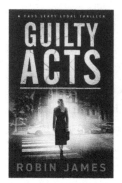

CLICK TO ORDER

Newsletter Sign Up

Sign up to get notified about Robin James's latest book releases, discounts, and author news. You'll also get *Crown of Thorne* an exclusive FREE bonus prologue to the Cass Leary Legal Thriller Series just for joining. Find out what really made Cass leave Killian Thorne and Chicago behind.

Click to Sign Up

http://www.robinjamesbooks.com/newsletter/

About the Author

Robin James is an attorney and former law professor. She's worked on a wide range of civil, criminal and family law cases in her twenty-year legal career. She also spent over a decade as supervising attorney for a Michigan legal clinic assisting thousands of people who could not otherwise afford access to justice.

Robin now lives on a lake in southern Michigan with her husband, two children, and one lazy dog. Her favorite, pure Michigan writing spot is stretched out on the back of a pontoon watching the faster boats go by.

Sign up for Robin James's Legal Thriller Newsletter to get all the latest updates on her new releases and get a free bonus scene from Burden of Truth featuring Cass Leary's last day in Chicago. http://www.robinjamesbooks.com/newsletter/

Also By Robin James

Cass Leary Legal Thriller Series

Burden of Truth

Silent Witness

Devil's Bargain

Stolen Justice

Blood Evidence

Imminent Harm

First Degree

Mercy Kill

Guilty Acts

With more to come...

Mara Brent Legal Thriller Series

Time of Justice

Price of Justice

Hand of Justice

Mark of Justice

With more to come...

Made in the USA
Monee, IL
11 August 2023

40858629R00225